ARTHUR

VENUS
PRIME ™

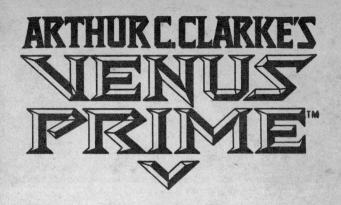

ARTHUR C. CLARKE'S VENUS PRIME™

VOLUME 5

THE DIAMOND MOON

PAUL PREUSS

A BYRON PREISS BOOK

AVON BOOKS • NEW YORK

ARTHUR C. CLARKE'S VENUS PRIME, VOLUME 5: THE
DIAMOND MOON is an original publication of Avon Books. This work
has never before appeared in book form. This work is a novel. Any simi-
larity to actual persons or events is purely coincidental.

Special thanks to John Douglas, Russell Galen, Alan Lynch, and Mary
Higgins.

AVON BOOKS
A division of
The Hearst Corporation
105 Madison Avenue
New York, New York 10016

Text and artwork copyright © 1990 by Byron Preiss Visual Publications, Inc.
Arthur C. Clarke's Venus Prime is a trademark of Byron Preiss Visual
Publications, Inc.
Published by arrangement with Byron Preiss Visual Publications, Inc.
Cover design, book design, and logo by Alex Jay/Studio J.
Front cover painting by Jim Burns
Library of Congress Catalog Card Number: 90-93162
ISBN: 0-380-75349-9

First Avon Books Printing: November 1990

AVON TRADEMARK REG. U.S. PAT. OFF. AND IN OTHER COUNTRIES, MARCA
REGISTRADA, HECHO EN U.S.A.

Printed in the U.S.A.

RA 10 9 8 7 6 5 4 3 2 1

ACKNOWLEDGMENTS

My thanks to Diana Reiss, founder of the Circe Project to investigate dolphin communication, who reminded me of the Dogon people and their beliefs about Sirius and its companion star. My apologies to Carl Sagan, a very plausible debunker of that and other intriguing myths—which, remarkably, I had managed to forget that I first read about in his writings—for pulling gently on his leg.

Data on the physical effects of near-instantaneous deceleration come from a paper of Colonel John Stapp in "Bioastronautics and the Exploration of Space," edited by Bedwell and Strughold, AFSC, USAF (GPO), 1965. And a grisly piece of work it is.
　　　　　　　　　　　　　　　　　—Paul Preuss

Prologue

All over the northern hemisphere of Earth, it was raining.

Forty minutes before the last episode of "Overmind" was scheduled to be sent throughout the solar system over open channels, Sir Randolph Mays appeared at London's Broadcasting House, water streaming from his Burberry, coming out of the night to insist that the episode's opening tease be re-recorded.

Hastily summoned from dinner at his club two streets away, a bedraggled and frantic program director confronted the interplanetary celebrity. "Sir Randolph, you can't possibly be serious. We've already loaded the finished chip for automatic transmission."

Mays pulled a blue-bound folder from his capacious leather satchel and brandished it in his huge right hand. "Kindly direct your *attention* to section *thirty-three*, paragraph *two* of our contract," he replied; he always talked as if underlining his key words. "Herein are set forth the *penalties* to be paid by the British Broadcasting Corporation in the event I am not granted absolute and total editorial *control* over the content of the series."

"Well, yes, but you also agreed to deliver a finished chip on a timely basis, following a script previously approved by us." The director didn't have to check the contract; the clause was standard. He allowed his old-fashioned steel-rimmed bifocals to slide down his long nose, the better to peer sternly at Mays. "*That* you have already done. And the time is, ah, no longer timely."

"You may *counter*sue. However, if you weigh the penalties specified by *contract*—what my breach will cost *me* as opposed to what your breach will cost *you*—I think you will agree that a simple substitution of the opening *two minutes* of tonight's program is the preferable solution." Mays was a gaunt man with a wide-stretched mouth, whose enormous hands chopped the air as he spoke, slicing out each emphasized word.

"I'll need a moment to . . ."

"Here is the timed *script* for the new section. All the visuals to be replaced are on this *chip.*"

The director pushed his bifocals back up. "Well . . . let me see, then."

Within five minutes Mays was ushered to an insert studio, where he sat in front of a matte screen facing a diminutive viddiecam and read half a dozen lines of narration in his unmistakably inflected voice.

Five minutes after that he was ensconced in a plush editing suite, peering over the shoulder of a hastily summoned video editor.

The editor was a pale, thin young man with glossy shoulder-length brown curls. After spending a few moments tapping keys with his delicate fingers he said, "All ready, sir. Old master on one, insert chip on two, unsynched reading on channel thirty, feeding to new master on three."

"I should like to see if we can do this in *real* time. Live to chip, as it were."

"All right, sir. You'll cue me."

"You may go ahead at any time. Begin on two."

On the flatscreen monitor an image appeared, familiar but still majestic, of Jupiter's clouds filling the screen, swirling in an intricate curdle of yellow and orange and red and brown—and in the foreground, the tiny bright spark of a swift moon.

"Reading," said Mays.

The editor tapped the keys again; May's recorded voice, a sort of harsh half-whisper filled with suppressed urgency, filled the upholstered room.

Jupiter's moon Amalthea. For more than a year, the most unusual object in our solar system—and the key to its central enigma.

The picture enlarged. Amalthea swiftly drew closer, revealing itself as an irregular lump of ice some scores of kilometers long, its major axis pointed toward nearby Jupiter. Too small to feel the internal sag and stretch of tidal forces and the resultant heat of friction—much too small to hold an atmosphere—Amalthea was nevertheless wreathed in a thin fog which trailed away behind it, blown to tatters by an invisible sleet of hard radiation.

"Good picture," the editor remarked.

Mays only grunted. This very image was the reason he had been insistent on revising the show opening; it was a classified Board of Space Control reconnaissance-satellite recording that Mays had acquired less than twenty-four hours earlier, by methods he did not care to discuss. The editor, with long experience of cutting together investigative news programs, understood Mays's diffidence and said nothing more.

The ever-enlarging video image now showed that upon Amalthea's surface, obscured by the clinging mist, hundreds of glittering eruptions were spewing matter into space. The voice-over continued: *The ice geysers of Amalthea have no known natural explanation.*

"Switch back to one," said Mays.

Abruptly the screen picture cut to Amalthea as it

had been known for the previous century—a dark red rubble-strewn chunk of rock 270 kilometers long, dusted with a few large patches of ice and snow. *Since the first views returned by robot spacecraft expeditions in the 20th century, Amalthea has been thought to be an ordinary, inert, captured asteroid.*

The scene dissolved, and now the image on the flatscreen was a view from deep within Jupiter's clouds, as recorded by the previous year's *Kon-Tiki* expedition. At center screen a giant floating creature, like one of Earth's many-armed jellyfish but several orders of magnitude larger in dimension, browsed quietly in cloudy pastures. Clearly visible on the side of its immense gas bag were peculiar markings, the checkerboard pattern of a meter-band radio array.

When the medusas that swim in the clouds of Jupiter were disturbed by the research vessel Kon-Tiki, the voice-over continued, *they began what some have called a "celestial chorus."*

"Cross to two," said Mays.

The screen dissolved to another of Mays's newly acquired illicit images, a false-color radio map of Jupiter's clouds, seen from Amalthea's orbit: concentric circles of bright red splotches indicating radio sources spread out over the paler graph lines like ripples on a pond, or the rings of a bull's-eye.

Six Jupiter days they sang their radio song directly toward Amalthea, commencing when that moon rose above their horizon, pausing when it sank. On the seventh day they rested.

The surface of Amalthea again: seen close, a column of foam stood up high above the slick surface. The geyser's orifice was veiled in tendrils of mist.

Surely it is no coincidence that these immense geysers suddenly began to spout everywhere on Amalthea at precisely the moment the medusas ceased to sing. So far, Amalthea has expelled more than one-third *of its total mass. Every hour it shrinks faster.*

"Insert my on-camera reading," Mays ordered. In the minute or two they had been working together, Mays and the editor had already fallen smoothly into synchrony; the editor had tapped the keys almost before Mays had spoken.

The image of Sir Randolph himself appeared, inserted neatly into a lower corner of the screen—the huge white geyser seemed to loom behind him, vaguely menacing. Three years earlier, few people would have known the face that stared from the screen—and in real life stared back at itself over a technician's shoulder. Once handsome, that face had grown pale and thin from half a century of disappointment with human nature, yet it betrayed no cynicism, and behind the staring gray eyes, under the drooping gray brows, a spark of faith seemed to burn hotly in Mays's brain.

Many more seeming unrelated events culminate on little Amalthea—events occurring in such far-flung locales as the hellish surface of Venus, the far side of Earth's moon, the deserts of Mars—and not least, at a lavish estate in England's Somerset countryside. These and other impossible coincidences will be the subject of tonight's program, the conclusion of our series.

Mays and his editor said the familiar words in chorus: "Music up. Roll titles," and the editor chuckled at their identical reflexes. Music swelled. Standard opening titles and credits flashed onscreen, superimposed on scenes from earlier "Overmind" episodes.

Both men stood. The editor stretched to get the tension out of his arms. "You had it timed to within a tenth of a second, sir," he said with satisfaction. "I'll just get this down to Master Control. We're on the air in seventeen minutes. Want to watch from the control room?"

"No, I'm afraid I have another appointment," Mays said. "Thank you for your assistance."

With that he strode out of the halls of Broadcasting House and back into the rainy night without another word to anyone—as if really, one did this sort of thing every day.

PART
I

TO THE SHORE OF
THE SHORELESS
OCEAN

1

Earlier the same day, on another continent . . .

"You aren't sure you are human," said the young woman. She sat on a spoke-backed chair of varnished pine.

In her oval face her brows were wide ink strokes above eyes of liquid brown, and beneath her upturned nose her mouth was full, her lips innocent in their delicate, natural pinkness. Her long brown hair hung in burnished waves to the shoulders of her summery print dress. "I believe that's where we left off."

"Isn't that where we always leave off?" Sparta's lips were fuller than the other woman's, perpetually open, as if testing the breeze; they did not curve easily into a smile.

"Certainly that is the question you hope to have answered. And until you do—or decide that some other question is more interesting—it seems we shall have to keep returning to it."

The room was unfurnished except for the chairs on which the two women sat facing each other from opposite corners. There were no pictures on the cream-painted walls, no rugs on the polished sycamore planks of the floor. The rain had stopped sometime in the night. The morning air was fragrant with the aroma of the greening woods, and

9

where sunlight came through the open casement, it was warm on the skin.

Sparta's straight blond hair just reached the high collar of her soft black tunic; together they framed her face, a smooth oval like Linda's. She turned her head to look out the single window. "They remade me to hear things no natural human can hear, see things no natural human can see, analyze what I taste and smell—not only with precision but consciously, specifying molecular structure—and calculate faster than any human being, and integrate myself with any electronic computer. They even gave me the power to communicate in the microwave. How can I be human?"

"Are the deaf human? The blind? Where does a quadriplegic's humanity end—somewhere in her spinal cord, or where her wheels touch the ground? Are such people dehumanized by their prostheses?"

"I was born perfect."

"Congratulations."

Sparta's pale skin brightened. "You already know everything I know and much more. Why is this such a difficult question for you?"

"Because only you can answer it. Do you know these lines?

Be still, and wait without hope
For hope would be hope of the wrong thing;
  wait without love
For love would be love of the wrong thing . . .
Wait without thought, for you are not ready
  for thought . . ."

The lines of poetry roused defiance in Sparta, but she said nothing.

"You have tried to think your way to an answer," Linda suggested. "Or feel your way, which in these circumstances is no better. What are feelings but thoughts without words? The answer to your question cannot be deduced or emoted. It will come when it comes. From history. From the world."

"If it ever comes."

"It's as good a question as any, but yes, you may lose interest in it."

Sparta picked at an imaginary bit of lint on the knee of her soft, close-fitting black trousers. "Let's change the subject."

"So easily?" Linda laughed, a girlish laugh, like the seventeen-year-old she appeared to be.

"My humanity or lack of it is not in fact the only thing that interests me. Last night I dreamed again."

"Yes?" Linda sat quietly alert. "Tell me your dream."

"Not of Jupiter's clouds, or the signs," Sparta said. "I haven't had those dreams for a year."

"That part of your life is past."

"Last night I dreamed I was a dolphin, racing deep under the sea. The light was very blue, and I was cool and warm at the same time, happy without knowing why—except that there were others with me. Other dolphins. It was like flying. It went on and on, deeper and deeper. And then I *was* flying. I had wings and I was flying in a pink sky over a red desert. It could have been on Mars, except there was air. I realized I was alone. And suddenly I was so sad I made myself wake up."

"What was your name?"

"I didn't . . . What makes you think I had a name?"

"I wonder, that's all."

Sparta paused, as if remembering. "When I was a dolphin, it was like a whistle."

"And when you were a bird?"

"A cry, like . . ." She hesitated, then said, *"Circe."* It came from her lips like a dolphin's squeal.

"Fascinating. Do you know what that means?"

"Circe? I don't know why I thought of that. In the *Odyssey* she changed men into animals."

"Yes. In the *Odyssey* she is the Goddess as Death. But the word literally means 'falcon.'"

"Falcon!" The previous year's *Kon-Tiki* expedition to Jupiter had been commanded by the airship captain Howard Falcon; in her madness, thinking him her rival, Sparta had tried to murder him.

Linda said, "A name not of death, but of the sun."

"I was happier under the sea," said Sparta.

"The sea is an ancient symbol of the subconscious. Apparently your subconscious is no longer barred to you. A propitious dream."

"But that came first. Then I lost it."

"Because a lonely, conscious task still calls you. A sunlike task. In the West, at least, the sun was a lonely god."

Sparta's expression set into stubbornness. "That task was imposed on me by others. *Empress of the Last Days*." She spoke the ritual phrase with contempt. "By what right did they elect *me* ambassador to the stars? I owe them nothing."

"True. But sooner or later you'll have to decide what to tell them. Whether yes or no."

Hot tears welled up in Sparta's eyes. She sat still and let them fall on her lap, to disappear in the soft black cloth. After a few moments she said, "If I were human I could refuse."

"Must you be sure of your humanity before you can refuse?"

Sparta evaded the question. "Then maybe I could be with Blake and do something normal, like live in a real house, have babies."

"Why is that impossible?"

"That was destroyed in me."

"You can be remade."

Sparta shrugged.

Linda tried again. "How does Blake feel?"

"You know."

"Tell me again."

"He loves me." Her voice was flat.

"And you love him."

"But I am not human," Sparta muttered.

Linda smiled dryly. "*Now* you are sure."

Trapped, Sparta stood up, her motion smooth as a dancer's. She moved toward the door, hesitated, then turned. "This is getting nowhere. I designed you as you are . . ."

"Yes?"

"Because when I was you—*was* Linda—I was human. Normal, almost. Before they turned me into *this,* I could have had anything I wanted."

"*Footfalls echo in the memory,*" Linda recited, "*Down the passage which we did not take. . . .*"

"What?" Sparta said irritably.

"Sorry, I seem to be iterating Eliot this morning. Do I understand you are disappointed that I am not in fact the girl you used to be?"

"I thought if I had them make you like this, maybe we could talk about things the way . . . normal women do."

"Alas, you are not normal, and I am certainly not a woman."

"As you insist on reminding me."

"The part of me you did not design for . . . user-friendliness . . . is a sophisticated ontologist, with many ways of testing what the world is, what a person is, how things are. Granted, the related epistemological questions are subtle, but at least my algorithms are explicit. Because you are who you are, however, you can never fully untangle what you know about the world and about yourself from how you know it."

"I'm no phenomenologist."

"No, and I don't mean to suggest that just because you have a human brain and not an electronic one there is no truth. Or that the universe is not consistent, or doesn't exist independently of your perceptions. I simply mean that—unaided by me or another therapist or teacher—it is doubtful that you, or anyone else, could ever free yourself from the web of your untested, culturally acquired assumptions."

"You haven't answered my question."

"I think I have. It's my job to help you see how things are. To become aware of *who* you are, Linda-Ellen-Sparta."

"We've been at this a year."

"I can hardly blame you for impatience."

"They took that stuff out of my belly. Fine—what do I need with a radio in my belly? As for my *seeing*, I personally killed that with Striaphan. Fine again. Those things were not really me. I feel strong now, I feel well now. Better than ever. But toward . . . oh, *meaning*, I suppose—a purpose of my own, decided on by *me*—what progress have I made?"

"To have completely recovered from your dependency on Striaphan seems like progress to me."

"Yesterday I was walking down by the cliffs, above the river, and I remembered that one of the boys from SPARTA was climbing in the Catskills one summer and the granite gave way beneath him and he fell and was killed. Just like that. And I thought, if that happened to me now, I . . . I wouldn't mind. That would be all right with me. Nothing that needs doing would be left undone."

"Do you miss Blake?"

Sparta nodded. Again the tears pooled in her eyes.

Linda spoke softly. "Perhaps there is something you need to do for your own sake."

From across the room, Sparta studied the simulacrum of her younger self sitting so placidly in the spring sunshine. Her reluctant lips formed a wry smile. "We always get to this place, too."

"What place?"

"Aren't we about to get to the place where you tell me I should talk to my mother?"

"I doubt that I have ever used the word *should*."

"For five years she let me believe she was dead. She tried to talk my father out of telling me the truth," Sparta said angrily. "She gave them permission to *do* this."

"Your reluctance to confront her is easy to understand."

"But you *do* think I should. Whether you use the word or not."

"No." Linda shook her head. The highlights in her brown hair gleamed in the sunlight. "It would be a place to start. But only one of many." The two women watched each other, unmoving, until Linda said, "Are you leaving already? The hour is young."

Sparta took a deep breath and sat down. After a silent moment, they continued their conversation.

2

Around the planet and throughout the solar system, a hundred million people gathered in front of their flatscreens. Only those in Great Britain would receive the final episode of "Overmind" at the comfortable hour of eight in the evening. Others, of whom there were many more—those who chose not to wait for local redistribution at a more convenient time—were fiddling with their satellite antennas as their clocks blinked to 3:22 A.M., or 11:43 P.M., or as close to the moment of original transmission from London as the speed of light allowed.

On the eastern seaboard of North America, it was almost three o'clock on an alternately bright and rainy afternoon, with the sun dodging in and out of the clouds. A tall man in a black leather topcoat mounted the porch of a stone house in the woods. He knocked on the door.

A woman in a wool skirt and leather boots opened the door. "Come inside, Kip, before you catch your death." Ari Nagy was spare and athletic and wore her graying black hair trimmed sensibly at the jaw line. She was among the few who called this man anything except Commander.

He did as she told him, shaking the water from his coat and leaving it hanging on a peg in the hallway beside yellow polycanvas slickers and down-filled parkas. He went into the long living room.

The house was larger than it looked from the outside. Through the windows at the south end of the room, beyond the woods, one could see a stretch of cloud-heavy sky ending in a horizon of low, gray green mountains—a monochrome landscape, punctuated by splashes of yellow forsythia and the pale white promise of dogwood blossoms among wiry wet branches.

Overhead, carved beams reflected warm light from bare planed surfaces; Native American rugs on the plank floor held in the warmth of an oak fire, which burned busily on the fieldstone hearth. The commander walked straight to it and held out his hands to collect the heat.

The woman returned from the kitchen, carrying a tea service. "Black tea? You've been known to have a cup on days like this."

"Thanks." He took a cup of tea from the tray and set it on the mantel; the porcelain saucer grated against the stone. "How'd you know I was coming?" His voice was so low and gravelly, it almost sounded as if it hurt him to speak. With his sun-cured skin and pale blue eyes he could have been a north woods lumberjack or fishing guide; he wore faded denims, and the sleeves of his plaid shirt were rolled back over his strong wrists.

"I called the lodge, looking for Jozsef. I was hoping he'd be with you."

"Soon. He wanted to put his report in the files."

"It's three o'clock. Just like him to miss the program—he thinks the world ought to take his schedule into account."

"We'll replay the important parts for him." He picked up iron tongs and poked fretfully at the burning logs until they crackled with heat.

Ari settled into a leather couch and arranged a red and green plaid blanket over her lap. "Turn on and record," she said in the direction of the pine-paneled wall—

—whereupon a hidden videoplate unfolded into a two-meter-square screen, thin as foil, and immediately brightened. "Good evening," said the voice from the screen, "this is the All Worlds Service of the BBC, bringing you the final program in the series 'Overmind,' presented by Sir Randolph Mays."

The commander looked up from the fire to see Jupiter's clouds filling the screen. Visible in the foreground was a swift, bright spark. "Jupiter's moon Amalthea," came the voice of Randolph Mays, in that half-whisper of suppressed urgency. "For more than a year, the most *unusual* object in our solar system—and the *key* to its central enigma."

Unlike most of the hundred million people watching "Overmind," who were sure their narrator would track down the truth wherever it led—indeed, most who had seen the earlier episodes were hoping Mays would solve "the central enigma of the solar system" this very night, before their eyes—the two watching in the house in the woods were hoping he wouldn't get too close to it.

"Good picture," Ari remarked.

"Heard about it on the way in—it was stolen from a Space Board monitor on Ganymede. Mays had re-edited the opening of his show within the last hour."

"Did someone in the Space Board give it to him?"

"We'll find out."

They watched in silence then, as Sir Randolph recited his litany of coincidences: ". . . events occurring in such far-flung locales as the *hellish* surface of Venus, the *far side* of Earth's moon, the *deserts* of Mars—and not least, at a lavish estate in England's Somerset *countryside*. These and other *impossible* coincidences will be the subject of tonight's program. . . . "

"Oh dear," murmured Ari; under her blanket she hugged herself tighter. "He's going to bring Linda into it after all, I fear."

The commander left off brooding by the fire to take a seat beside her on the couch, facing the screen. "We've put up as high a stone wall as we can."

"How does he know these things?" the woman demanded. "Is he one of them?"

"They're finished—we knew it when we went into Kingman's place and found the destruction."

"But he's spilling secrets they killed to keep."

"Probably the man has his hooks into some poor disillusioned soul who repented and wants to tell all. Whoever it is needs a better confessor."

"No one below the rank of the knights and elders could connect Linda to the Knowledge." Her voice betrayed her fear.

On screen, the title sequence faded. The final episode began. . . .

Sir Randolph Mays was a formerly obscure Cambridge historian whose title derived not from his scholarship but from the lavish charity of his youth, when he had given a good part of his inheritance to his college. Popular with his students, he had become an overnight star, a veritable viddie nova, with his first thirteen-part BBC series, "In Search of the Human Race." Mays had seemed to move through the widespread locations of his show as if stalking elusive prey, gliding on long, corduroy-clad legs past the pillars of Karnak, up the endless stairs of Calakmul, through the jumbled maze of Çatal Hüyük. All the while his great hands sawed the air and, perched atop the neck of his black turtleneck, his square jaw worked to deliver impressively long and vehement sentences. It all made for a wonderful travelogue, thickly slathered over with a sort of intellectual mayonnaise.

Mays took himself quite seriously, of course; he

was nothing if not opinionated. Like Arnold Toynbee and Oswald Spengler before him, he had reduced the whole of human history to a recurrent and predictable pattern. In his view, as in his predecessors', the elements of that pattern were societies having their own life cycles of birth, growth, and death, like organisms. And like organisms—but with the aid of rapid cultural change rather than sluggish biological adaptation—societies evolved, he claimed. Just what human society was evolving toward, he left as an exercise for the viewer to determine.

The historical and ethnographic establishments assailed him for his primitive ideas, his dubious interpretations of fact, his loose definitions (What distinguished one society from another? Why, for Mays, did Jews constitute a society wherever they lived but not, for example, expatriate Hungarians?), but a dozen eminent scholars mumbling in their dewlaps were not enough to deflate public enthusiasm. Randolph Mays had something better than academic approval, something better than logic; he had an almost hypnotic presence.

That first series ran to numerous repeat screenings and set record videochip sales; the BBC begged him for another. Mays obliged with the proposal for "Overmind."

The proposal gave even its BBC sponsors initial pause, for in it Mays set out to prove that the rise and fall of civilizations were not, after all, a matter of chance evolution. According to him, a superior intelligence had guided the process, an intelligence not necessarily human, which was represented on Earth by an ancient, most secret cult.

The first dozen programs of "Overmind" adduced evidence for the cult's existence in ancient glyphs and carvings and papyrus scrolls, in the alignments of ancient architecture and the narratives of ancient myth. It was a good story, persuasive to those who wanted to believe. Even unbelievers were amused and entertained.

As Mays knew, and as his immense audience was about to find out, tonight's episode went well beyond ancient texts and artifacts. It brought Grand Conspiracy into the present day.

But Randolph Mays was nothing if not a shrewd showman. His viewers were forced to sit through almost the whole ensuing hour of review, during which Mays rehearsed all the evidence he had developed in preceding weeks, thriftily using the same locations and replaying bits of preceding shows; only the skeptic viewer would have noted that his thesis was thus reduced from thirteen hours to one.

Finally he came to his point. "They *called* themselves the Free Spirit, and by a dozen *other* names," Mays asserted—appearing in person now, close up, swiping at the air. "*These* people were almost certainly among them."

The next image was static, taken by a photogram camera: a fit but aging English gentleman in tweeds stood in front of a massive stone house, a shotgun crooked in his arm. His free hand stroked an aviator's flamboyant mustaches.

"Rupert, Lord Kingman, heir to ancient St. Joseph's Hall, *director* of a dozen firms—including Sadler's Bank of Delhi—who has not been *seen* for three years . . ."

Next, a woman with sleek black hair and painted red lips glared at the camera from astride a sweating polo pony, its bridle held by a turbaned Sikh.

"Holly Singh, M.D., Ph.D., chief of neurophysiology at the Board of Space Control's Biological Medicine Center, who *disappeared* at precisely the same time as Lord Kingman . . ."

Next the screen showed a tall, lugubrious man whose fine blond hair fell across his forehead.

"Professor Albers Merck, noted xeno-archaeologist,

who attempted to *murder* his colleague, Professor J.Q.R. Forster—and in the same attempt killed *himself*. He failed to kill Forster, of course; he *succeeded*, however, in destroying the unique Venusian fossils housed on Port Hesperus. . . ."

Next, a publicity still showed two strapping big blond young people in technicians' smocks, smiling at the camera from their instrument consoles.

"Also on the same date, astronomers Piet Gress and Katrina Balakian both committed suicide after *failing* to destroy the radiotelescope facility at Farside Base on the moon. . . ."

Next, a square-built man with a sandy crewcut, wearing a pinstripe suit: he was caught scowling over his shoulder as he climbed into a helicopter on a Manhattan rooftop.

"And again on the same date, the Martian plaque *disappeared* from the town hall of Labyrinth City on Mars. Two men were killed. Later the plaque was *recovered* on the Martian moon Phobos. Within hours, Mr. John Noble, founder and chief executive of Noble Water Works of Mars, whose space plane was used in the attempted theft, *vanished* and has been *missing* ever since. . . ."

The next image was not of a person but a spacecraft, the freighter *Doradus*. The camera slowly tracked the big white freighter where it lay impounded in the Space Board yards in Earth orbit.

"This is the *Doradus*, whose crew attempted to remove the Martian plaque from Phobos—it was called a pirate ship by the media, but I assert that the *Doradus* was in fact a Free Spirit warship—although the Space Board would have us believe the vessel's true ownership has never been *traced* farther than a bank. Yes, Sadler's Bank of Delhi . . ."

When the next image came on the screen, Ari put a hand on the commander's arm—giving support, or seeking it.

"Inspector Ellen Troy of the Board of Space Control," Mays reminded his audience, although there could have been few who did not recognize the woman's picture. "Not long ago, a household name because of her extraordinary exploits. *She* it was who rescued Forster and Merck from certain death on the surface of Venus. *She* it was who prevented the destruction of Farside Base, and *she* who snatched the Martian plaque from the grasp of *Doradus*. Then she too *vanished*—to reappear, under circumstances that have never been explained, at the very moment of the *Kon-Tiki* mutiny—only to vanish again. Where is she now?"

The haunting image of Amalthea reappeared on the screen; in Jupiter's reflected light, the moon was swathed in mist the color of buttermilk.

"The Space Board have declared an absolute *quarantine* within 50,000 kilometers of the orbit of Amalthea. The only exception granted is on behalf of *this* man, of whom we have already heard so much."

The media had often described J.Q.R. Forster as a banty rooster, but the newsbite Mays showed of him made him look like a jaunty miniature astronaut, breezily bounding up the steps of the Council of Worlds headquarters in Manhattan, ignoring the mediahounds who pursued him.

"Professor Forster is now on Ganymede Base, in the final stages of preparation for his expedition to Amalthea—an expedition *approved* by the Space Board only a few short months *before* that moon revealed its idiosyncratic nature."

Sir Randolph returned to the screen in person. For a moment he was quiet, as if gathering his thoughts. It was a bold actor's moment, showing his mastery of the medium, focussing the attention of an enormous audience on his next words.

He leaned forward. "Is Inspector Ellen Troy there too, on Ganymede, a part of Forster's plan?"

He lowered his voice further, as if to force his

watchers to lean even closer, his huge hands pulling at the air with spread fingers to draw them further into his intimate net. "Is Amalthea the focus of centuries of Free Spirit scheming? Is the mighty Board of Space Control itself a party to this grand conspiracy? I believe so, and though I cannot *prove* it tonight"—Mays drew back, straightening his gaunt frame—"I give you my word of honor that I will discover the common thread that links these events which I have brought to your attention. And having done so, I shall *expose* these ancient secrets to the light of reason."

Ari said, "Turn off," her voice loud in the quiet cabin. As the final credits were rolling up the screen, the image faded to black and the videoplate folded itself into the paneled wall.

Rain fell steadily on the porch roof; brick-red coals crumbled in the fireplace. The commander broke the silence. "A bit anticlimactic."

"He got one thing wrong, at least," Ari said. She didn't have to say what she meant: Ellen Troy was not on Amalthea.

Footsteps scraped on the boards of the porch. The commander stood up, alert. Ari threw her lap robe aside and went to open the door.

3

The man who came into the room was damp and tweedy; his thinning gray hair stuck out in wet clumps, giving him the look of a baby bird just emerged from the egg. He gathered Ari into his arms and hugged her enthusiastically; she laughed and stroked his wet hair. They were not much alike, but they looked well together, he in his tweeds and she in her flannel. They'd been married for decades.

"Something to warm you, Jozsef? We are having tea."

"Thank you. Kip has told you of our adventures?"

"Not yet," said the commander.

"We watched Mays pontificate. The final episode of 'Overmind.' "

"Oh no, am I so late?" Jozsef was stricken.

"When has it been otherwise?" Ari said. "Don't worry, I recorded it."

"A waste of your time," said the commander.

Jozsef sat heavily on the couch. Ari handed him a cup and moved the tea tray to the low pine table in front of him. "Except for one thing. Mays has connected Linda with the Free Spirit."

"With Salamander?"

"He doesn't know anything about Salamander," said the commander.

"It's all speculation," Ari agreed.

"Nevertheless he'll be on his way to Amalthea on *Helios*, to poke around."

"You can confirm that?" Jozsef asked the commander, who nodded. Jozsef slurped a mouthful of the hot tea and carefully resettled the cup on its saucer. "Well, it can hardly make a significant difference. Half the reporters in the solar system, it seems, are already there, eager for news."

Ari settled beside him and rested her hand on his knee. "Tell me about your trip."

"It was quite wonderful." Jozsef's eyes lit with enthusiasm. "If I were a jealous man, I should be jealous that Forster came unaided to his great discoveries. He fired me with his own enthusiasm—I believe he is a *heroic* figure."

"He was hardly unaided." Ari was defensive on her husband's behalf. "You—and Kip and I—have been of critical help to him."

"Yes, but he had nothing like the Knowledge to guide him. By himself he deciphered the Venusian tablets, and then the Martian plaque—and from that he deduced the nature of Amalthea."

"Its presumed nature," said Ari.

"All without hints from any ancient secrets," Jozsef insisted, "which confirms our own belief that the truth needs no secrets."

Ari looked uncomfortable, but like the commander she said nothing, unwilling to contradict Jozsef's version of the creed.

"But let me tell you what I saw," Jozsef said, recovering his enthusiasm. He settled himself deeper into the couch cushions and began to speak in the relaxed manner of a professor opening a weekly seminar.

"What we North Continentals call Ganymede is popularly known to those who live there as Shoreless Ocean, a poetic way of referring to a moon whose surface consists almost entirely of frozen water. The same name applies to Ganymede City, and it's written over the pressure portals in half a dozen languages. I was in trouble almost before I'd gotten through the gates.

"As I left the formalities at entry control—all on my own, and somewhat bewildered—a strange young Asian persistently beckoned to me from beyond the barrier. His eyes showed a pronounced epicanthic fold, his hair was glossy black, pulled straight back into a ponytail that reached below his waist, and he was sporting quite a diabolical mustache. With that and his costume of tunic and trousers and soft boots, he could have been Temujin, the young Genghis Kahn. I tried to ignore him, but once I was through the gates he followed me through the crowd, until I turned on him and loudly demanded to know what he wanted.

"He made noises about being the best and least expensive guide a stranger to Shoreless Ocean could find, but between these declarations—for the benefit of the people around us—he commanded me in an urgent whisper to stop drawing attention to myself.

"As you have guessed, it was Blake. His remarkable disguise was necessary because, as he picturesquely phrased it, a pack of newshounds had driven Professor Forster and his colleagues to ground and now kept them in their den. Blake, being the only one of them who could speak Chinese, was the only one who could move freely in the town.

"I had thought I would need no disguise, of course; no one had the slightest idea who I was or how I had got here, the Board of Space Control having smoothed my passage. Blake took my luggage—which weighed very little, for although Ganymede is larger than Earth's moon it is still less massive than a planet.

"The city of Shoreless Ocean is less than a century old but appears as exotic—and as crowded—as Varanasi or Calcutta. We were soon lost in the crush. After pushing through corridors which, as it seemed to me, became narrower and louder and smellier with every turn, it was all I could do to keep up with Blake, and I suspect he became somewhat exasperated with me. He hailed a pedicab and whispered something to the rangy boy who drove it. Blake pushed my bags into it, then me, and said he would meet me where the cab let me off; I need say nothing to the driver, for the fare had already been arranged.

'The cab took me through corridors which grew rapidly less crowded as we moved away from the commercial and residential quarters of the city. A final long run down a dim, cold tunnel—whose walls, seen through bundles of shining pipe, were slick with ice—brought me to my destination, a plain plastic door in a plain plastic wall with a single caged red light burning above it. There was nothing to indicate what sort of place this might be, except that it had some industrial purpose. As soon as I got myself and my luggage out of the cab the boy pedaled away, blowing his breath in clouds before him, anxious to be out of the cold.

"I shivered alone for several minutes, peering about me at the vast steel manifolds that formed the ceiling and walls of the ill-lit tunnel. Finally the door opened.

"Blake had brought me a heavy parka. Once I was dressed for the cold he led me inside the plant, along clacking plastic-mesh catwalks and up ladders, through other doors, other rooms. Pressure hatches and sealed doorways warned of possible vacuum, but our route had been fully pressurized.

"Through a little hatch we entered a huge drain-

pipe of shiny metal, titanium alloy by the look of
it, and climbing up I found that we were in a cav-
ernous space, bizarrely sculpted into what seemed
like a great curving watercourse of black ice. I was
reminded of the dripping ice caves that feed streams
running beneath glaciers, like those I entered on the
alpine treks of my youth, or of a polished limestone
cave, the bed of an underground river. Unlike a gla-
cial cave, these ice walls did not radiate the brilliant
blue of filtered sunlight, nor did their frozen surfaces reflect the warmth of smooth limestone, but
instead absorbed all the light that fell upon them,
sucking it into their colorless depths.

"We clambered over the scalloped edges of a frozen waterfall into a bell-shaped hall, and suddenly
I understood that the cavern had not been carved
out by running water, but by fire and superheated
steam. We were inside the thrust-deflection chamber
of a surface launch facility. Its walls, fantastically
swashed by repeated bursts of exploding gases, were
draped in veils and curtains of transparent ice.

"High above us the pressure dome was sealed,
trapping air and cutting off any view of the bright
stars and moons and the disk of Jupiter. Inside the
dome, lowering over our heads like a stormcloud
made of steel, was a Jovian tug. The vessel squatted
on sturdy struts and was webbed about with gantries, but what commanded my gaze were the triple
nozzles of the main rocket engines and the three
bulging spherical fuel tanks clustered around them.

"Beneath this intimation of the refiner's fire—this
sword of Damocles poised to flash downward—
stood Professor J.Q.R. Forster and his crew, bundled against the cold. Over titanium deflection
scoops a scaffold of carbon struts and planks had
been erected; tool benches and racks of electronics
stood about, and someone had draped a large hardcopy schematic over a lathe. As Blake brought me
into their midst, Forster and his people were bent

over this diagram in spirited discussion, like a Shakespearean king and his lords debating their battle plan.

"Forster turned on me almost fiercely—but I quickly realized he was displaying a smile, not a grimace. I was familiar with holos of him, of course, but since Kip had thought it wise to keep us from meeting before this moment, I was unprepared for the man's energy. He has the face and body of a thirty-five-year-old, a man in his prime—a result of the restoration they did on him after Merck's attempt on his life—but I venture that his authority stems mainly from the experience gained whipping several decades' worth of graduate students into line.

"He introduced me to his crew as if each were a mythic hero: Josepha Walsh, pilot, an unruffled young woman seconded from the Space Board; Angus McNeil, engineer, a shrewd and portly fellow who studied me as if reading gauges inside my head; Tony Groves, the dark little navigator who had steered Springer to his brief, glorious rendezvous with Pluto. I solemnly shook hands with them all. All of them are as well known in their own circles as Forster in his—and none of them is Asian—and therefore all are sentenced to shiver in hiding so long as Forster wishes to avoid the press.

"Indeed, when I remarked on the tortuous paths through which Blake had led me to reach him and asked why he didn't simply place himself under the protection of the Board of Space Control, Forster told me that the launch pad we stood in was actually inside the Board's surface perimeter, but that he did not wish his connection with the Board generally known. It was enough that he and he alone had been granted a permit to explore Amalthea, and that the Space Board were still honoring it despite the subsequent spectacular events there. Professor Forster left many things unsaid, but it was clear to me that—with the possible exception of you, Kip—he trusts no one in the bureaucracy. We broke off then, deferring a deeper conversation until later.''

Jozsef paused in his narrative. Ari leaned forward to pour more tea for the three of them. Jozsef sipped thoughtfully, then continued.

''Forster's camp inside the ice cave resembled that of a military expedition preparing for battle. The pit was piled high with supplies and equipment—food, gas bottles, instruments, fuel tanks—most of it intended for an unmounted strap-on cargo hold, still at ground level and split open like an empty sardine tin. Blake showed me where I was to stay: it was a foam hut built against the wall of the blast chamber, quite warm inside despite its primitive appearance. Not long afterward the work lights dimmed, indicating the approach of night.

''In the largest temporary shelter, the quartermaster's hut, I joined the little group for a European-style dinner, accented by selections from Professor Forster's excellent store of wines—and quickly learned to appreciate Walsh's wry wit, Groves's penchant for debate (learning that I was a psychologist, he was eager to take me on about the latest theories of the unconscious, of which he knew very little—but still more than I, since you and I gave the subject up as hopeless, Ari, twenty years ago), and McNeil's astounding store of salacious gossip (the man may be a noted engineer, but he has the tastes and narrative gifts of a Boccaccio).

''After dinner, Forster and I went alone to his hut. There, after I had sworn him to secrecy—over glasses of his superb Napoleon brandy—I brought out the holo projector and revealed to him what we had prepared: the distillation of the Knowledge.

''He watched without comment. He has had a lifetime's practice defending his academic priority. Nevertheless, he showed less surprise than I might have expected; he told me that he had had glimmerings of the truth as long ago as the discovery of the Martian plaque—long before he had managed to decipher its meaning, long before it was possible to know anything at all about its makers, which he himself had first dubbed Culture X.

"The conventional theory—intentionally promulgated, as we know, by the Free Spirit—was that Culture X had evolved on Mars and had died out a billion years ago, when the brief Martian summer ended. Forster's ideas were different, and far more ambitious: he was convinced that Culture X had entered the solar system from interstellar space. The fact that no one else believed this annoyed him, though not very much, for he is one of those people who seem happiest when in the minority.

"When he learned that an Ishtar Mining Corporation robot had stumbled into an alien cache on Venus, with great energy and dedication he organized an expedition to explore and if possible retrieve the finds. Although his mission was cut short and the material artifacts still rest buried on Venus, he came back with the records"—Jozsef paused and allowed himself a small smile—"I'm retelling these events as I think he views them—at any rate, less than a year elapsed before he proved that the Venusian tablets were translations of texts dating from Earth's Bronze Age. He was now convinced that representatives of Culture X had visited all the inner planets, had perhaps tried to colonize them.

"Shortly thereafter he was able to apply his translation of the Venusian tablets to a reading of the Martian plaque, with its references to 'cloud-dwelling messengers' and a 'reawakening at the great world.' Thus through his own research he skipped over millenniums of our hoarded secrecy, arriving instantly at a very substantial part of the Knowledge.

"But logic suggested to him—and *Kon-Tiki* later

proved—that the clouds of Jupiter, the 'great world,' could hide no creatures capable of having fabricated the material of which the Venusian tablets and the Martian plaque were made, much less of doing the great deeds the plaque commemorates. And decades of on-site exploration of Jupiter's satellites had uncovered no trace of a past alien presence.

"Despite this, Professor Forster told me, a single clue convinced him that a more thorough search of one of Jupiter's moon was justified: it had long been observed that Amalthea radiated almost one third more energy into space than it absorbed from the sun and Jupiter together. It had been assumed that bombardment from Jupiter's intense radiation belts made up the deficit, but Forster looked up the records and noted that, when the radiation flux had been accounted for, a discrepancy at radio wavelengths remained—duly noted by planetary scientists but small enough to be ignored as uninteresting, much as the precession of the orbit of Mercury was considered a minor anomaly, not a threat to Newton, until Einstein's theory of gravitation retroactively yielded its precise quantitative value two centuries later.

"Then the medusas of Jupiter sang their song, and Amalthea erupted. With characteristic spirit, Forster insisted upon pressing ahead with his exploration as already planned and approved, without announcing any design changes that might require bureaucratic meddling. He did make some design changes en route to Ganymede, however, and when I met with him three weeks ago, he and his crew were beginning to implement them—clandestinely.

"What I had to tell him confirmed the correctness of his vision and underscored the need for the changes he had already made in his mission plan. But of course, the Knowledge implies more. . . ."

Ari could not contain her distress. "It implies that any attempt to proceed without Linda will meet with disaster."

"So I told Professor Forster, and he did not deny the force of the evidence," Jozsef replied quietly. "Nevertheless he is determined to go ahead, with or without her."

"Then he—and all of them, Blake Redfield with them—are doomed to death and worse. He must be stopped . . . that was why you went to Ganymede, Jozsef! Why did you so easily allow him to dissuade you?" But Jozsef returned her demanding stare with nothing better than soft-eyed resignation. "Kip—*you* can stop him," she said.

"Not even if I wanted to."

"*If* . . . ?" Ari looked at him in despairing unbelief.

"Ari, the Space Board hasn't the will or—so the people in the line departments claim—the resources to maintain the quarantine of Amalthea much longer. The Indo-Asians are applying tremendous pressure at Council level." He sighed impatiently. "They talk about safety, about energy resources, even about basic science. Meanwhile they're counting lost tourist dollars."

"What does that have to do with Forster?" she demanded.

"He's got a narrow window of opportunity. With or without Ellen—Linda, I mean—somebody's going to land on Amalthea. And soon."

"We'd rather it be Forster," Jozsef said. "All of us would, I think."

"No." Ari stiffened. "Not without her."

"But that's not . . ." Jozsef cleared his throat noisily and left the sentence unfinished.

The commander said it for him. "That's up to her, Ari. Not you."

4

Blake Redfield forced his way through crowded winding corridors, past stalls selling carved jade and translucent rubber sandals in the many colors of jujubes, past shelves of bargain-priced surveillance electronics, past racks of spot-lit fresh-killed ducks with heads and feet attached—while people pushed him from behind, elbowed him aside, and blocked the way in front of him, none maliciously or even with much force, for gravity here was a few percent of Earth's and too vigorous a shove was as awkward for the shover as for the shovee. More people sat huddled in circles on the floor throwing dice or playing *hsiang-ch'i* or stood bargaining excitedly before tanks of live trout and mounds of ice clams and piles of pale, wilted vegetables. Students and old folk peered at real paper books through thick rimless glasses and read flimsy newspapers printed in what to most Euro-Americans were indecipherable squiggles. Everyone was talking, talking, talking in musical tones most North Continental visitors heard only as singsong and jabber.

Usually auburn-haired—even handsome, in a fresh-faced, freckled way—Blake had disguised himself well, looking less like young Ghengis Khan than a Pearl River dock rat. He was in fact half Chinese on his mother's side, the other half being Irish, and although he did not know more than a few useful phrases of Burmese or Thai or any of the dozens of other Indochinese languages common on Ganymede, he spoke eloquent Mandarin and expressively earthy Cantonese—the latter being the favorite trade language of most of the ethnic Chinese who made up a substantial proportion of the Shoreless Ocean's non-Indian population.

From the low overheads hung paper banners which fluttered endlessly in the breeze of constantly turning ventilator fans; these did their inadequate best to clear the corridors of the smell of pork frying in rancid oil and other, less palatable odors. The stall owners had rigged up awnings against the flickering yellow glare of the permanent lighting; the awnings billowed ceaselessly, waves in an unquiet sea of cloth. Blake pushed ahead, against the tide. His destination was the contracting firm of Lim and Sons, founded in Singapore in 1946. The Shoreless Ocean branch had opened in 2068, before there was a sizable settlement on Ganymede; a generation of Lims had helped build the place.

The firm's offices fronted on the chaotic intersection of two busy corridors near the center of the underground city. Behind a wall of plate glass bearing the gold-painted ideograms for health and prosperity, shirt-sleeved, bespectacled clerks bent studiously to their flatscreens.

Blake stepped through the automatic door; abruptly the corridor sounds were sealed out, and there was quiet. No one paid him any attention. He leaned over the rail that separated the carpeted reception area from the nearest clerk and said in careful Mandarin, "My name is Redfield. I have a ten o'clock appointment with Luke Lim."

The clerk winced as if he'd had a gas attack. Without bothering to look at Blake he keyed his commlink and said, in rapid Cantonese, "A white guy dressed like a coolie is out here, talking like he just took Mandarin 101. Says he has an appointment with Luke.''

The commlink squawked back, loud enough for Blake to overhear. ''See what happens if you tell him to wait.''

''You wait,'' said the clerk in English, still not looking up.

There were no chairs for visitors. Blake walked over to the wall and studied the gaudy color holos hanging there, some stiff family portraits and wide-angle views of construction projects. In one, pipes as tangled as a package of dry noodles sprawled over a kilometer of surface ice; it was a dissociation plant, converting water ice to hydrogen and oxygen. Other holos showed ice mines, distilleries, sewage plants, hydroponic farms.

Blake wondered what role Lim and Sons had played in the construction of these impressive facilities; the holos were uncaptioned, allowing the viewer to assume anything he or she wished. Unlikely that Lim and Sons had been principal contractor in any of them. But one in particular captured his attention: it depicted a big-toothed ice mole cutting through black ice, drilling what was presumably one of the original tunnels of the settlement that had become Shoreless Ocean.

For twenty minutes Blake patiently cooled his heels. Finally the clerk keyed the link and muttered ''Still standing here . . . no, seems happy as a clam.''

Another five minutes passed. A man appeared at the back of the room and came to the railing, hand extended. ''Luke Lim. So sorry, Mr. Redfield''— *Ruke Rim. So solly, Missa Ledfeared*—''Most unavoidably detained.'' Lim was tall even for the low gravity of Ganymede, almost emaciated, with sunken cheeks and burning eyes. On the point of his chin a dozen or so very long, very black hairs managed to suggest a goatee. Unlike his facial hair the hair of his head was thick and glossy, long and black, hanging to his shoulders. He had inch-long nails on the thumb and fingers of his right hand, but the nails of his left were cut short. He was wearing blue canvas work pants and a shirt patterned like mattress-ticking.

"No problem," said Blake coolly, giving the outstretched hand, the dangerous one, a single short jerk. A curious fellow, thought Blake: his accent was as phony as they come, straight out of an ancient Charlie Chan movie-chip; the fingernails were not a Mandarin affectation but apparently for playing twelve-string guitar, and the work clothes suggested that the guy wanted to present himself as a man of the working class.

"So glad you not in big hurry," said Lim.

"You have something to show me?"

"Yes." Lim's voice was suddenly low and conspiratorial, his expression almost a leer. "You come with me now?" Ostentatiously, he held the gate of the railing open and waved Blake through it.

Blake followed him to the back of the office and into a low dark passageway. He caught glimpses of small, dim rooms on either side, crowded with men and women bent over machine tools.

A slow ride in a big freight elevator brought them out into a huge service bay, its floor and walls carved from ancient ice. The excavation of the bay wasn't finished; there was a hole in a sunken corner of the floor as big as a storm drain, to carry off the melt as ice was carved away.

In the middle of the bay, inadequately lit by overhead sodium units, a spidery flatbed trailer supported a big load, securely tied down and wrapped in blue canvas. "There it is," Lim said to Blake, not bothering to move from where he was standing by the elevator.

Two middle-aged women bundled thickly into insulated overalls looked up from the engine of a surface crawler; most of the machine was in pieces, scattered over the ice. "One of the rectifiers in that thing is still intermittent, Luke," said one of the women in Cantonese. "Supply is supposed to send a rebuild over this afternoon."

"How long can this one run?" Lim asked her.

"An hour or two. Then it overheats."

"Tell Supply to forget it," Lim said.

"If your customer wants to take delivery . . ."

"Ignore the foreigner, go back to work," Lim said, his breath steaming in the orange light.

Blake went to the flatbed and released the tie-down catches. He yanked at the canvas, patiently circling the rig until he had all the cloth piled on the floor. The machinery thus revealed was a cylinder compounded of metal alloy rings, girdled by a universal mount and carried on cleated treads; its business end consisted of two offset wheels of wide, flat titanium teeth, each cutting edge glistening with a thin film of diamond.

An ice mole—but despite its impressive size, it was a mere miniature of the one Blake had seen pictured on the office wall.

Blake jumped lightly onto the flatbed. He pulled a tiny black torch from his hip pocket and switched on its brilliant white light; from his shirt pocket he took magnifying goggles and slipped them on. For several minutes he crawled over the machine, opening every access port, inspecting circuits and control boards. He checked bearing alignments and looked for excessive wear. He pulled panels off and studied the windings and connections of the big motors.

Finally he jumped down and walked back to Lim. "Nothing visibly broken. But it's as old as I am, seen a lot of use. Maybe thirty years."

"For the price you want to pay, surplus is what you get."

"Where's the power supply?"

"You pay extra for that."

"When somebody tells me 'like new,' Mr. Lim, I don't think they mean thirty years old. Everything made in this line in the last decade has built-in power supply."

"You want it or not?"

"With power supply."

"No problem. You pay five hundred IA credits extra."

"Would that be new? Or 'like new'?"

"Guaranteed like new."

Blake translated the figure into dollars. "For that much I can buy new off the shelf in the Mainbelt."

"You want to wait three months? Pay freight?"

Blake let the rhetorical question pass unanswered. "How do I know this thing isn't going to break down as soon as we get it to Amalthea?"

"Like I say, guaranteed."

"Meaning what?"

"We send someone to fix. Free labor."

Blake seemed to consider that a moment. Then he said, "Let's take it for a test drive."

Lim looked pained. "Maybe too much to do this week."

"Right now. We'll add some space to your work area here."

"Not possible."

"Sure it is. I'll borrow the power supply and commlink from that crawler"—he indicated the machine parts scattered on the floor—"since nobody's going to need them for a while." Blake picked his away among the scattered parts in the corner; he hefted one of the massive but lightweight units, jumped onto the trailer, lifted a cowl, and wrestled it into place.

The women, who hadn't really been concentrating on their work, now watched Blake openly—meanwhile trying to remain impassive, with cautious and uncertain glances at Lim. Reluctantly, as if he were playing without enthusiasm a role that required him to come up with some protest, however feeble, Lim said, "You can't just do what you want with our . . . this equipment."

Blake ignored him. He took a pair of heavy rubber-insulated cables from a spring-loaded spool on the wall and shoved their flat, copper-sheathed heads into a receptacle in the rear of the mole; he locked them in place. Then he slipped into the mole's cockpit and spent a moment fiddling with the controls. With a whine of heavy motors, the machine came to life, its red warning beacon whirling and flashing. The warning horn hooted repeatedly as it backed off the trailer on its clattering cleats. Blake pushed the levers ahead and the mole moved toward a blank spot in the wall of ice.

Lim watched all this as if stupefied, before shaking himself to action. "Hey! Wait a minute!"

"Climb on, if you're coming!" Blake shouted, slowing the machine's wall-ward progress long enough for Lim to scramble up the side of the machine and sling himself into the open cockpit. The door sealed itself behind him; Blake checked the dashboard to see that the little compartment was sealed and pressurized. Then he shoved the potentiometers forward again, all the way to the stops.

Transformers sang; the giant bits on the mole's nose spun in a blur of counter-rotating blades. Blake drove the machine squarely into the ice, and there was a sudden screech and rumble; ice chips exploded in an opaque blizzard outside the cockpit's cylindrical polyglas window.

Inside the machine, the air was rank with ozone. False color displays on the dashboard showed a three-dimensional map of the machine's position, built from stored data and updated with feedback from the seismic vibrations generated by the whirling bit. The void in the ice they were enlarging was at the edge of the settlement, only twenty meters below the mean surface, and adjacent to the spaceport. The dashboard map displayed the region of ice beneath the port in bright red, with a legend in bold letters: RESTRICTED AREA.

The machine moved ahead, shuddering and plunging toward the red barrier at top speed—which for the old machine was a respectable three kilometers per hour. Unseen by the riders, a river of melted ice flowed out the rear of the machine and through the tunnel behind them, to pour down the drain.

"Watch where you go." Lim's accent showed signs of slipping. "Cross that barrier, the Space Board impounds us."

"I'll turn here, take the long way back. Let's see how it holds together after an hour or so."

"Must go back *now*."

Blake pulled back on one of the potentiometer levers and the machine skewed, skittering and squirming like a hand drill with a dull bit. "Thing bucks like a wild horse—kind of hard to steer. Say, you smell something hot?"

"Don't turn so hard," Lim said in alarm. "Not good to abuse fine equipment."

A panel light on the dashboard began to glow, dull yellow at first, then bright orange.

"Looks like we're overloading something," Blake observed equably.

"Go slow, go slow!" Lim shouted. "We'll be stranded!"

"Okay." Blake straightened the machine and eased off the drilling rate. The overload warning light dimmed. "Tell me about that guarantee again."

"You see yourself, if not abused, machine in very good condition. It breaks, you bring it in and we fix."

"No, I'll tell you what, if it breaks out there on Amalthea we'll come get your top mechanic. We'll take that person and whatever parts we need back with us, right then. You pay for everything, including the fuel." Fuel was gold in the Jupiter system; because of the depth of the giant planet's gravitational well, the delta-vees between Ganymede and Amalthea were practically the same as between Earth and Venus.

Lim's nervous expression vanished. He glared at the man beside him, no more than a few centimeters away. "You not stupid, so you must be crazy."

Blake smiled. In fluent Cantonese he said, "Besides an intermittent rectifier, what else did your mechanics find wrong with this bucket?"

Lim snorted in surprise.

"Answer my questions, Mr. Lim, or you can look for somewhere else to unload this antique."

Caught out, Lim looked as if he might just throw a temper tantrum and let the deal go. Then, suddenly, his extravagant features stretched themselves into a gleeful grin. "Aieeee! You one foxy character, Led-feared. I lose much face."

"And you can drop the Number One Son accent. I don't want to get the idea you're making fun of me."

"Hey, I *am* my daddy's number one son. But never mind, I take your point. My people will tell your people whatever you want to know. If anything needs fixing we'll fix it." Lim leaned back in his seat, obviously relieved. "But then you sign off. And we forget all this nonsense about guarantees. And rocket fuel."

"Okay with me," Blake said.

"Take me back to the office. You can write me a check and drive away."

"Throw in the power supply?"

Lim sighed mightily. "The white devil is merciless." But in fact he seemed to be taking pleasure in Blake's hard-nosed attitude. "Okay, you win. Get us back in one piece, I'll even take you to lunch."

* * *

Late the same evening, Blake returned to the Forster expedition's secret camp under the ice.

The rocket nozzles of the ship that would carry them to Amalthea loomed over them, beneath the frozen dome. Forster had leased the heavy tug for the duration; he couldn't legally change its registration, but he could call it anything he wanted. He had named it the *Michael Ventris* after his hero, the Englishman who'd been the co-decipherer of Minoan Linear B and who'd tragically been killed at the age of thirty-four, not long after his philological triumph.

The uneven icy floor of the exhaust-deflection chamber was less cluttered than it had been a few weeks earlier, when Professor Nagy had paid Professor Forster a visit. By now the cargo needed for the month-long expedition had been loaded and the clip-on cargo hold secured to the frame of the big tug. The equipment bay still stood open and empty, however. There was room in it for the ice mole and more.

Blake knocked at the door of Forster's foam hut. "It's Blake."

"Come in, please." Forster looked up from the flatscreen he'd been studying as Blake ducked into the hut. He peered shrewdly at Blake and knew the news was good. "Success, I assume."

Blake's expression sagged only slightly; he wished Forster wouldn't *assume* so easily. Finding and leasing a working ice mole, and keeping the search reasonably confidential, was not so straightforward that success could be *assumed* in advance.

But Blake had been successful, after all, and Forster—who looked only a few years older than Blake, but who had actually been at this game for decades—was accustomed to compromise and improvisation and had probably developed a sixth sense for the problems that were really hard and the ones that only seemed that way. "Lim's machine will do the job," Blake acknowledged.

"Any particular problems?"

"Lim tried to cheat me. . . ."

Forster frowned, affronted.

"So I asked him to be our agent."

"You did what?" One of Forster's bushy brows shot up.

Good, that got a rise out of him. Blake smiled— mild enough revenge for Forster's assumptions. "We played a little game of bargaining. He played by the rules, so I decided to trust him to help us locate the other machine. He's got unique contacts in the community. My problem is that, even though I can pass, nobody knows who I am. That's what's taken me so long to get this far."

"Sorry if I've been presumptuous." Forster had finally heard some of his young colleague's hitherto unstated frustration. "You've been carrying a heavy load. As soon as it's safe for the rest of us to show our faces, we'll be able to relieve you."

"I won't count on any help until the day we blast off, then," Blake said, smiling wryly. "According to my informants, guess who's about to descend on us from *Helios.*"

Forster's cheerful expression folded into gloom. "Oh dear."

" 'Fraid so. Sir Randolph-Call-Me-Arnold-Toynbee-Mays."

5

After weeks in space, planetfall. The
great fusion-powered passenger liner
Helios, all its portholes and glassy
promenades ablaze, was inserting itself
by the gentlest of nudges into parking
orbit around Ganymede.

And in the Centrifugal Lounge, a celebration: passengers chattering at each other, drinking from tall
flutes of golden champagne, some of them dancing
tipsily to the music of the ship's orchestra. Randolph Mays was there, although he firmly believed
no one recognized him or even knew he'd been
among them, for it suited him to travel incognito—
as he had been since before *Helios* had left Earth—
thus to see but not be seen. He was one of those
men who liked to watch.

And to listen. The curve of the Centrifugal
Lounge's floor-walls, designed to maintain a comfortable half-g of artificial gravity for the comfort of
the passengers, also made a good, quasi-parabolic
reflector of sound waves. People standing opposite
each other in the cylindrical room—thus upside
down with respect to each other—could hear one
another's conversations with perfect clarity.

Randolph Mays craned his neck back and peered
upward at a striking young woman, Marianne
Mitchell, who stood momentarily alone directly

over his head. A few meters away a young man, Bill Hawkins, was trying to work up his nerve to approach her.

She was certainly the prettiest woman on the ship, slender, dark-haired, green-eyed, her full lips glossy with bold red lipstick. For his part, Hawkins too was passably attractive, tall and broad-shouldered, with thick blond hair slicked straight back—but he lacked confidence. He'd managed no more than a few inconsequential conversations with Marianne in weeks of opportunity. Now his time was short—he would be leaving *Helios* at Ganymede—and he seemed to be trying to make up his mind to have one last go at it.

Through one of the thick curving windows that formed the floor, Marianne watched as, far below, the Ganymede spaceport swung into view on the icy plains of the Shoreless Ocean. Beneath her feet paraded what seemed like miniature control towers, pressurized storage sheds, communications masts and dishes, spherical fuel tanks, gantries for the shuttles that plied between the surface and the interplanetary ships that parked in orbit—the practical clutter that any working port required, not much different from Cayley or Farside on Earth's moon.

She let out a disconsolate sigh. "It looks like New Jersey."

"Beg pardon?" Bill Hawkins had lifted a bottle of champagne and two glasses from a circulating waiter and, having detached himself from the knot of partygoers, was finally moving toward her.

"Talking to myself," said Marianne.

"Can't believe my luck, finding you alone."

"Well, now I'm not alone." Her cheer seemed forced. What was there to say to him? Aside from the obligatory exchange of life stories, they hadn't had much success conversing.

"Whoops. Shall I go away again?"

"No. And before you ask," she said, eyeing the champagne, "I'd be delighted."

Hawkins poured it—the real thing, from France, a fine Roederer *brut*—and handed her a glass.

"*À votre santé,*" she said, and drank off half the glass.

Sipping his own, Hawkins raised a questioning eyebrow.

"Oh, don't look at me like that," she said. "It's consolation. Six weeks on this tub and we might as well be back at Newark shuttleport."

"Couldn't disagree more. For my money it's quite a sight. The largest moon in the solar system. Surface area bigger than Africa."

"I thought it was supposed to be *exotic,*" Marianne complained. "Everybody said so."

Hawkins smiled. "Wait and see. Not long now."

"Be mysterious, then."

Indeed, Ganymede did have a romantic reputation. Not because of all the major settlements in the solar system it was the most distant from Earth. Not for the weird landscapes of its ancient, oft-battered, oft-refrozen crust. Not for its spectacular views of Jupiter and its sister moons. Ganymede was exotic because of what humans had done to it.

"When *are* they letting us off?" Marianne demanded, gulping more champagne.

"Formalities always take a few hours. I imagine we'll be down below by morning."

"Morning, whenever that is. Ugh."

Hawkins cleared his throat. "Ganymede can be a bit confusing to the first-time visitor," he said. "I'd be glad to show you around."

"Thanks, Bill." She favored him with a heavy-lidded glance. "But no thanks. Somebody's meeting me."

"Oh."

His face must have revealed more disappointment than he realized, for Marianne was almost apologetic. "I don't know anything about him. Except *my* mother is very eager to impress *his* mother." Marianne, twenty-two years old, had left the surface of Earth for the first time only six weeks earlier; like other children of wealth—including most of her fellow passengers—she was supposed to be making a traditional year-long Grand Tour of the solar system.

"Does this fellow have a name?" Hawkins asked.

"Blake Redfield."

"Blake!" Hawkins smiled—partly with relief, for Redfield was rather famously involved with the notorious Ellen Troy. "As it happens, he's a member of Professor Forster's expedition. As am I."

"Well, lucky for both of you." When he made no reply, she gave him a sidelong glance. "You're looking at me again."

"Oh, I was just wondering if you're really going to stick out this whole Grand Tour. You spend two weeks here—which is not enough to see anything, really. Next stop, San Pablo base in the Mainbelt— and anything more than a day there is *too* much. Then Mars Station and Labyrinth City and the sights of Mars. Then on to Port Hesperus. Then on to . . ."

"Please stop." He'd made his point. For all that the ship would make many ports of call, she would be spending most of the coming nine months en route, in space. "I think I'd like to change the subject."

Besides being the ship's youngest passenger, Marianne was its most easily excited and most easily bored. Most of the others were new graduates of universities and professional schools, taking the year off to acquire a thin coat of cosmopolitan varnish before settling down to a life of interplanetary banking or stock brokerage or art dealing or fulltime leisure. Marianne had not yet found her calling. None of the undergraduate majors she'd undertaken had proved capable of holding her interest; pre-law, pre-medicine, history of art, languages ancient or modern—nothing had lasted beyond a romantic first encounter. Not even a real romance—she would tell this part delicately, hinting at a brief affair with a professor of classics—had carried her past the midterm in the subject. Semester after semester she'd started with A's and ended with incompletes.

Her mother, possessed of a seemingly inexhaustible fortune but beginning to balk at financing Marianne's ongoing education without some glimmer of a light at the end of the tunnel, had finally urged Marianne to take time off to see something of the rest of Earth and the other inhabited worlds. Perhaps *somewhere* in Europe or Indonesia or South America or out there among the planets and satellites and space stations, *something* would capture her daughter's imagination for longer than a month.

Marianne had spent the year after her twenty-first birthday wandering Earth, acquiring clothes and souvenirs and intellectually stylish acquaintances. If she lacked discipline, she was nevertheless gifted with a restless intelligence and was quick to pick up the latest in *modes pensées*—among which the ideas of Sir Randolph Mays figured prominently, at least in North Continental circles.

"You're actually working for Professor Forster? You didn't tell me that before." Her customary boredom was overcome. "You don't look much like a conspirator type to me."

"Conspirator? Oh . . . don't tell me."

"What?"

"You're *not* one of those who take Randolph Mays seriously."

"Several million people do." Her eyes widened. "Including some very intelligent ones."

" 'The ultimate spiritual *presence* that is the dweller in the *innermost,* besides being the *creator* and sustainer of the *universe'*—do I quote him correctly?''

"Well . . .'' Marianne hesitated. "Why *is* Forster going to Amalthea, if he doesn't know something he's not telling?'' she demanded.

"He may suspect he knows something, but he's going for pure research. What else?'' Hawkins, a postdoc in xeno-archaeology at the University of London, was a blind loyalist where his thesis advisor was concerned. "Remember, Forster applied for his grants and permits long before Amalthea got into the news; that anomalous radiation signature has been known for over a century. As for this warmed-over conspiracy business—really, that too belongs back in the 20th century,'' Hawkins said a bit huffily.

Marianne was uncertain whether to be miffed; having formed few opinions of her own, she found herself at the mercy of people who claimed authority. She struggled bravely on. "So you think there's no such thing as the Free Spirit? That aliens never visited the solar system?''

"I'd be a right fool to say that, wouldn't I? Seeing as how I'm one of less than half a dozen people who can read Culture X script. So is Forster, which is how I know him. Which has nothing to do with Mays and his theories.''

Marianne gave it up then, and drained the last of her champagne. She studied the empty flute and said, "There's a lot I don't know about you.'' She was stating a fact, not starting a flirtation.

Panic creased his brows. "I've done it again, launched into a lecture. I always . . .''

"I like to learn things,'' she said plainly. "Besides, you shouldn't try to be somebody you aren't.''

"Look, Marianne . . . if you don't mind my tagging along with you and Redfield, maybe we could talk more. Not about me,'' he said hastily. "I mean about Amalthea and Culture X . . . or whatever you'd like.''

''Sure. Thanks,'' she said, with an open and thoroughly charming smile. ''I'd like that. Got any more of this?'' She wiggled the glass at him.

Watching from over their heads, Randolph Mays observed that Hawkins, having offered to continue his conversation with her later, soon ran out of things to say; when his bottle was dry he awkwardly retreated. Marianne watched him thoughtfully, but made no effort to stop him.

Mays chuckled quietly, as if he'd been privy to a confidential joke.

6

Under the ice of the Shoreless Ocean, night passed by the artificial count of the hours, and morning came like clockwork. Morning changed imperceptibly to afternoon.

Luke Lim, having skipped breakfast and then lunch in order to pursue his commission into the commercial corridors and back alleys—it was one of the ways he maintained his skinny charm—tugged pensively at the straggling hairs on his chin while he studied the holographic nude Asian female on the wall calendar. She was kneeling, leaning forward with an innocent smile on her red-painted lips, and she held a pure white lotus blossom in her lap, its golden heart ablaze with the date and time. Luke's stomach growled.

Lowering his gaze a few centimeters from the calendar, Luke could stare into the sweating face and evasive eyes of an overfed blond man who sat in a swivel armchair rearranging yellow slips of paper on his desk. For half a minute the two men sat wordlessly, almost as if they were a pair of music lovers trying to concentrate on the clash and wail of the Chinese opera that filtered through the thin wall between them and the barber shop next door. Then the faxlink on the credenza beeped and spit out another hardcopy.

The fat man grunted and leaned perilously over the starboard rail of his armchair to snag the paper from the tray. He glanced at it and grunted again, leaning to port across the littered desktop to hand it to Luke, who folded it and stuck it in the breast pocket of his work shirt.

"Pleasure doing business with you, Von Frisch." Luke got up to leave.

"For once I can say the same," the fat man grumbled. "Which suggests you are spending somebody else's money."

"Better if you keep your guesses to yourself."

"Gladly, my friend. But who else in our small village will believe that Lim and Sons needs a submarine just to fulfill a municipal reservoir maintenance contract?"

"Nobody needs to believe anything, if they never hear about it." Luke paused at the door in the opaque wall and as if on impulse groped in the back pocket of his canvas pants. He brought out a worn leather chip case and extracted a credit sliver. "I know we took care of your bonus, but I almost forgot your *bonus* bonus."

He reached over and grabbed the fingerprint-smeared black plastic infolink unit on the desk and stabbed the sliver into the slot. "Let's say two percent of net, payable one month from delivery"—Luke withdrew the sliver and put it back in his wallet—"if I haven't heard whispers in the corridors about the sale of a Europan sub by then."

"Your generosity overwhelms me," said the fat man, although he did a creditable job of hiding his surprise. "Rest assured that anything you hear won't have come from *my* people."

Luke jerked his head toward the surveillance chip in the corner of the ceiling. "Just the same, I'd fry that peeper."

The fat man grunted. "Doesn't work anyway."

"Yeah?" Luke grinned his mocking grin. "Your money." He turned and pushed through the door.

Von Frisch instantly calculated the amount of Luke's attempted bribe; he thought he knew where he could sell the information for more. At least it was worth a try, and with luck and a bit of discretion, Luke would never hear of it.

The fat man waited until Luke had had a chance to leave the brokerage and disappear into the crowd outside. He touched a button to de-opaque the partition; in the outer office his staff of two, harried-looking middle-aged male clerks who were suddenly aware that they were once more under the eye of the boss, crouched in painful concentration over their flatscreens.

He keyed the office interlink and offloaded the contents of the surveillance chip onto a sliver, then erased the previous twenty-four hours' surveillance. Fingering the black sliver in one pudgy hand, he punched keys on the phonelink with the other; like those of most businesses, his phone was equipped with one-way scrambling to prevent, or at least impede, tracing.

"This is the Ganymede Interplanetary Hotel," said a robot operator. "How may we assist you?"

"Sir Randolph Mays's room."

"I'll see if he's registered, sir."

"He's registered. Or he will be soon."

"Ringing, sir."

Fresh from two days of quarantine, Marianne Mitchell and Bill Hawkins found themselves crushed together in a corner by an over-full load of passengers, riding an elevator car down into the heart of Shoreless Ocean city. The last thirty meters of the slow descent were in a free-standing glass tube through the axis of the underground city's central dome. The view opened out suddenly, and

Marianne gaped at the startling mass of people on the floor far below.

The crowd spilled in and out through four great gates, outlined in gold, set in the square walls upon which the dome appeared to rest—although the masonry shell was really a false ceiling suspended in a hollow carved from the ice. As the elevator car moved lower, she could see upward to the vast, intricate, richly painted Tibetan-style mandala that covered the inner surface of the dome.

"You can't see the floor for the crowd," Hawkins said, "but if you could, you'd see an enormous Shri-Yantra laid out in tile."

"What's that?"

"A geometric device, an aid to meditation. Outer square, inner lotus, interlocking triangles in the center. A symbol of evolution and enlightenment, a symbol of the world, a symbol of Shiva, a symbol of the progenitive goddess, the yoni . . ."

"Stop, my head's spinning."

"At any rate, a symbol Buddhists and Hindus are both happy with. By the way, this elevator shaft is supposed to represent the lingam in the yoni."

"Lingam?"

"Another object of meditation." He coughed.

"Somehow these people don't seem like they're meditating. Shopping, maybe."

The heavenly car came to rest and the doors slid open.

"If we're separated, head for the east gate—that one over there." Hawkins barely got the words out before the two of them were expelled into the mob.

Marianne kept a vice grip on his arm. She was glad he knew where he was going; she was sure she could never have found the restaurant Blake Redfield had named without Hawkins to guide her.

Finding the right current in the human stream, they plunged through the east gate into a narrow passage, which soon bifurcated, then divided again.

They were in what seemed a rabbit warren or ant's nest of curving tunnels and passages, jammed with people, spiraling up and down and crossing each other at unexpected and seemingly random intervals. For Marianne the yellow and brown faces around her evoked no comparisons with rabbits or ants, however—she was too much a child of the widely (if shallowly) tolerant 21st century for the easy slurs of 19th-century racism to hold any metaphoric force for her—she was merely overwhelmed by dense humanity.

After twenty minutes of effort and many questions, which Hawkins insisted upon bawling out in a sort of pidgin, they found the restaurant, a Singaporean establishment aptly named the Straits Cafe.

Inside, it was as busy as the jam-packed little alley-wide corridor it fronted. The air was rich with a compound aroma—sharp spices, hot meats, steamed rice, and undercurrents of other, unidentifiable odors. Hawkins hesitated in the doorway. A teenage girl wearing a viddie-inspired version of the latest interplanetary fashions—orange and green baggies were in this year—started toward them, tattered menus in hand, but Hawkins waved her off, having caught sight of Blake Redfield at a table for four next to a wall-sized aquarium.

Marianne hadn't been expecting much from the son of her mother's friend, so Blake was an interesting surprise: handsome, freckle-faced, auburn-haired, an American with continental airs and too much money—it showed in his clothes, his hairstyle, his expensive men's cologne.

And when he spoke, it sounded in his English-flavored accent. "You're Marianne, nice to meet you," he said, getting to his feet, a bit distracted.

There was another man at the table, an emaciated Chinese in work clothes who barely glanced at Hawkins but positively leered at Marianne. "This is Luke Lim," Blake said. "Marianne, uh, Mitchell. Bill Hawkins. Thanks for taking over for me, Bill. Sit down, everybody sit down."

Hawkins and Marianne exchanged glances and sat down side by side, facing the aquarium wall, their faces lit by the greenish light that filtered through its none-too-clean water.

Menus arrived. Hawkins barely glanced at his. The expression on Marianne's face conveyed her bewilderment—

—not lost on Luke Lim. "The rock cod is fresh," he said to her. "Also nervous." He tapped the glass and grinned, an appalling display of yellow teeth and goatee hairs.

She returned a feeble smile and found herself staring past him at the ugliest fish she'd ever seen, all flaps and wrinkles and stringy parts the color of mucilage, floating at Lim's eye level where he leaned his head against the aquarium glass.

Man and fish studied her in return.

"Uh, I think . . ."

"On the other hand, you might prefer the deep-fried shredded taro," said Lim. "Very . . . crunchy."

She couldn't believe he was licking his lips at her like that. She stared at him, fascinated.

"Until you start chewing it," Bill Hawkins warned. "Then it turns into one-finger poi, right in your mouth."

"What's poi?" Marianne asked softly, almost whispering.

"A Polynesian word for library paste," Hawkins said grumpily. "Blue gray in color. One-finger is the gooiest sort."

Luke Lim had turned his wild leer full upon Hawkins. "Apparently Mr. Hawkins doesn't appreciate our Singaporean cuisine."

"When were you last in Singapore?" Hawkins asked—mildly enough, yet enough to cause tension; he and Lim had taken an instant mutual dislike.

"Oh dear," Marianne murmured, turning back to the menu. Surely she would find there a few familiar words, like beef, potatoes, spinach. . . .

"Forster's off with the others tonight," Blake said to Hawkins, diverting his attention. "He wants to see you tomorrow morning. You've got a room waiting in the Interplanetary. You can sit in it, or in the bar, or wander 'round the town, but don't expect to find anybody in our so-called office." Blake hadn't even glanced at Marianne since she and Hawkins had sat down. "Luke and I—we'll be in touch, don't worry—we've recently concluded arrangements for the delivery of, uh, the first item."

"The what?"

"Item A," Lim said meticulously. "He paid me to call it that. At least in public."

"We're working on the second," said Blake.

"Item B," Luke said helpfully.

"Why all the damned secrecy?" Hawkins asked.

"Forster's orders," Blake said. "We're under observation."

"I should bloody well think so. By about three-quarters of the population of the inhabited worlds."

"Dressed like this, in fact," Blake said, "I'm a *bloody* neon sign, but I think it would be even odder if I were to greet Ms. Mitchell in my customary get-up these days."

"What's that mean?"

"Did you notice Randolph Mays with you on *Helios*? No? I'm not surprised."

"Mays?" asked Marianne, perking up.

"Would you like to know how Randolph Mays managed to get himself comfortably ensconced in the Interplanetary Hotel for two days during which all the rest of you have been detained in quarantine?"

"Sir Randolph Mays is in our hotel?" Marianne asked.

Blake was still ignoring her, fixing a stern eye on Hawkins and barely restraining himself from tapping a forefinger on the tabletop. "Mays has contacts, informants, friends in places high and low. He knows customs types and hotel managers and maitre d's and all that sort, knows what they like, which is clean money—which he's also got. The man's *not* just a fatuous old Oxbridge don, Bill, to whom the BBC mistakenly offered a pulpit from which to spout bull. He's a damned good investigative reporter, stalking history on the hoof. And we have the misfortune to be his quarry of the moment." Blake reached for the sliver of paper covered with handwriting that indicated his and Lim's bill. "Luke and I have already had lunch. If you wouldn't mind carrying on with Marianne here, Bill . . . I mean . . ."

"Quite, delighted to," Hawkins said quickly, before Blake could make it worse. "Assuming that's all right with you, Marianne."

Two bright red patches had appeared high on Marianne's cheeks. "Why waste another minute on me? I'm capable of looking after myself."

"Marianne," Hawkins said fervently, "I can think of nothing I would rather do—much less *need* do—than spend the next few hours in your company."

"Catch you at the hotel in the morning, then." Blake had already stood up. He looked at Marianne, his eyes unfocused. "Sorry, really I am. This way it works out for everybody."

Lim followed Blake to the counter. "Did I hear you say you were paying, my friend?" He was talking to Blake, but he couldn't resist a final, over-the-shoulder leer at Marianne.

Hawkins watched them go. "Extraordinary!" He seemed genuinely astonished. "Before today I couldn't have imagined Redfield behaving in other than the most exemplary fashion. Perhaps things aren't going well for him—Forster seems to have put the fear of God into him.''

''He was certainly being obscure,'' said Marianne.

''Yes, as in some cheap spy novel. When really, there's no mystery. The professor plans a thorough exploration of Amalthea. I know he counted on acquiring an ice mole—a mining machine—here on Ganymede. That must be Item A.''

''Item A, Item B. Worse than this menu.''

Hawkins took the hint. ''May I order for both of us?''

''Why not? If we were in Manhattan, I'd do the same for you.''

But Hawkins paid no attention to the menu. Instead he absently studied the fish swimming in the huge aquarium. ''I suppose Item B would be a submarine.''

''What would Professor Forster want with a submarine?''

''Only guessing.'' He waved for the waitress. ''Those geysers, you know . . . could be that under the ice, there's liquid water. *Well,* let's see what this place has to offer.''

Marianne glanced toward the doorway through which Blake and his friend Lim had disappeared into the throng. Depending on one's mood, all this could be viewed as intensely mundane or intensely exciting. Why not hope for the best? Marianne moved perceptibly closer to Hawkins.

If anyone had said to Marianne that she might someday blossom into an intellectual, she would have been shocked; she thought her own record of academic failure proved nothing but the opposite. But in fact she had a powerful hunger for information, a powerful attraction to schemes of organization, and a sometimes too-powerful critical sense that kept her hopping from one such flawed scheme to another. And they were all flawed.

Sometimes her lust for knowledge got mixed up with her liking for people and her own physical wants. At the beginning of any relationship, people see what they want and hear what they want and take as clues what may be nothing more than accidental gibberish or cant. She knew that. On the other hand, it did help that Bill Hawkins was big and strong and nice looking. She allowed her warm thigh to brush his as he made a great show of studying the menu. Marianne was no intellectual yet, but she was a young woman of ambition, at a stage of her life when men who knew something she didn't know were the sexiest men of all.

7

All afternoon, after their awkward luncheon with Blake Redfield and his odd local friend, Hawkins and Marianne wandered through the corridors of the exotic city, unburdened by an itinerary. They visited the more famous tourist sights—a stroll through the crowded ice gardens, a ride on a sampan through steaming-cold canals lined with tourist shops—and they talked about what Hawkins knew of the worlds: about his earliest desire to be a full-fledged xeno-archaeologist, his vacation trips to Venus and Mars, his studies under Professor Forster. The history of Culture X was virtually a blank, he told her, although it was known that beings who spoke—or at least wrote—their language had visited Earth in the Bronze Age, while other references made it seem they had been around at least a billion years before that.

And the language of Culture X presented far more difficulties than the layperson would believe, in this day of computer translation. For the computer translated according to rules that had been programmed into it, no matter how well it might understand what it was saying (and some computers were bright enough to understand a lot); different rules based on different assumptions yielded different meanings, and thus each translation was like the invention of a new language. What relationship Forster's program for the speech of Culture X bore to the lost language, and especially to its sounds, was a matter of continuing discussion.

"Forster discusses it?" Marianne asked shrewdly.

"Other people's discussions," Hawkins said, smiling. "He, of course, considers the matter closed."

Evening came. Miraculously, they were both staying at the same luxurious hotel, and Marianne had not let Hawkins run out of things to talk about by dinner time, or even afterward.

"Come upstairs with me," she said, when they'd put down their empty coffee cups.

"Well, of course I'll ride up with you. Aren't we both staying on the . . . ?"

"Oh shut up, Bill. Think about it a minute, if you want to—that's all right, that's the kind of person you are. Then say yes or no." She smiled wickedly. "I prefer yes."

"Well, of course." He blushed. "I mean, yes."

The Interplanetary's rooms were small but lavish, with piles of soft cotton carpets covering woven-reed floors and screens of pierced sandalwood in the corners; warm yellow light, turned low, came through the myriad openings in the fretwork like patterned stars. In a gossamer net of light, wearing nothing, her limbs long and smooth and muscular, with glistening darkness flowing in her hair and shining in her eyes and touching the mysterious places of her body, Marianne was so beautiful Bill Hawkins could think of absolutely nothing more to say.

But much later, she started murmuring questions again. They passed the night in bouts of mutual interrogation.

"You are Mrs. Wong?" Randolph Mays asked the woman in the high-collared green silk dress.

She gave him a hard stare, then forced a sincere if unaccustomed smile. "Sir! I am very honored making your acquaintance, Sir Randolph Mays."

"The honor is *mine,*" said Mays, taking her small, muscular hand. "Do I understand that you are the *owner* of this handsome establishment?" He threw his hands wide, indicating the interior of the Straits Cafe. At the midmorning hour it was empty, except for a girl sullenly mopping the floor.

"Since my husband died almost ten years ago, I am sole proprietor." She crushed out a half-smoked, lipstick-smeared cigarette that had been perched on a thick glass ashtray on the counter. Smoking was a rare habit in controlled environments, banned in some, but Mrs. Wong owned the air inside these four walls.

"Come, sit down." Her manner betrayed an edge of impatience. "I will have tea brought. We can talk."

"Delighted."

"What kind do you like?"

"Darjeeling," Mays said. "Or whatever you might recommend."

Mrs. Wong said something in Chinese to a girl at the charge machine. She took Mays to a round table in front of the aquarium wall. He and the ugliest fish he had ever seen stared at each other; Mays blinked first, and sat down.

Mays's unannounced arrival at the Ganymede Interplanetary Hotel had thrown the local gossip mongers into a fury of speculation, but they quickly realized he must have traveled on *Helios* under an assumed name, presumably in disguise. Having registered at the Interplanetary under his own name, wearing his own face, it had taken only hours for the news to circulate throughout the community.

The hotel's bolder guests approached him for autographs whenever he appeared in public; he obliged them and answered their questions by explaining that it was his purpose—no, his sworn *duty*—to investigate Professor J.Q.R. Forster and every aspect of the expedition to Amalthea. Word of Mays's intentions traveled as fast as the news of his arrival.

For show, Mays did make one or two attempts to contact the Forster expedition, who had set up official headquarters in the town's Indian quarter, but no one answered their phonelink except the office robot, who always claimed everyone was out. As Mays quickly learned from his acquaintances among the interplanetary press corps, Forster and his people hadn't been seen since their arrival; most of the reporters had come to the conclusion that Forster wasn't on Ganymede at all. Perhaps he was on some other moon, Europa for example. Perhaps he was in orbit. Perhaps he'd already left for Amalthea.

Mays was unsurprised and unperturbed. His fame was a magnet, and sure enough, people with information to offer soon began calling *him*. . . .

Mrs. Wong lit another cigarette and held it between fingers that boasted inch-long, red-lacquered nails. "They were sitting right at this table," she told him, leaning back and blowing smoke at the cod. "Mr. Redfield, I know he works for the professor, he was talking with that Lim person. They were talking in Chinese. Mr. Redfield speaks very good Cantonese."

Although Mrs. Wong considered this an unusual feat, Mays showed no surprise. "Who is that Lim *person?*" he asked.

"Luke, son of Kam, Lim and Son Construction. Long hair, dresses like cowboy. No good."

Mays lifted an impressive eyebrow, inviting more, but Mrs. Wong was either reluctant to give examples of Luke Lim's bad behavior or had none specific to give. "What were they talking about?" he asked.

"From what they said, I think Lim sold Mr. Redfield their old ice mole."

"Ice mole?"

"Tunnelling machine designed special for here—where ice is very cold, gravity very low. And they talked about something else the professor is buying someplace. I didn't hear what. Then two others came in." Mrs. Wong picked at a tobacco crumb on the tip of her tongue.

"Please go on."

"A Mr. Hawkins, I think he works for the professor too, and a young girl named Marianne. Just visiting."

"Ah, Marianne," Mays said.

"You know her?"

"Not well," he said. He leaned back in his chair to avoid a new emission of asphyxiating cigarette smoke. "What did the four of them have to say to each other?"

"Mr. Redfield was unhappy, I think. Didn't want to talk at all. In a few minutes he left with Lim. Then Mr. Hawkins was trying to impress the girl. He said probably the professor wanted to buy an ice mole to explore under the surface of Amalthea. Also a submarine."

Mays's expression stiffened for a moment— "Ahh?"—then he nodded judiciously. "*Submarine*, of course. Then what?"

"Then they ate. Talked about sightseeing, other things. About you and your video programs."

"Really."

"Mr. Hawkins did not like your programs. He talked so much about how you are wrong and the professor is right, after a while he bored the girl. I think he is not very successful with girls."

Mrs. Wong went on a few minutes longer, but Mays soon realized he had gotten everything she knew worth repeating. When he left the Straits, a pile of well-worn, old-fashioned North Continental paper dollars—in denominations of hundreds and thousands, untraceable through the credit net—stayed on the table behind him.

A Buddhist festival was in progress in the corridors. The town seemed to hold a festival of some sort every other day, and most were not for tourists; the place crawled with religionists. Mays made his way through passages echoing from strings of exploding firecrackers, through air thick and blue with acrid smoke; wreaths and garlands of smoke were sucked into the laboring exhaust fans. Excited children coursed past his long legs. He reached the central square. A sea of saffron-robed monks parted before him, and suddenly there was the fake stone facade of the Interplanetary, bristling with finials and encrusted with ponderous statuary, an imitation Angkor Wat.

The lobby was a cooler, quieter place, but not by much. He ducked past the concierge and into the lift, dodging a pride of businessmen with autograph-lust in their eyes to seek the privacy of his room. But no sooner had he let his door lock itself behind him than his phonelink chortled.

"Randolph Mays here."

"Mr. Von Frisch, sir, of Argosy Spacecraft and Industrial Engineering. Shall I put him through?"

This Von Frisch person had called twice before, but he was as elusive as Forster, and they had not yet made contact. "By all means put him on."

The voice on the phonelink was distorted by a one-way commercial scrambler; the screen remained dark. "We meet at last, Sir Randolph."

"Under the circumstances that's putting it rather *strongly*, Frisch . . . I beg your pardon, Mr. *Von* Frisch."

"Yes, well. A hard world, Sir Randolph. Better safe, and all that."

"What's your business, sir?"

"Argosy are equipment brokers, among other things."

"With *me*. Your business with me."

"I've lately participated in a rather interesting transfer of property to someone who is planning an expedition to Amalthea. I think it might be worth your while to learn more about it."

"Let me *guess*. You've sold the professor a submarine."

Von Frisch, obviously no amateur, managed to contain whatever surprise he may have felt. "Guess if you like, Sir Randolph. If you want facts, we should talk."

"All right, then. Where and when?"

The arrangements made, Mays keyed off. He leaned back on the bed and lifted his large feet onto the cover. With his long fingers knitted behind his head, he stared at the ceiling and considered his next move.

From Mrs. Wong, Mays had learned that Hawkins had been told to take a room in this very hotel. It wouldn't be long before the mediahounds got hold of *that*. Indeed, Forster and friends had very likely thrown Hawkins to the hounds deliberately—the professor's people evidently didn't have a lot for him to do, except deflect attention from themselves. Mays was a few hours ahead of his, mm, *colleagues* with these tidbits, but he was playing a deeper game than they were. And he was after bigger game than Hawkins.

Nothing he knew suggested that Hawkins was any but the least important member of Forster's team, a former student of the professor's who'd most probably been recruited primarily for his family's wealth and connections—and perhaps secondarily for his strong back—but only incidentally for his knowledge of the language of Culture X, which he'd learned to read from Forster himself. Hawkins, naturally, believed that his linguistic ability and scholarly acumen were the reasons for the honor his former teacher had conferred upon him.

He was a bright enough young man, but he was mightily opinionated and, as was often the case with such people, fundamentally shy. He didn't so much talk as lecture; if he were wound up in his subject, he could even be rather charming at first. But he didn't know when to stop talking—or how to stop, once he'd run out of things to say. Thus what social advantages he had often turned into liabilities. He was vulnerable.

Marianne Mitchell was also staying at the Interplanetary. In managing an effective introduction to a woman more than two decades younger than he was, it helped Mays to know that she was already among his fans. And that she had a thirst for knowledge.

It was essential that he approach them together. Mays staked out the hotel bar, making no attempt to hide; as a consequence, for most of one day and a good part of the next he signed books and cocktail napkins, even stray bits of lingerie, until the current crop of autograph seekers was sated. His patience was rewarded: late on the second day of his watch, Hawkins and Marianne entered, sat down, and ordered cocktails. He gave them ten uninterrupted minutes. Then . . .

"You're Dr. William *Hawkins*," he said, looming suddenly out of the shadows, wasting no time on subtlety.

Hawkins looked up from what did not seem a happy conversation with Marianne. "Yes . . . oh! You're . . ."

"If one were to *count* the number of people who can even *begin* to read the infamous Martian script, one would need only *one* hand to do it. And there *you* would be," Mays said, sounding immensely pleased with himself. "But *sorry*, my name's Mays."

"Of course, Sir Randolph"—Hawkins almost knocked his chair over, standing up—"won't you sit down? This is my friend, Miss . . ."

"*Terribly* rude," Mays said. "You will *forgive* me."

". . . Mitchell."

"Marianne," Marianne said sweetly. "It's an honor to meet you, Sir Randolph."

"Why, *really.*"

"Really, yes. Bill and I have talked about you a great deal. I think your ideas are so fascinating."

Mays threw Hawkins a quick look; upon hearing this from the woman he'd been trying to impress by cataloguing Mays's follies, Hawkins suddenly realized how incongruous were his own obsequious noises. Abruptly he straightened his chair and sat down.

"How *good* of you to say so . . . Marianne?" A quick nod of her glossy brunette head confirmed that Mays had permission to use her first name. "If there is *any* secret to my success with the public, it is simply that I have managed to *focus* attention on some great thinkers of the past, too *long* neglected. Toynbee, for example. As of course *you* know."

"Oh yes. Arnold Toynbee." She nodded again, more vigorously. She'd definitely heard of Toynbee—mostly from Bill Hawkins.

"You're suggesting, Sir Randolph," Hawkins suggested for him, "that like Newton, if you have seen farther it is because you stand on the shoulders of giants?"

"Mmm . . . well . . ."

Hawkins was all heavy humor and undisguised resentment. "I've heard that Isaac Newton intended that remark to insult his rival, Robert Hooke—who was a dwarf."

"In that case, apparently I am even *less* like *Hooke* than like *Newton.*"

Marianne laughed delightedly.

Hawkins flushed; she was not laughing with *him*. "I'll find a waitress." He jerked his hand up and looked about.

"Bill says you're here to investigate Professor Forster's expedition to Amalthea," Marianne said to Mays.

"That's right."

"Bill says they aren't doing anything except making an archaeological survey."

"Perhaps the professor hasn't told Bill everything," said Mays.

She persisted. "But do you *really* think the professor is part of a conspiracy?"

"I say, Marianne," said Hawkins worriedly, his hand still in the air.

"I'm afraid my views on that subject have not been accurately reported," Mays replied. "I haven't accused Professor Forster of being part of a *conspiracy*, only of knowing more than he's telling the public. Frankly, I suspect he has discovered a secret that the Free Spirit have jealously guarded for centuries."

"The Free Spirit!" Hawkins exclaimed. "What could some centuries-old superstition possibly have to say about a celestial body that was unknown until the 1880's?"

"Just so," Mays said amiably.

The waitress appeared, dressed in an elaborate Balinese temple dancer's costume.

"What will you have?" Hawkins asked Mays.

"Ice tea, Thai-style," said Mays.

"Two more here," said Hawkins, indicating the tall rum drinks he and Marianne had been sipping.

"Not for me," Marianne said. Her glass was still more than half full. The waitress bowed prettily and left.

"You were asking about centuries-old superstitions, Dr. Hawkins," Mays said suavely, turning his attention full on Hawkins. "Before I address your question, let me first ask if you can tell me *why* the underground temples of the Free Spirit cult have the southern constellation *Crux* depicted on their ceilings—when at the time the earliest of them were built no one in the *northern* hemisphere knew the configuration of the *southern* sky? And just what *secrets* were those two astronomers on the moon trying to keep when they plotted to destroy the Farside radiotelescopes, which were then trained upon Crux?"

"That the aliens are from Crux, and they're coming back," Marianne said with satisfaction.

"Oh, Marianne," Hawkins groaned.

"A very reasonable hypothesis," Mays said, "one among several."

"Including coincidence, which in a probabilistic world is not only possible but inevitable." If Hawkins had not been so flustered, he would have stopped there—"And what clues could Professor Forster have concerning these living aliens . . . that he wouldn't share with the rest of his team?"—realizing too late that there were all sorts of things someone in Forster's position would want to keep secret from his academic rivals.

But again Mays declined a frontal attack. "As to that, I really don't know. I assure you, however, there will be no *secrets* when I discover what the professor is keeping to himself." Mays knitted his furry brows, but there was a kind of mockery in his challenge. "Perhaps you should consider this fair warning, sir. I intend to follow every *clue.*"

"There won't be many clues to a nonexistent secret."

"Dr. Hawkins, you are such a . . . *straightforward* man, I'm sure you would be surprised at what I have uncovered already. For example, that Professor Forster has acquired both a small ice mole and a Europan submarine—tools that give your expedition capabilities well beyond the scope of its stated survey goals."

Hawkins was indeed surprised, and failed to hide it. "How did you know that?"

Mays answered with another question. "Can you offer a straightforward explanation for these rather odd acquisitions?"

"Well, certainly," said Hawkins, although he was unsure how he'd been maneuvered into defending himself. "Amalthea is obviously a different place than it seemed when the professor wrote his proposal. The subsurface geology . . ."

". . . could be understood with conventional seismographic imaging techniques. Perhaps already *is* understood. The Space Board has kept watch on Amalthea for more than a year," Mays said. "No, Dr. Hawkins, Professor Forster wants more than a survey of Amalthea's surface or a picture of its interior. He is looking for something . . . something *beneath* the ice."

Hawkins laughed. "The buried civilization of the ancient astronauts from Crux, is that it? Quite imaginative, Sir Randolph. Perhaps you should be writing adventure viddies instead of documentaries." It was a juvenile retort. To Hawkins's evident dismay, Marianne did not bother to hide her contempt. . . .

Days later, Mays could still smile triumphantly at the memory of that moment. When Hawkins left the table a few moments later, he'd recovered just enough of his dignity to avoid making false excuses. "It's clear that you have more to talk about with Sir Randolph than with me," he'd said to Marianne. "It would be churlish of me to interfere."

And indeed they did have more to talk about. Much more.

PART
2

GANYMEDE CROSSING

8

Two weeks earlier . . .

"You were right. I can't leave Blake and the others out there floundering. I'm probably the only one alive who knows what to do."

"*I* was right?" Amusement touched Linda's calm features. "Did *I* tell you all that?"

"You got me to think it, and then to say it. Which is the same thing."

Linda nodded. "I suppose so." The faint smile remained.

Sparta nervously paced her end of the room, her boot heels knocking softly on the bare polished boards. "Maybe I gave you the wrong impression. I'm not here for our regular session."

"Somehow I sensed that. For one thing, you haven't sat down."

"I wanted to tell you what I've decided."

"And I'd like to hear it."

"Yes . . . Yes." Sparta stopped pacing and stood at something resembling parade rest, her feet spaced apart, her hands clasped behind her. "I've made arrangements to join Forster. A fast cutter will take me to Ganymede. Planetary alignments are almost ideal. It should take a little over two weeks."

Linda said nothing, only sat upon her plain pine chair and listened. The light from the window was fitful, brightening and dimming with the swift passage of clouds before the sun, causing Linda's and Sparta's shadows to shrink and swell on the polished floorboards and enameled walls.

"And there are some other . . . details," Sparta said.

"Which you wish to discuss with me."

"That's right. What we talked about before."

"We've talked about a lot of things."

"Specifically about . . . humanness. What it is to be human."

"Oh."

"Well, I don't think I can define it for you—for myself—any better than I ever could." In struggling to express concepts that seemed self-evident to the majority of those who ever thought of them at all, Sparta seemed younger than her years. She swiped at the short blond hair that fell below her eyebrows. "But I think I know now that . . . I mean, I don't think it has anything to do with what's done to the body. After a person is born, anyway." Quickly she added, "I'm speaking generally."

"Of course." Linda showed no amusement; Sparta's statement, which in the abstract was so general as to be virtually without content, coming from her was a major concession. "Do I take it you no longer feel that you were robbed of your humanity by those who altered you?"

"More than that," Sparta said. "I think . . . I mean, I've decided that nothing others do to me *can* rob me of my humanity."

"Say more about that."

"Nothing done to me, that is, so long as I can remain conscious of my own feelings."

Linda smiled. "To hear you say so makes *me* feel very good."

Sparta, startled, laughed abruptly. "You claim you can feel?"

"Oh yes. You're the one who taught me that feelings are thoughts that need no words. Granted I'm not human; I'm the projection of what we agree is a machine. Nevertheless I have both thoughts and feelings."

Sparta was momentarily confused. She had come here to tell Linda about matters of profound importance and intimacy; Linda seemed to be confusing the issue with these remarks about herself . . . *it*self.

But perhaps Linda had anticipated the rest of what Sparta intended to reveal. Sparta pushed on. "What they did to me wasn't arbitrary. Some of it was a mistake; still they . . ." But she quickly floundered again; it was difficult to find straightforward language for what she was trying to express.

Linda tried to help her. "We've talked about the mission they planned for you."

"The mission remains." Sparta took a sharp breath. "To fulfill it I will require certain modifications. Some that they anticipated, but that I . . . that have been . . . damaged. I need to restore the capacity to *see*, microscopically and telescopically— and the capacity to image the infrared. And other modifications, specific to the anticipated environment . . ."

Linda interrupted her before she could begin busily listing them. "You intend to change yourself?"

"The arrangements have been made." Sparta seemed edgy, defensive. "The commander is cooperating. I haven't said anything to my mother and father . . . yet. But I will, really."

Linda was still; she gave the impression that she was lost in thought.

She was quiet so long that Sparta sniffed noisily and said, "I don't have a lot of time before . . ."

"You have made vital progress," said Linda, abruptly cutting her off. "I applaud and admire your courage in deciding to *choose* this difficult task, which others tried to thrust upon you without your consent, but which nothing now compels you to undertake. You have mastered your groundless fears and faced up to one or more fundamental questions that must eventually confront all people of sensitivity and imagination.'' She paused only a moment before she added, ''I worry about only one thing.''

''What?''

''No one can make progress by running away.''

''Meaning?'' Sparta demanded.

''You must interpret what I say in your own words. You are aware by now that I am little other than what is potential in you.''

With that, as if to underscore her Sibylline message, a blue flash of light and a soft ''pop'' emanated from the center of Linda's persuasively solid body, and she vanished. Sparta stared at the empty room, shocked and a little offended.

Then she smiled. Linda really was—had been— the perfect psychotherapist. One who knew when it was time to stop.

9

Even in this age of microminiaturization, of tailored artificial proteins and nucleic acids, of nanomachines, some radical procedures still began and ended with the scalpel.

Sparta was continuously under the diamond-film knives for forty-eight hours before she began her swim back to consciousness. Rising to be born again through dim and surging depths toward a circle of lights, she burst like Aphrodite from the foam—

—in her case, a froth of bloody bubbles the surgical nurses bent quickly to clean away from the multiple incisions in her thorax. She had taken them by surprise, willing herself to wake up even while still in the operating theater.

They handled the emergency competently, and within moments were wheeling her away. By the time she was fully alert, multiple growth factors had done their job: her skin was pink and unscarred, her internal organs unbruised; her many changes were virtually undetectable.

For another twenty-four hours she stayed under observation, allowing the doctors to keep watch on her for the sake of their professional ethics and their personal consciences, although with her acute self-awareness Sparta monitored her internal states better than they could.

From the window of the private room in the high security wing of the Space Board clinic she looked east, across a pea-soup river of algae with huge stainless steel harvesters poised upon it like delicate waterbugs, across the ruins of Brooklyn in the midst of the greenbelt, to a gray urban mass beyond, barely visible in the smog. One morning she watched through the murk as an orange-purple sun wobbled into the sky, and she knew the moment had come; she was fit and ready.

The door chimed softly. She saw on the flatplate that the commander was standing outside in the hall. "Open," she told the door.

He was wearing his blue Space Board uniform, with the insignia of rank and the thin rows of ribbons and the collar pips that signified the Investigations Branch; its reflected blue made the hard eyes that studied her even bluer. His expression softened. "You look good, Troy. They tell me no complications."

She nodded.

He looked as if he wanted to say something more. But he'd never been one to make speeches. And their relationship had changed, even if she was still officially Inspector Troy of the Board of Space Control and he was still officially her boss.

"Chopper's ready when you are. Your parents should be on the way to the lodge."

"Let's go."

Wordlessly, he stood aside. She walked through the door without looking at him. She knew the pain she caused him, but it had been a year at least since she had allowed herself to show any outward sign that she cared what he or the rest of them felt.

After thirty-five years of marriage, Jozsef Nagy still sometimes behaved toward his wife like the youthful student he had been when they met. In those days, meeting his new beloved under the spring trees in Budapest, the mode of transportation had usually been bicycles. Today he'd called a gray robot limousine to their retreat in the North American forest.

He held the door open for Ari while she got in and arranged herself on the leather cushions, just as formally as if it were a horse-drawn cab he'd rented with a month's allowance to take them to the theater. The day was cold and fresh, the sunlight bright, the shadows crisp on the dewy branches. For several minutes the car rolled down the narrow paved roadway that looped through the springtime woods before she spoke. "So she has agreed to see us at last."

"It's a sign, Ari. Her recovery has been gradual, but I think it is now almost complete."

"She talks to you. Do you know something you haven't told me?"

"We talk about the past. She keeps her plans to herself."

"It can only mean that she has come to her senses." Ari spoke with determined confidence, refusing to acknowledge doubt.

Jozsef looked at her with concern. "Perhaps you should not assume too much. After all, she could be planning to quit. Perhaps she merely feels she should tell us in person."

"You don't believe that."

"I don't want to see either of you hurt."

Suddenly her voice was edged with anger. "It is your exaggerated concern for her *feelings*, Jozsef, that has cost us this past year's time."

"We must agree to disagree upon that point," Jozsef said calmly. His wife had been his professional colleague for most of their married life; he had acquired the knack of keeping their strategic differences separate from their personal ones early on, but it was a discipline she had never bothered to try. "I worry about *you*," he said. "What if you learn that she will not do what you expect of her? *And* about her—what if you refuse to accept her as she is?"

"When *she* accepts herself as she is, she and I cannot help but agree."

"I wonder why you continue to underrate our daughter, when she has never failed to surprise us."

Ari stifled the tart reply that came naturally to her tongue; for all her ways—the ways of that intelligent, too-pretty, spoiled young woman Jozsef had fallen in love with four decades ago—she was fair-minded, and what Jozsef said was true. However much Ari might be irked by her daughter's unorthodoxy, Linda had never failed to surprise them, even when she was carrying out her parents' wishes.

Iron gates loomed before them. The car slowed only slightly as the gates slid open on well-oiled tracks.

"I will say only this much more; if she wants to be released, you must let her go freely. It is not so much from her destiny as from your will that she must declare her independence."

"That I will *not* accept, Jozsef," Ari said sternly. "I can never accept that."

Jozsef sighed. Once his wife had been one of the world's most acclaimed psychologists, yet she was blind to what drove her love for the people she loved the most.

An unmarked white helicopter waited on the roof of the Council of Worlds building, its turbines keening. Seconds after Sparta and the commander climbed aboard, the sleek craft lifted into the sky and banked northward, heading up the valley of the broad Hudson River, leaving behind the glistening towers and marble boulevards of Manhattan.

Sparta made no conversation with the commander, but peered fixedly out of the canopy. Soon the Palisades of the Hudson were passing beneath them. Below her spread soft waves of green, flowing northward with the lengthening days; the forests of the Hendrik Hudson nature preserve were hurrying toward springtime.

The white helicopter turned and swiftly crossed the broad river, swooping low over the trees that guarded the cliff tops. A broad lawn opened before it, and there on the lawn a massive stone house. The silent craft settled to a landing in front of it. Sparta and the commander stepped out, not having exchanged a single word, and the helicopter lifted off behind them. No record of their visit to the house on the Hudson would appear in any data bank.

As they walked across the springy grass, she thought of the months she'd spent in this place, Granite Lodge. Not a Space Board facility, the lodge belonged to Salamander, the association of those who had once been among the *prophetae* of the Free Spirit and were now their sworn enemies. Salamander objected to the authoritarian, secretive leadership of the Free Spirit and to its bizarre practices, but not to its underlying beliefs—not to the Knowledge. By necessity, Salamander too was a secret society, for the Free Spirit regarded its members as apostates and had sworn to kill them.

The two organizations had struck many murderous blows at each other. Not even knowing the identities of the combatants, Sparta had been in the front lines; her wounds were deep. But for the past year, she had been safe from all that.

"I wanted you to believe we were dead. Then nothing could come between you and your purpose." Ari sat placidly in her armchair as if enthroned, her clasped hands resting on top of her lap robe. She glanced sidelong at Jozsef, who sat stiffly on a straightback chair nearby. "I was right to do so."

"After everything that's happened . . ." Sparta broke off, moved fitfully around the room, stopped to stare aimlessly at the spines of the library's old books, avoiding her parents' eyes.

"You should have seen yourself as I saw you," said Ari. "You burned with vengeance. You bent all your extraordinary powers to seeking out and destroying the enemy. You thought you were doing it on our account, but in the process you were able to recover your *real* purpose." She was stirred by her own words. "You were magnificent, Linda. I was immensely proud of you."

Sparta stood motionless, fighting back anger. "I almost died, an addict of Striaphan. I would have died, having accomplished nothing—except several murders, of course—if Blake hadn't come after me."

"We should not have let things go so far," Jozsef said softly.

But Ari contradicted him. "You would *not* have died. In the end, nothing would have been different—except that you would not have lost your will to go on."

Sparta looked at Jozsef. "The night you came to us, Father, you said Mother was sorry. I believed you."

"He should not have apologized for me," Ari said.

"Ari . . ."

"Let us be honest, Jozsef. When you revealed that we were alive, you were interfering. Against my wishes."

Sparta said, "And you still haven't forgiven him for it?"

Ari hesitated; when she spoke her tone was cool. "It's no secret that I think it was a serious mistake. But it's not too late to correct it."

For the first time Sparta faced her mother directly.

"You call them the enemy, but you were one of them."

Jozsef said, "That was before we realized the depths of their error, Linda, the extent of their corruption . . ."

"You gave them your *permission*, Mother," Sparta cried. "Worse, you helped *design* the thing I was."

"Long before that, I gave birth to you."

Sparta flinched. "You mean to say you *own* me?"

When Ari looked momentarily confused, Jozsef said, "She didn't intend to suggest any such thing, Linda. She means that she has loved you and cared for you all your life."

"You apologize for her again." It cost Sparta an effort to draw breath. "How can you talk about me as if I were an object?" she said to her mother. "Even one you claim to love."

Ari said, "Please be sensible, that's not what . . ."

Sparta cut her off. "Really, I shouldn't . . . shouldn't have anything more to do with you."

"You want me to say I was wrong. Believe me, if I thought I were wrong . . ." Ari still anticipated her daughter's eventual capitulation, but she forced herself to acknowledge Linda's understandable concerns. "I'm afraid I can't say something I don't believe. Any more than you could."

When Sparta turned away without replying, Ari tried again. Surely Linda—a wonderful child, possessed of quick intelligence and sound instincts—could see not only the necessity but the grandeur of the evolutionary process they all served. "I love you, Linda. I believe you were chosen for greatness."

"Chosen by you," Sparta said tiredly. "Is that why you decided to have me in the first place?"

"Oh darling, you were not chosen by me or by any human. I believe history brought us to this point. And that you are history's focus."

"History as controlled by the Pancreator?"

Jozsef said, "We don't use that word—it is *their* word. The realization of your role came later, please believe us. Not until you were six or seven. We had already begun SPARTA." The SPecified Aptitude Resource Training and Assessment project had been founded by Jozsef and Ari to prove that every ordinary human is possessed of multiple intelligences, not a single something called I.Q., and that with the right kind of education many intelligences can be optimized. Their own daughter was the first subject of the experimental program, and in her they believed they had succeeded to the full extent of their grandest hopes.

"At first we were reluctant. We tried to guard against our own wishful thinking. But the signs were unmistakable." Ari's tone was almost soft, fully acknowledging her daughter's need to understand. "When Laird came to us, we saw that we were not alone in recognizing your potential."

"So you sent me to the devil."

"I am not too proud to admit . . ." Her voice faded.

She looked at her husband, who nodded. "Go on."

"That we have made mistakes," Ari said.

"Many profound mistakes, Linda, for which we are both sorry."

"Mother, you are still blind to the biggest mistake of them all. Why do you think I finally agreed to see you? What did you think I would say to you today?"

Ari lifted an eyebrow. "Why, that you have thought about these matters and come to the necessary conclusion. That you are ready to go on."

"What do you think *going on* involves?"

"To those of us who have striven to understand it, the Knowledge is explicit about what's needed." It was the very question Ari was best prepared to answer. "First, of course, we must restore your powers. You must be able to *see* as we define seeing, and *listen,* and sense and understand chemical signals, sense and communicate directly by microwave . . ."

"Save me the whole weary catalogue. It's true that what I came to tell you is that I will go on."

Ari said nothing, but her eyes gleamed. Jozsef cleared his throat nervously.

"I resisted the decision until now for . . . for a lot of reasons. The humiliation of this moment probably deterred me as much as anything"—Sparta's gaze drifted upward and she tilted her head back as if she'd found something fascinating to look at on the ceiling; she was trying to keep the tears from rolling down her cheeks—"and what a pathetic comment on my confused priorities! Putting my reluctance to face my mother's insufferably superior attitude ahead of the general welfare."

"I hardly . . ."

"Don't interrupt me, Mother. I've decided that I can't leave Blake and the others out there floundering."

"Linda, whatever you think of me, I'm very proud . . ."

Again Sparta cut her off. "You don't understand the Knowledge any better than the Free Spirit, Mother. You and Father—and the commander and the rest—can imagine nothing grander than the return of the Pancreator. You can't think beyond that, what it might imply. The Free Spirit want to keep it secret, keep Paradise for themselves. You want to make it public—on your own terms, of course. But I'll tell you this much: this whole business is far more complex and serious than you think."

Jozsef studied his daughter curiously, but Ari's smile was patronizing.

Sparta caught her look. "I'm wasting my breath

on you. Some things will only become obvious in hindsight.''

"Your insolence isn't very becoming, dear," Ari said quietly.

Sparta nodded. "My therapy program would probably call it a sign of humanity. Not that my personal humanity makes any difference now." She swallowed. "Any meddling could seriously endanger the mission. And my life. I said that none of you understand the Knowledge. Your ignorance has been the source of much confusion. That ghastly stuff they put under my diaphragm . . . one of your so-called improvements, which I almost died for: microwave was perfectly useless, the medusas knew what to look for. And some things that should have been done weren't."

Ari said coolly, "Be that as it may, the best surgeons are available to us as soon as you . . ."

"For the past three days I've been in the clinic. Everything that needs doing has now been done. I've told the commander to see to it that neither Father nor you—especially you—make any effort to communicate with the surgeons. My life is my own."

Ari stiffened. "Linda, you cannot talk to me like that." Her hands left her lap; her fingernails dug into the leather chair arms. "My role in these matters, like yours, is clearly defined."

"You and I won't be discussing this subject again until my mission is complete. Whether you want to see me—whether you think we have anything else to talk about—I'll leave to you. Now I should go." She turned away. But then her steel mask slipped. "Unless there's anything . . . you think I ought to know."

"Linda, please!" Ari's confusion had overwhelmed her anger, but she realized there was nothing to be gained by arguing now. Perhaps later . . . She stood up, rising from her chair as if abdicating her throne. "My darling, what's become of you?"

In Sparta's mind, compassion and cruelty competed to make an answer; she resisted both. With set shoulders she turned her back on her parents and walked quickly out of the library.

10

Beyond the radiation perimeter of Earth the white cutter's fusion torch lit and the ship, oddly aerodynamic for an interplanetary spacecraft, accelerated on a column of unbearably bright fire.

During the fortnight's passage Sparta kept to herself, saying as little to the single other passenger and the three-person crew as she needed to. She ate alone in her little cabin. She stretched and lifted and exercised and practiced solitary unarmed combat until the sweat poured from her dancer's slim body, hours a day, every day. She read and watched viddie chips, few of which had any obvious application to the mission she was undertaking—Eliot and Joyce and good translations of the epic of Gilgamesh and African folk tales. She read a thousand pages of *Genji Monogotari* before she became mired in its famous sticking place, which was to novice humanists as the *pons asinorum* was to novice geometers.

She slept ten hours a day.

At the halfway point, acceleration became deceleration. Finally the torch shut off, and the cutter slid smoothly into orbit around Ganymede. Again the blue band and gold star of the Board of Space Control had descended upon the moons of Jupiter.

* * *

Blake insisted upon greeting her personally. He hired *Kanthaka*, a fat round shuttle—an energetic little tin can, really—and took the co-pilot's seat on the boost up to parking orbit, which was reached in under an hour.

He'd thought about her, the woman he loved, almost without a moment's pause since he'd lost her three years ago and regained her and lost her again. He did not know how she felt about him, for the simple reason—she'd finally made it plain—that she did not know how she felt about herself. If a person cannot speak with some little grain of confidence in herself, then she cannot be trusted or understood, cannot be depended upon even to say, honestly and knowledgably, no.

Now she had said, in the precise but cryptic way that had become more than a pleasant joke between them, that she was joining him. Not meeting or observing or going along with, but joining. Not joining the expedition, but him.

He wanted nothing more in time and the worlds. But there was so much now between them, so much strange and private, belonging to what had virtually become their alternate universes, that he no longer knew if he could trust her or his own desire. For she had warned him (or was it a promise?) that she had changed.

Kanthaka came into orbit. He went back into the passenger cabin as the cutter's pressure tube snaked out of the lock and fastened itself over the shuttle's hatch with a solid clunk of magnets. There was a suck of air and the throb of pumps, equalizing pressure. Then the inner hatch opened with a pop. Inside the lock Ellen floated alone, carrying a duffle almost as small as it was weightless. He felt his heart catch.

"You look good, as a Mongol," she said, with a tiny smile.

"You look beautiful." He reached out to her.

Hugging needs caution in microgravity, and he had to keep one hand through the safety strap. "It's been a long time."

Did she seem resistant to his touch, or was it only his imagination? He wanted to cry out against his fear. Disappointment flooded his senses . . . then he felt her stiffness melt, and in a moment she was clinging to him as if he were the only solid thing in the world's vortex.

"Isn't he coming? Are you alone?" he asked.

"He's staying with the cutter for now."

Blake risked letting go of the strap. They rolled slowly in mid-air in the padded cabin. He only half heard her whispered words when she said, "I needed to touch you more than I let myself know."

For answer, he held her tighter.

They were interrupted by a jolly shout. "Whenever you're ready, folks." A small brown female face, the pilot's, peered at them through the flight-deck hatch.

Sparta reluctantly detached herself from Blake. "Does anyone know I'm here yet?"

He hesitated before answering. "A Space Board cutter brings out all the busybodies. There've been rumors ever since they broke off the quarantine. Forster didn't think there was any point in trying to hide you."

"But he didn't . . ."

Blake nodded. "He called a press conference."

She sighed.

"The professor's been under a lot of pressure," Blake said. "Randolph Mays has been on Ganymede for over a month. Raising hell with the Space Board and the Culture Committee because Forster won't give him an interview. Forster hasn't given an interview to *anybody*. He's been in hiding so long most of the hounds finally got bored and went away. But Mays has whipped them all up again."

"So . . ." Sparta nodded, unsurprised. "Forster's

decided to throw *me* to the hounds.'' She found a seat and started buckling herself into it.

Blake looked acutely embarrassed. ''Just one press conference. Then it's over. He'll be there too.''

''The difference is, *he* loves this sort of thing.''

''You can handle it.'' In a less than enthusiastic voice he called to the pilot, ''Need me up there?''

''Don't be ridiculous,'' the woman replied, and closed the flight-deck door firmly behind her.

A minute later the retrorockets rumbled, beginning an unusually slow and gentle burn. Blake and Sparta, sitting side by side with safety harnesses in dangerously loose condition, failed to notice the smooth deceleration, which they owed to their pilot's weakness for romance.

After a wild ride by moon buggy, involving two transfers to escape prying telescopes, Sparta reached the ice cave under the pressure dome where the *Michael Ventris* still waited. The ship's cargo hold and equipment bay were sealed, and its tanks smoked with liquid fuel. The cave was empty except for the huts of the little encampment; the *Ventris* was poised to blast off.

Sparta met the crew. It was almost a homecoming for her—she knew not only Forster, but Walsh, who had piloted cutters that had carried her to the moon and Mars. And then there was McNeil . . .

''Angus, it really is you.'' She grabbed the burly engineer's hand in both hers, keeping him at arm's length while she looked him in the eye. ''Found yourself a captain with a grand wine cellar, did you now?''

He returned her knowing look. ''Still in the inspectin' business, Inspector?''

''And haven't made lieutenant in all these years, is that what you're askin', McNeil?''

''Wouldna ha' crossed my mind.'' Both their Scottish accents were growing thicker, as they tried to outdo each other. "I'm mightily pleased to see you, whate'er your rank may be."

She let go of his hand and hugged him. "And I'm pleased to be working with you."

In the supply hut Forster mounted one of the lavish dinners that made their lives in the ice cave tolerable. Sparta sat between Forster and Tony Groves, and learned something more of Groves than the quick navigator suspected, for as usual he was asking most of the questions. As she told him the standard tale of Ellen Troy's "lucky" exploits, she inspected him with a cold macrozoom eye and an ear trained in the inflections of speech, confirming his restlessness and daring. But it was on the basis of his nice smell that she decided he was a person to be trusted.

The other new face at the table was poor Bill Hawkins, who sat enveloped in gloom and had to struggle just to get out the pleasantries; he said he was pleased to meet her, but Sparta suspected he could not have given an adequate description of her five minutes later, so absent were his thoughts. When he excused himself early, Groves leaned over and told Sparta, in an unnecessarily low voice, what she already suspected.

"Lovesick. Poor boy was dumped for another fellow. He was rather gone on the girl, and I don't blame him. She was a looker. Oh, and very intelligent, to hear him tell it."

"We'll take his mind off such things soon enough," growled J.Q.R. Forster. "Now that the Inspector has joined us, there is no reason to delay another day."

Sparta shared Blake's dark, warm hut and its narrow bunk.

"Just think," she whispered, "within twenty-four hours this little place will be swept away in a torrent of fire . . . or maybe sooner.'' She muffled his laughter with her mouth.

They struggled to find room. ''Just one thing,'' she said, hesitating. ''There are some places you have to be careful.''

''I'll be careful of everyplace.''

''I'm serious. Here, and here . . .'' She showed him the results of her surgery. ''They're sensitive.''

''Hm. Are you going to explain all this to me, or do I have to take it on faith?''

''I'll explain everything. Later.''

Much later Blake sat on the end of the bunk, dangling a leg over the edge and watching her in the light from the single torch, turned down to less than a candle's glow. Even completely exposed, there was nothing visible in this eccentric light to reveal that her long-limbed, small-breasted body was other than simply human.

To her infrared-sensitive vision, Blake presented a much brighter image, for he glowed with heat wherever the blood coursed through his veins. She amused herself, watching the heat slowly redistribute itself.

''Sleepy?'' she asked.

''No. You?''

She shook her head. ''You wanted me to explain. It's a very long story. Some parts you've already heard, but not in the same order.''

''Tell me a long story. Any order you want.''

On the far side of the ice cave, Bill Hawkins lay alone on his bunk and stared with open eyes into pitch darkness. With the imminent arrival of Inspector Troy, and thus of the launch of the *Ventris*, Forster had finally brought poor Hawkins out of the glare of the spotlight and into hiding with the rest of the expedition. He was grateful. He was a shade less miserable once he'd gotten away from the Interplanetary, which now held nothing but bitter associations.

He repeatedly replayed his few hours with Marianne in his mind, noting that the same events looked a bit different each time he analyzed them. Each time, his behavior looked worse.

It began the very morning after their first night, when they met at a *dim sum* place in the square and she arrived with a smile that lit up her green eyes—straight from the travel agency. She announced to him that she'd canceled the rest of her Grand Tour. He'd turned her smile to anger with his disapproval; what, after all, did she intend to do with herself without him? She'd answered that she would find something to do until he came back from Amalthea. So he'd given her a lecture on broadening her knowledge of the worlds, etc., and she'd thrown in his face his own remarks about how two weeks wasn't enough to get to know Ganymede. . . . He'd had the sense to retreat, but not until she'd accused him of sounding like her *mother*, for God's sake. . . .

It got worse. Hawkins was the sort who got himself twisted into moral knots over whether to speak up every time somebody said something that was well known but untrue—for example, that Venus had once been a comet, or that ancient alien astronauts had bulldozed runways in the Peruvian desert—and some imp of the perverse wouldn't let him keep his mouth shut whenever she made a petty mistake, even ones far less egregious than these. She took this treatment longer, perhaps, than she should have, for she was acutely aware of the scattered nature of her education.

But eventually she had to stand and fight, for her own self-respect. And it was Hawkins's bad luck that she chose to make her stand upon the theories of Sir Randolph Mays. Something about Mays sent her into raptures—so many piles of facts, perhaps, his truly extraordinary erudition, as if somehow he had read five times as much as any other man alive—and that same something sent Hawkins into paroxysms of offended rationalism—perhaps because Mays's facts, taken individually, were unassailable: it was just the cockamamie way he stacked them up. . . .

The more she defended Mays, the more Hawkins attacked him. Hawkins always won the arguments, of course. But in retrospect it seemed inevitable that Randolph Mays would show up in person during one of their little debates.

Now Hawkins could brood at leisure upon his disastrous success in reducing Marianne to silence.

11

A huge stupa-like dome dominated the port's striated icy plain; big curving black-glass windows took in the panoramic view. Through one of them, Randolph Mays idly watched a pressurized moon buggy bound across the ice.

Mays stood slightly apart from the crowd of mediahounds who'd gathered to slice newsbites out of Inspector Ellen Troy and Professor J.Q.R. Forster. His new production assistant craned her neck to see the door, at present firmly shut, where the media victims were scheduled to appear. "Shouldn't we be closer?" Marianne fretted. "They'll be here any minute."

"We're quite well situated," Mays replied, speaking into the microfiber that tight-linked him to the pick-up unit Marianne wore in her ear. When the time came to take his pictures and ask his questions, his great height and unmistakable voice would make it unnecessary to actually come in contact with the squirming mass of his fellows.

"I can't see very well," Marianne complained.

"I can," said Mays, putting an end to the discussion. His assistant didn't need to see in order to do her job—such as it was. Having decided he could use her help, Mays had been prepared to put up with bare competence in some areas provided he got complete cooperation in others. To his surprise, Marianne had proved far from useless; indeed, she had shown herself quite adept at making travel arrangements and appointments and generally keeping his schedule in order, using the phonelink in that half-efficient, half-sexy, American college girl voice of hers as if she'd been born to the device. She didn't even balk at carrying his luggage; in his workmanlike old leather satchel she'd brought along his recorders and extra chips and the old-fashioned notebook he sometimes used as a prop.

If Mays were given to such thoughts, he would have had to credit Bill Hawkins with his good luck. But Mays wasn't the sort to give credit to others, unless forced to it. After all, he'd decided to seduce Marianne no matter what; Hawkins had just made it that much easier. . . .

"Here they come, Randolph," said Marianne. There was hissing and jostling in the pack of newshounds. She handed him the camera and microphone pick-up he'd specified.

Mays slipped into the rig and expertly framed the shot in time to catch the opening of the door. Professor Forster was first through it, followed by the rest of his crew. Last onto the dais was Inspector Ellen Troy, trim in her Space Board blues. Marianne stood by, thrilled, watching the scene unfold on her tiny auxiliary remote monitor.

"Good morning, ladies and gentlemen," Forster began. "I would like to start by . . ."

"Why have you been avoiding the media, Forster?" someone yelled at him.

"What have you got to hide?" another screamed.

"Troy! Inspector Troy! Isn't it true—"

"You, Troy! What about reports that you—"

"—that you've been locked up in an asylum for the past twelve months?"

"—tried to kill Howard Falcon and sabotage the *Kon-Tiki* expedition?"

Forster closed his mouth with an almost audible snap, tucked in his chin, and glared from beneath gingery brows, waiting for the questioners to wear themselves down. Finally there was a lull in the cacophony. "I'll read a brief statement," he said, clearing his throat with a growl. "Questions afterward."

There were renewed shouts, but the majority of the reporters, realizing that Forster would go on ignoring them until he'd been given a chance to read his prepared remarks, turned on their fellows and shushed them smartly.

"If he says anything of the slightest *interest,* please make sure I'm *awake* to record it," Mays drawled into his microlink.

"Thank you," said Forster into the sullen and expectant silence. "Let me introduce the members of the Amalthea expedition. First, in charge of our vessel, the *Michael Ventris,* our pilot, Josepha Walsh; our engineer, Angus McNeil; and our navigator, Anthony Groves. Assisting me in surface operations will be Dr. William Hawkins and Mr. Blake Redfield. Inspector Ellen Troy represents the Board of Space Control."

"I'll wager she represents rather more than *that,*" whispered Mays.

"Our mission is two-fold," Forster continued. "We wish to determine the geological structure of the moon. More particularly, we hope to resolve certain persistent anomalies in the radiation signature of Amalthea. For over a century—until the termination of the *Kon-Tiki* expedition last year— Amalthea was observed to radiate more energy than it receives directly from the sun and by reflection from Jupiter. Almost all of the excess heat could be attributed to the impact of charged particles in Jupiter's radiation belt—almost all, but not quite all. We should like to learn where that extra heat came from."

"*Especially* now that the heat's been turned *up*," Mays kibbitzed.

"The question has become more urgent since Amalthea became geologically active. It now reradiates *much* more energy than it absorbs. What kind of heat engine is driving the ice geysers that are causing Amalthea to lose almost half a per cent of its original mass each twelve hours—every time the moon orbits Jupiter?"

"Oh, do *tell* us," Mays pleaded, *sotto voce.*

"Finally, of course," Forster said, speaking hurriedly, "we hope to learn what connection may exist between the recent events on Amalthea and the creatures called medusas which live in the clouds of Jupiter." He glared at the audience of ostentatiously bored reporters. "We'll take questions."

"Troy! Where did you spend the past year?" shouted one of the loudest of the hounds.

"Is it true you were in an asylum?"

She glanced at Forster, who nodded. He knew who the real media star was. "I've been involved in an investigation," she said, "the nature of which, for the time being, must remain confidential."

"Oh, come on," the man groaned, "that doesn't . . ."

But other questioners were already shouting him down: *What about the aliens, Forster? Aren't you really going to Amalthea to find Culture X? You and Troy talking to these aliens, is that it?*

A piercing female voice cut through the babble: "You claim your expedition is *scientific*, Professor Forster. But Sir Randolph Mays claims you're part of the Free Spirit *conspiracy*. Who's right?"

Forster's grin was feral. "Are you sure you're quoting Sir Randolph correctly? Why not ask him? He's right there, in back."

The whole pack of them turned to stare at Mays,

who muttered, "What's *this* then?" even as he continued to aim his photogram camera at the odd spectacle. "Be *ready*, my dear," he addressed Marianne, "we're going to have to spring our little *surprise* earlier than I'd hoped."

"What about it, Sir Randolph?" the woman reporter called in his direction. "Don't you think Forster's one of them?"

He held the camera to one side, still pointed at the newshounds—enjoying their resentful attention—and at the crew of the *Michael Ventris* waiting uneasily on the dais beyond them. "I never said you were *part* of the conspiracy, Professor," he called out cheerfully, a huge grin stretching his voracious lips over his sturdy white teeth. "Nevertheless I throw the question *back* to you. You know *something* known to the Free Spirit and unknown to the rest of us. Tell us the *real* reason you are going to Amalthea. Tell us the *reason* you are taking an *ice* mole. Tell us *why* you are taking a Europan *submarine*."

Ice mole!

Submarine!

What's all this in aid of, Forster?

"As for this Free Spirit of yours, Sir Randolph, I am wholly in the dark." Forster's grin was as fierce as Mays's; they could have been a pair of feuding baboons disputing the leadership of the pack. "But as to the moon Amalthea, it seems you have chosen not to hear what I have just been saying. Amalthea is expelling its substance into space through immense spouts of water vapor. Therefore this moon must consist very largely of water, some of it solid—for which an ice mole is a useful exploratory tool—and some of it liquid, the sort of environment for which the submarines of Europa were designed."

Josepha Walsh leaned forward to tap Forster on the shoulder; Forster paused to listen to his pilot's whispered words, then returned his attention to the assembled reporters. "I'm informed that the count-down for our departure has already begun," he said with gleeful malice. "Unfortunately that is all the time we have for discussion. Thank you for your attention."

The cries of rage from the frustrated newshounds were frightening enough to justify the precaution of spaceport guards, who emerged from the doorway to protect the retreat of Forster's crew; none but Sparta and Forster himself had said a word to the assembled media.

"Is that all they're going to say?" Marianne asked, frustrated that her questions—thousands of them—were still unanswered.

Mays tore off his comm rig. "He *mocks* me." He stared over the heads of his milling colleagues, seemingly lost inside himself. Then he looked down at his assistant. "We have only *begun* to report this story. But to carry on will require imagination . . . and *daring.* Are you still committed, Marianne?"

Her eyes shone with dedication. "I'm with you all the way, Randolph."

PART 3

THE MANTA,
THE MOON CRUISER,
AND THE OLD MOLE

12

Everyone not on duty gathered in the wardroom of the *Michael Ventris* to watch the final approach on the viewscreens. At first, Amalthea appeared as a tiny gibbous moon hanging in space, its night sector lit up faintly by the reflected glory of Jupiter.

Jupiter seemed to expand forever, until finally it filled the sky, rolling overhead at an incredible rate as the ship smoothly matched orbits with its bright, swiftly moving target. What had been a lump of dark rock 270 kilometers long, blotched with a few snowy patches, was now a shorter ellipsoid of gleaming ice, as polished and abstract as a Brancusi sculpture, its long axis pointed straight at the curdled orange and yellow clouds of Jupiter, its principal.

Even if they had not had the aid of the viewscreen optics, they were close enough now to see hundreds of plumes of vapor dotting the sculptured ice surface, a celestial Yellowstone of fizzing soda-water geysers. Instead of falling back to the ground, these geysers all gracefully curved away into space, dissipating in fairy veils of mist that made it look as if Amalthea were caressed by gentle winds, rather than racing into stark vacuum.

The only "atmosphere" this far from Jupiter—

despite its awesome size, still almost 110,000 kilometers distant—was the horde of particles in its radiation belts. Like the tail of a comet approaching the sun, the tenuous gases of Amalthea were set aglow and blown backward by radiation pressure alone.

It was into this misty slipstream that Josepha Walsh steered the *Ventris*—into the only region of space close to Jupiter that was shielded from lethal trapped radiation. Here, a little over a year ago, *Garuda* had waited while Howard Falcon descended into the clouds in the balloon-borne *Kon-Tiki*. *Garuda*'s task had been easy by comparison to that of the *Ventris*, for it had only to wait the few short days until Falcon returned. The mission of the *Michael Ventris* was open-ended, and the object of its study changed shape with each passing minute.

Jo Walsh maneuvered as close to the moon as she dared without actually touching down upon it. Finally Jupiter disappeared from the viewscreens, setting beyond the close, sharply curved horizon of Amalthea; a few minutes more, and the *Ventris* sidled so close that from the main hatch it would be only a little jump into the mists that shrouded the surface below.

Long before the ship stopped moving, the watchers in the wardroom had seen the strange black markings on the moon. Hawkins blurted out the question on everyone's minds: "What are those? Craters?"

Groves and McNeil soon joined Blake and Bill Hawkins and the professor in the wardroom. The whole crew was there except Walsh, who still had things to attend to on the flight deck, and Sparta, who had not been seen since shortly before launch from Ganymede.

The biggest viewscreen was playing back in extreme slow motion the sequence of images from the *Ventris*'s final approach. At three places on the side facing them, clearly visible through the tenuous surface mist, were huge, sharply defined circles—black lines inscribed as if with a fine nib, India ink on white rag paper—circles within circles, too mathematically precise and too regularly spaced to have been the product of random cratering.

"Professor, did you already know about this?"

"Let's say it isn't as much of a surprise to me as it is to you." Forster's shiny young face with its old man's eyes looked very smug as he fielded their questions. "The Space Board have managed to keep most of its remote satellite observations under wraps. Only one slip—that image Mays somehow got hold of, which was too distant to give away anything of consequence—and these patterns only showed up in the high-resolution visuals within the past month. We're the first to get a close look."

As the image sequence continued, with the point of view sinking closer to the surface, it was obvious to the onlookers that the rings were not inscriptions, not something incised in a smooth surface; on the contrary, they stood out in relief. They were structures of some kind, delicate black traceries of metal or some composite material, standing a few meters above the icy plain.

"Anybody got any ideas about what we're looking at?" Forster asked.

"Well, sir, I'd venture . . ."

"No fair, Angus, you can tell at a glance. Bill? Tony? Any guesses?"

Tony Groves shook his head and smiled. "No idea. Although they do look a bit like giant dartboards."

"Some dartboards," McNeil snorted. "Some darts."

"Bill?" the professor prompted.

Bill Hawkins said rather sullenly, "I'm a linguist, not a planetologist." He seemed genuinely hurt by

Forster's evident decision to withhold his prior knowledge of the markings.

"What about you, Blake?"

Blake smiled. "Could they have something to do with the fact that when Falcon aroused the medusas, they aimed a radio blast right at Amalthea?"

"Is that really true?" Hawkins asked sharply. "Mays claimed it, but the Space Board never confirmed it."

"It's true, Bill," Forster said. "I'll show you my analysis of that signal. I think you'll come to the same conclusion about its meaning I did."

"Which is what?" Hawkins demanded.

"A message that translates, 'They have arrived.' I believe the medusas were announcing the arrival of visitors in the clouds of Jupiter."

"The medusas!" Hawkins protested. "They're not intelligent, are they? Aren't they merely simple animals?"

"Well, we really have no idea how intelligent they are. Or even how to apply the concept of intelligence to alien lifeforms. But given the right sort of training, or programming, it takes no particular intelligence for an Earthly organism to emit a complex-seeming behavior, upon the right stimulus. Trained parrots for example."

"Assuming the medusas *were* signalling, there would have to be receivers to pick up the signal," Blake said.

"*Radio* antennas, you mean?" said Hawkins, incredulous.

"So I'd bet," said Forster.

Angus McNeil nodded. "That's just what they are, by the look of 'em. Suitable for meter wavelengths, same as the markings on the medusas. What I wonder is why nobody ever noticed 'em before."

"Until a year ago—until the geysers erupted—Amalthea was covered with reddish black dirt,"

Forster said, "the color of a carbonaceous body rich in organics, and incidentally the perfect color to hide these artificial structures."

"You think they were deliberately disguised, then?" asked Tony Groves, sounding skeptical.

"I don't know," Forster replied simply. "I suppose the dirt layer could have accumulated over the millenniums from random collisions with meteoroids." He looked at Blake. "What do you say?"

"What seems irrational to a human might make perfect sense to an alien," Blake answered. "Yet I don't see the point in hiding the antennas, if the idea is to alert some . . . *presence* on Amalthea that visitors have arrived at Jupiter. What difference would it make if the visitors saw these things and chose to land on Amalthea before going to Jupiter?"

"Unless this presence, as you call it, didn't want to be discovered accidentally," said Forster.

"What does that mean?" Hawkins blurted, still nursing his resentment.

"A year ago nobody knew there were medusas living in the atmosphere of Jupiter," Forster said to him, "despite a century's worth of probes—over three hundred robot probes. Until somebody goes back down there and tries to interview a medusa, we won't know how intelligent they are—your point, Bill—or what kind of intelligence we're dealing with. Perhaps this—*presence*—doesn't want to talk to robots. Or to trained parrots. Perhaps it doesn't want to talk to entities that have merely stumbled upon some sign or mark of artifice on the surface of Amalthea. Perhaps this presence only wants to talk to those who know exactly what they're looking for."

"Those who've found and deciphered the Martian plaque?" Hawkins asked, adding a bit acidly, "People like yourself?"

Forster smiled disingenuously. ''The Martian plaque—or its equivalent.''

''According to Sir Randolph-Bloody-Mays, the Free Spirit claims to have preserved from antiquity such an *equivalent.*'' Hawkins almost spat the words. ''They call it the *Knowledge.*''

''I'm not one of the Free Spirit, Bill, and I'm not in league with them,'' Forster said quietly. ''Whatever Mays may claim.''

Blake broke the awkward silence that ensued. ''Our turn to quiz you, Professor. What *are* we looking for out there?''

''Good question.'' Forster paused, tugging at a stray hair in one of his thick brows. ''Answering it is the essence of our task. I have my notions, but in fact I don't know anything with certainty. No more than any of you,'' he added, with a nod to Bill Hawkins. ''We'll begin with a close-in survey from orbit.''

They flew through a fantastic cloudscape, a corona of gases standing straight out from the surface of the moon like electrified hair. Instead of entangling itself in these evanescent tresses, the *Ventris* sailed through them without leaving so much as an eddy, except where the cage of its superconducting radiation shield temporarily bent the charged particles around the ship in curves of mathematical precision.

Coming over the leading half, blown bare of gas, they looked down upon a blinding whiteness that appeared as smooth and hard as a billiard ball; but when they bounced radar signals off the surface, a mushy signal came back. They charted the locations of the geysers and found that while they were not exactly equidistant from one another, they marked out the interstices of a regular imaginary grid pattern over the entire ellipsoidal surface of the moon. They found six of the giant ''dartboards,'' one at each pole of the long axis, and four evenly spaced around the equator.

When they were safely parked back in the radiation shadow, Tony Groves, who was in charge of the survey, neatly summed up the results: "Friends, there's absolutely nothing natural about this so-called moon."

The first exploratory team—Blake, Angus McNeil, and Bill Hawkins—went out twelve hours later. In that time Amalthea and its flea-sized parasite, the *Michael Ventris*, had raced all the way around Jupiter once and come back approximately to where they had been with respect to Jupiter and its planet-sized, slower-moving Galilean moons, when they'd first made moonfall.

The hatch swung open and the three explorers, spotlighted by a circle of yellow light from the airlock, floated out into the shadow of Amalthea. McNeil had done this sort of thing more times than he could count, on hundreds of asteroids and moonlets, although he'd never done it quite like this—

—diving into a white fog as bright and opaque as dry ice vapor but more tenuous, gauzier, harder to disturb, less skittish; it was as if the fog were no more substantial, no easier to cup in the hands or disturb with a vigorous swing of the arm, than the diffuse and omnipresent light that had existed in the photon era of the early universe.

When Forster had announced the roster, McNeil had muttered to Tony Groves that Hawkins was too inexperienced for the tricky extravehicular activity. But Forster made it clear that he wanted Hawkins to be on the first team.

Nor was Blake exactly an old hand; his experience in space was, putting it politely, eclectic. He'd once had fun jumping around on Earth's moon, and he'd had plenty of practice with Martian pressure suits, but aside from one brief episode in an old-fashioned soft-suit near the Martian moon Phobos, he was new to work in deep space.

McNeil was appointed their shepherd. In thirty years of space travel, there were few emergencies he had not faced and managed.

When they got close enough to the surface they discovered beneath their booted feet a froth of pure and delicate water ice, fantastically carved by forces no more powerful than sublimation into a fluffy crystalline universe of branching miniaturized snowflake-structures—the scale and complexity of deep coral reefs, yet as insubstantial as a puff of talc.

The gravity of Amalthea was so microscopic that walking was out of the questions; they were all roped together like mountaineers, and they blew themselves across the plain with gentle bursts from their backpack maneuvering systems.

"What's it like down there?" came Forster's impatient query in their suitcomms.

"Like an Italian ice," said Blake.

"The closer one looks, the more extraordinary the formations," Hawkins said. "Infinitely recursively structured, probably down to the limit of the water molecule."

"What did he say?" McNeil muttered audibly.

Blake and McNeil were at the two ends of the tether, so that any unwise eagerness on Hawkins's part—he'd established a reputation as one given to disruptive enthusiasms—was restrained. After his companions had had to yank him back into line for the second time, Forster's voice came over the commlink again. "How are you feeling, Bill?"

"I know that some people think it must be very entertaining to walk around on an airless, low-gravity planet in a spacesuit. Well, it isn't."

McNeil grumbled, "Strain getting to you?"

"All these checks and precautions."

"Just think about the main points. Know where you are?"

"What does it matter when I'm on this bloody rope?"

"Have enough air?"

"Well of course, Angus, really . . ."

"Then just don't forget to breathe."

For five minutes they moved on in silence until their objective, one of the arrays of black circles they had seen from space, was a quarter of a kilometer away, and they could just make out a hazy sketch of lines in the mist.

McNeil said, "Maybe we're dealing with a relay, an amplifier. Maybe some of these antennas are aimed at the home star of the ones who built them."

"Why six antennas?" Hawkins asked. "Even with one to point at Jupiter—seems like four extra to me."

"Rotation," said Blake.

"It couldn't have taken long for Amalthea to become tidally locked to Jupiter," Hawkins protested. "So it must have been in this orientation a billion years."

"You're overlooking its revolution around Jupiter."

"Right," McNeil said. "With six arrays, they can cover the whole sky all the time."

"Well, whatever it is, *there* it is," Hawkins said.

The line of half-drifting, half-flying spacesuited men rebounded to an awkward halt, like a Slinky toy falling off a stairstep. Out of the white mist ahead of them the thing loomed up, black and spidery, furred with icicles weirdly splayed in every direction.

It was unquestionably an artificial object—very possibly a radio antenna, as seemed likely—but it was unutterably foreign in its details. It could have come from beneath the sea.

* * *

An hour went by. Blake exhausted himself trying to prize a chunk of stuff off the structure, but there was nowhere to get a purchase. Nothing was rusted; the thing didn't appear to be made of iron or any metal susceptible to corrosion, but of something resembling an indestructibly tough black plastic. There were no seams big enough to slip a knife-blade into. He couldn't unscrew anything or shear off anything, because there were no screws or bolts or rivets. As for the base of it, that was apparently still buried meters deep in the ice.

The huge circular rig was a shallow, bowl-shaped mesh more than a kilometer across, a paraboloid with a central mast terminating at its focus. But Angus McNeil pointed out that it seemed the wrong shape, too flat in the Z-axis, for the electromagnetic radiation it was supposed to detect. "If it's an antenna, okay, but it would be damned inefficient," he said. "I can't believe these aliens were sophisticated enough to set up a listening post here but not sophisticated enough to design an efficient receiver or transmitter."

"Maybe it's not a transmitter. Maybe they didn't worry about the home star," said Blake. "Maybe Amalthea houses some kind of memory device, recording data intended to be picked up later."

"But this whole thing was supposed to be under ice for a billion years, right?" Hawkins said.

Looking at the huge construction which loomed like a spider web in the mist, it was hard to remember that the fragile snow around them hadn't always been there, that not long ago the surface of Amalthea had been higher than their heads—high enough to completely engulf the alien antenna.

"You mean its geometry compensates for the speed of light in water?" McNeil's tone conveyed what he left unsaid: either you don't know anything at all about physics, young Dr. Hawkins—or you're not so dumb after all.

"Did I say that?" Hawkins asked.

The former, McNeil decided. Ah, well. "Radio waves don't travel far in water," he growled.

"It wasn't *that* far under water," Blake said, siding with Hawkins. "Only a few meters."

"Well, it's a hypothesis," McNeil said. "I'll have to run some calculations."

"Still . . . if these are antennas, where's the power source?" Hawkins added, still playing devil's advocate, taking delight in complicating matters further.

"If this were my rig, I'd make it self-contained, fit it with superconducting batteries and capacitors," McNeil said. "Field measurements will tell us. If you want to worry about power, think about whatever's driving those geysers."

"Could be, their power source isn't on Amalthea at all," Blake said.

"What do you mean, Blake?" Professor Forster's voice sounded in their helmets.

"Until a year ago, Amalthea was thought to be a rigid body. If the rigidity was artificial, maybe the medusas' signal somehow turned off the gizmo—so now Amalthea is feeling the tidal forces from Jupiter. In that case Jupiter would be the heat engine."

"As with the volcanoes of Europa," Forster said.

"Yes sir," Blake said. "If Amalthea is really mostly water, expansion and contraction as it whips around Jupiter would be enough to start it boiling away, so long as nothing prevents it."

"Meaning we still don't know what we're looking for," Angus McNeil grumbled.

Later, when it was arbitrary night aboard the *Ventris*, McNeil displayed the results of his measurements and calculations on the graphics plate. Indeed, the structures had just the right geometry to function as antennas under a moderate layer of ice.

The team was supposed to use the night hours to sleep, but the day's events left few of them calm enough. After dinner in the wardroom, Blake left the others arguing about how and with whom the antennas communicated and went back to the ship's cramped but well-equipped laboratory.

Having finally resorted to a laser probe and an ion trap to get a few sample molecules from the alien structure, he spent the early evening hours trying to find out what the stuff was. Spectrometry didn't help him much: no exotic elements showed up in the peaks and valleys of the spectrum—a few common metals, plus carbon and oxygen and nitrogen and other light elements—and not even any unusual ratios among them. Whatever had given the structure its extraordinary strength and durability was surely due to its crystalline structure—but that had been reduced to molecular chaos when Blake blasted it with his laser.

He gave up and turned to the ice cores they had collected. These were more . . . suggestive.

He was peering at the readouts, shaking his head glumly, when he became aware that Forster was watching him from the hatch of the cramped, padded laboratory.

"Hello," Blake said, "have you come to watch me learn basic college chemistry?"

"What are you doing?" Forster asked, eyebrows vibrating.

"Well, sir, I could give you a list of failed experiments. Structure and composition of the ice. Age of the ice—trying to do age determinations on these core samples we took today and not succeeding."

The surface of Amalthea, subliming into space, was constantly exposing fresh layers of material. The long-buried ice had been affected by particles in Jupiter's radiation belt and by solar and cosmic rays. By measuring isotope ratios in the fresh ice, it was theoretically possible to calculate how long each layer had rested undisturbed.

"What's the problem?"

"The readings are crazy. Neighboring samples give values that differ by five or six orders of magnitude."

"You've calibrated the instruments?"

"Yes sir. Maybe I'm misreading the manuals—maybe they were translated from Eskimo or Finno-Ugrik or something."

"Why not believe the instruments? One sample's old, another's young."

Blake said, "We're not talking old and young here, sir, we're talking young and *very* young. Most of the samples date this ice to a billion years BP. Compare that to ice from Ganymede or Callisto or Europa, which is a respectable four-point-five billion years BP."

Forster sounded gruff, but there was a smile in his voice. "Meaning Amalthea didn't form as part of the Jupiter system. Perhaps it was captured later."

"Meaning Amalthea didn't form as part of the *solar* system." Blake grunted. *"Listen* to me, I sound like Sir Randolph-Loudmouth-*Mays."*

"And the other sample?" Forster demanded.

"Somewhere between a thousand and ten thousand years old."

"Not *quite* as old as the solar system," Forster said, smiling openly now.

"Well sir, if you were a Creationist . . ."

"Where did that sample come from?"

"Right under the alien antenna," Blake said.

"Might be an interesting place to start looking." Forster sighed softly. "Too bad Troy's not with us. Could be, that cult of hers would have something to say about these matters."

"She wouldn't like to hear you call the Free Spirit *her* cult, Professor."

"Salamander, then, or whatever you call yourselves. Professor Nagy attempted to enlighten me, but I'm afraid I was never able to get it all straight."

"Besides, the Knowledge is hardly complete. It doesn't make any reference to Amalthea," said Blake, evading the topic.

"Rather odd, then, that Troy always seems to know more than this so-called Knowledge. Too bad she never stays in one place long enough to make herself useful."

Blake felt his ears glowing. "She usually manages to arrive when she's needed," he said defensively. Forster of all people knew that better than most.

"Quite. What *is* she about, back there on Ganymede? Did she drop any hints in your hearing?"

"Sorry. I don't know any more about it than you."

"Hm, well . . . I wish she'd let us know earlier. Saved ourselves a week or two in that gloomy cavern." Forster turned his attention to the lab bench, tapping the laser spectrometer's little flatscreen. "What else have you got to show, my boy?"

"Take a look at the basic composition of this stuff. Look at these ratios." Blake first showed Forster close-ups of ice crystals on the big screen, then a chemical analysis of the foreign minerals trapped in the crystals.

Looking at the colored graphics and spiky charts on the flatplate, J.Q.R. Forster's face broadened into a truly happy grin. "Golly, Mr. Wizard."

"What are you onto, sir?" Blake demanded, for it was obvious the older man was not surprised.

"You first, young man—what does it all mean to you?"

"Well, the crystalline structure's common enough. Ordinary Ice I, so we know it froze at low pressure."

"Surely that's what you'd expect."

"Yeah, unless Amalthea was a leftover chunk of the core of a much larger ice moon."

"You considered that, did you?" Forster said appreciatively.

"It crossed my mind. See, I don't think this stuff froze in vacuum. How could you explain these dissolved minerals—salts, carbonates, phosphates, others. . . . " He pointed to the graphic on the plate.

"What does it look like to you?" Forster prodded.

"How about frozen seawater?"

13

The *Michael Ventris* slowly settled out of orbit under the feathery tug of Amalthea's gravity, until its flat tripod feet sank deep into the frothy surface. In the equipment bay the ice mole hung lightly in its shackles, lit by the metallic glare of worklights. Blake and Forster pulled themselves into its cockpit and methodically strapped themselves in. The gingery professor was seething with impatience.

"Quaint old gadget," Blake muttered placidly, regarding the gaudy display panel now lit up like a carnival midway. He fiddled interminably with the instruments while Forster, who had been edgy throughout the tedious pre-launch, grew increasingly tense.

"Got an *old* mole here, do we?" came Josepha Walsh's hoarse and cheerful voice over the comm.

"This Old Mole's still got plenty of get up and go," Blake said at last. "Diagnostics give us a clean slate. Ready to launch."

"Let's get *on* with it," Forster said.

"All set, Jo?" Blake said in the general direction of the mike.

For a moment there was silence on the commlink before Walsh replied. "That's a roger. You may proceed."

Blake brought the clear bubble down over their heads and sealed it. "Confirming full atmospheric pressure, no discernible leaks."

"You'll be fine as long as you've got your E-units," came Walsh's reply. Against sudden pressure loss they wore emergency soft-suits, with the faceplates of their head-fitting helmets left open. The mole was of too early a vintage to be equipped for Artificial Reality suits, with which a pilot could feel wholly a part of the machine.

"I hardly think we're going to die of depressurization," Forster said sharply.

Blake gave him a quick glance. Perhaps it was the sense of separation, the need for layers of protection and interpretation between him and the environment, that made the professor so irritable. Perhaps he was reminded of his near-disastrous expedition to Venus.

"I'll not hold you up any longer then," said Walsh. The clamshell doors of the equipment bay peeled away—

—opening upon stars above and unearthly white mist below, and on the horizon a ruddy glow, Jupiter itself riding unseen beneath the moon's edge.

The whine of a miniature electric crane conveyed itself through the grapple to the roof of the vehicle as the mole was lifted ever so slowly out of the hold and held poised, outside the ship. The whine ceased. There was a click as the last magnetic grapple let go. Then another click, as springs uncoiled and gently propelled the machine away from the ship. Almost but not quite weightless, the massive machine slowly began to drop, nose down. It fell a long time into the mists, like a sagging helium balloon, interminably.

An edge of the huge alien antenna came out of the milky whiteness on the port side. The *Ventris* had purposely dropped the mole beside the antenna, for here the ice samples showed patches anomalously younger than Amalthea's otherwise uniform age of a billion years.

Blake and Forster hardly felt the slow collision with the delicate ice when they hit the surface—but outside there were sudden snowdrifts, halfway up the cockpit window.

Above and behind them, barely visible through the frosty window, two white shapes gleamed like portly angels, drifting down the black sky—Hawkins and Groves, checking the fat, half-coiled electrical cables that would power the mole from the *Ventris*'s auxiliary power units. They did what they had to behind the ice mole, securing the cable attachments.

"Okay, you should be mobile," came Hawkins's jolly voice over the commlink. He had gotten over his awkwardness in spacesuits; indeed, with a day's practice he'd become quite the athlete of the vacuum.

"We're all go here," Blake reported to the *Ventris*.

"And all links look good on our boards," said Walsh from the flight deck.

Forster said tensely, "You may go ahead when ready."

Blake eased the pots forward.

Below them opposed twin bits began an intricate dance, slowly at first, then with rising speed. A cloud of ice crystals engulfed the mole. The top ten or twelve meters were spongy froth, then there was a bump, and the machine abruptly descended through a pocket of vacuum-pocked ice. Finally, with a screech, diamond-edged titanium blades engaged old, hard ice, and the mole began to drill straight into the heart of Amalthea.

Forster suddenly relaxed, releasing a long sigh, as if he'd been holding his breath. The center of Amalthea tugged at his heart, harder the closer he got to it—like gravity, the force of his obsession increased with decreasing distance from his goal. But at least he was moving as fast as he could toward the object of his desire.

The big screen in the middle of the console gave Blake and Forster a clear three-dimensional image of their sector of the moon's structure—where they were and where they were going. Along with information from a year's worth of passive observation by Space Board satellites, the results of the *Ventris*'s recent seismic studies had been fed into the mole's data banks. Had Amalthea been anything but a thoroughly surprising place, the image on the screen might have been unexpected. . . .

For over a century, since it was first photographed close up by the primitive robot probe *Voyager 1*, Amalthea had been thought to be low in volatile substances—certainly a reasonable hypothesis, for the moon had no atmosphere, was rigid, seemed inert. By contrast, its much larger neighbor, Io, was a moon so rubbery, so rich in mutable liquids and gases, that remarkable sulfur volcanoes had been in constant eruption somewhere upon its surface ever since they had been discovered by the same *Voyager 1*, the first artificial observer to reach Jupiter's orbit and the first, upon returning images of Io to its controllers, to reveal that the Earth was not alone in the solar system in being geologically active.

But Amalthea was in fact about as volatile as a small body can be, consisting almost entirely of water; yet even while bathed in Jupiter's radiation belts and racked by the tidal forces of the giant—a planet so massive it fell not far short of self-ignition into a star, and thus had often been described as a failed rival to the sun—Amalthea had remained frozen solid.

It takes energy to keep water frozen when the surroundings are hot. After all pertinent data had been fed into the *Ventris*'s computers it was learned that the apparent discrepancy in Amalthea's energy budget was due not to anything so paltry as a leakage of electrical energy from its radio antennas but to the considerably larger output of what, for want of better name, the expedition called its "refrigerator."

A refrigerator is really a heater that heats one part of the thing to be cooled until it is hotter than its surroundings, moving heat from the source to a sink or a radiator. The dark red dust of classical Almathea made a fine radiator, a surface from which the moon could rid itself of the heat it removed from its underlying ice. Most of the heat loss was disguised in the flux of Jupiter's radiation belts; for more than a hundred years no one had suspected that diminutive Amalthea was adding measurably to the total energy of the belts themselves.

But where was the source?

The Old Mole's graphics program had its limits— one had to severely restrain it from pretending to more certainty than it really had, when the input was from soft data—so the computer-generated map only sketchily showed that a spheroid of uncertain composition and dimension lay in the core of the moon. For a billion years, presumably, this object had produced the energy necessary to keep Amalthea frozen solid.

A year ago Amalthea had begun to unfreeze. But the moon was melting far faster than radiation belts or tidal forces could account for. Amalthea was melting because the core object had increased its heat output by several orders of magnitude. The refrigerator had turned into a stove.

This was what the seismologically generated map of Amalthea on the console displayed: a rind of solid ice, pierced by vents of gas and liquid, its surface subliming into vacuum. A mantle of liquid water, thirty kilometers deep. A core of hard, hot matter, composition unknown, but hot enough to boil the water that touched it.

The ice mole would come nowhere near that hot inner core, of course. The mole's function was simply to pierce Amalthea's frozen crust.

A slurry of sludge and chips blown back from the blades clumped and writhed over the Polyglas canopy, making it seem as if something out there was alive, but beyond the walls of the smooth-cut shaft there was nothing but dense ice.

"Almost there," said Blake.

"Don't slow down," Forster said, as if anticipating some uncharacteristic caution on Blake's part. Forster tugged at his nose and muttered little ruminative wordless bleats, watching the image of the ice mole boring closer to the bright boundary of ice and water.

Forster was sure he knew what that thing in the middle of Amalthea was, although he hadn't known a thing *about* it until they'd finally started getting the hard data a few days ago. Years had passed since his conviction had started him on the difficult path to these discoveries.

The view through the window was almost total blackness, relieved only by reflected light from the cockpit instruments; the view on their screen vividly depicted the mole grinding its way straight down through the ice. Behind it, liquified ice flashed into vapor and was propelled up the shaft. But to Forster's imaginative eye, the deeper they got the more the surrounding ice seemed to glow with some faint and distant source of radiance.

Up on the flight deck of the *Ventris*, the same reconstructed graphic from the mole's mapper was available on the big screens, alongside the projection of the *Ventris*'s more powerful and sophisticated seismic-tomography program. Here there was nothing uncertain—within the limit of resolution of sound waves in water—about the size and shape of Amalthea's crust or the object at its core. On these screens were incorporated the dimensions, temperature, density, and reflectivity, at every depth, of multiple imaginary slices through the moon. Yet even on *Ventris*'s screens the core was represented as a black hole. For the core object was almost perfectly absorptive of sound waves.

The boiling hot water around it was pictured with perfect clarity, in false colors that showed the intricate eddies and jets surrounding the core. But no image of the inside of the core was possible; whatever it was made of either did not transmit ordinary vibration or somehow actively damped the vibrations of the seismic disturbance that buffeted it on every side.

Over Jo Walsh's shoulder, Tony Groves watched in fascination as the mole descended. "Caution now, caution now." His voice was almost a whisper.

Walsh pretended to take him at his word. "The navigator urges caution," she said into the commlink.

Groves reddened. "Now Jo, we don't want . . ." He let his sentence dribble away.

"What's that, Tony?" she asked.

"Silly thing . . . watching the screen I was afraid for a moment . . . that when they broke through the ice they might fall."

"No danger of that." She reached up and rotated the graphic 120 degrees. "Sometimes this is a helpful reminder, when up and down aren't too significant."

"You're making fun of me, Jo," Groves said disgustedly.

But a moment later he exclaimed "Oh!" in excitement and hope, for on the screen the ice mole had finally punctured the skin of Amalthea.

Unfortunately live visuals were missing: the

mole's original designers had not thought it sensible to put a camera on a machine that was meant to spend its working life surrounded by solid ice. "Blake. Professor. Can you see anything? Tell us what you see," Walsh said.

Blake's voice was delayed, coming over the comm. "Well, it's kind of weird. We don't have outside lights on this thing, but it doesn't seem as dark. . . ."

"We're in the water," said Forster. "The lights of our cockpit are having a definite effect on the surroundings."

"What are you talking about, sir?" came Blake's puzzled voice over the commlink—

—as Walsh added her dry request, "Please be good enough to specify what the hell you're referring to, Professor."

Forster's voice came back to those who waited in the *Ventris,* satisfied and unmistakably thrilled. "Swarming all around us. *Life.* The water is full of it. . . ."

Lazy spirals of cable descended as slowly as smoke wreaths from the bulk of the *Michael Ventris.* Power cables and safety cables slithered across the ice toward the hole and disappeared into the vapor plume, following the mole inward. To Hawkins and McNeil, hovering nearby on the surface, the sign of the mole's progress was a plume of agitated vapor in the mist.

They heard the reports from the mole over their suitcomms, and for a moment Hawkins shared the thrill of the impossible discovery. *Life.* For that moment, at least, he was able to stop thinking about Marianne Mitchell and Randolph Mays.

14

Randolph Mays knew damned well
that spectacular discoveries were being
made on Amalthea, and—as he made
clear to Marianne—sitting still on
Ganymede waiting to hear about them
was driving him *crazy*.

Even in the midst of his self-described insanity he
retained his charm, however. Whether he had really read her so completely, or whether it was just
wonderful luck, Marianne found that he exerted a
powerful attraction upon her. He was almost old
enough to be her father—though not so old as her
real father, which perhaps lowered that particular
psychological barrier—and he was far from conven-
tionally handsome. Nowhere near as handsome as
. . . well, Bill Hawkins, for example. But his . . .
rugged looks and, mm, *rangy* physique were kind
of sexy if you thought about it, and his *mind* . . .

She loved working with him. She wouldn't have
minded something more than work. But he had
treated her with nothing but professional courtesy.
She did her best to live up to all his expectations in
that category, and at first she trotted after him as
faithfully as a pet. . . .

Marianne was not the only woman on Ganymede who was trying to read Randolph Mays's

mind. Sparta had hardly stopped thinking about him since Forster's press conference, on the eve of the launch of the *Ventris*. She had never seen him in person before. So intrigued was she by the stagy presence of the historian-reporter, in fact, that she had decided not to be aboard the *Ventris* when it blasted for Amalthea.

"You need to go openly now," Sparta said to the commander. "Find out more about this broker Von Frisch. See if Luke Lim is what he claims to be. Be obvious about it—it will take the pressure off of me."

"Everyone thinks you're with Forster."

"You'll get me there later. When I need to be there."

"You think I'll get you wherever you need to be whenever you need to be there, don't you?"

"Not always. Only if you can."

He said nothing, only stared morosely at the wall. He was sitting on a sprung plastic-covered couch, legs stretched out and arms crossed, and she was pacing the scuffed tile floor of the visitors' area in the Space Board's headquarters on Ganymede, a grim, cramped room in a grim, bulging, pressure-structure hidden from casual view among blast domes and fuel storage tanks in a remote corner of the spaceport—a structure whose low domed profile and windowless, government-gray skin were a reflection of the uneasy relations between the Space Board and the Indo-Asian communities of the Galilean moons.

"This is a small settlement," she continued. "All it takes is one curious person to spread the news. I'll have to dress up like a Balinese dancing girl or something."

He emitted a gravelly chuckle. "You'll be on every videoplate in Shoreless Ocean if you dress up like a dancing girl."

"Like a Tibetan nun, then," she said. "I know how to be invisible, Commander. With your help."

"Not that you really need it."

"Mays mustn't suspect I'm watching him."

The commander shifted uneasily on the broken springs of the steel-backed couch. "Why do you want to bother with Mays? He's got no way of interfering with Forster now, no way of getting to Amalthea. We have him right where we want him, under observation."

"He strikes me as a very clever man," she said. There was nothing flip or clever about the way she said it.

Ganymede had an electromagnetic cargo launcher like the two on Earth's moon—proportionally longer, of course, some fifty kilometers overall, to accommodate Ganymede's greater gravity. In addition to freight services and routine transportation to parking orbit, the Ganymede launcher offered something Earth's moon couldn't—self-guided tours of Jupiter's spectacular Galilean moons.

But the delta-vees required to send even an essentially free-falling capsule around the Jovian system and get it back again didn't come cheap, and selling tour tickets at several hundred new dollars a pop wasn't a cinch. Over the years the hucksters had evolved a graduated pitch:

Free!—and available at any of the numerous agencies with offices on the main square—was an informational slide show, a minichip's load of two-and-a-half-dimensional views of the Galilean moons as seen through the portholes of automated tour cruisers, with an accompanying narration consisting mostly of astronomical facts—cleverly presented by leading industrial psychologists to instill in the viewer the conviction that there was something interesting out there, and whatever it was wouldn't be learned from *this* feeble presentation.

"What'd you think, Marianne?" Mays asked her after they'd watched it.

"If there's something interesting out there, you wouldn't know it from *that* feeble presentation," she replied.

For only a few new cents more, one could view a three-dee-feelie in the big Ultimax theater, just off the Shri Yantra square. Breathtaking fly-bys of Callisto, Ganymede, Europa, Io! See Grooved and Twisted Terrain! See History in the Craters! See the Largest Active Volcano in the Solar System! Outside the theater, buy sackfuls of Greasy Dim Sum and Fried Won Ton!

"What'd you think of that, dear?"

"Well—it seemed kind of flat."

And for just one new dollar more, you could ride Captain Io's Mystery Tour, which mimicked a close pass right through the plume of Io's biggest sulfur eruption. The tilting, vibrating seats, the high-speed, high-definition images, the screaming music and sound effects made a thrilling ride for adults and even for very young children.

"How did that strike you, darling?"

"My spine hurts."

When all else failed, there was the real thing.

"Countdown's under way! Let's get the next couple of folks aboard. Move along smartly please!"

Randolph Mays and Marianne Mitchell were led through the boarding stages of the Rising Moon Enterprises tour by brightly uniformed young men and women who all seemed to have been cloned from the same pair of traditionally golden-haired Southern Californians—Ken 'n' Barbies who might have seemed strangely out of place in this Asian culture, were it not for the ancient Disneyland tradition, much admired in Earth's Mysterious East. If any thoughts lurked behind these white-toothed, blue-eyed smiles, the customer would never know it; these kids were paid to stay *cheerful.*

"Doesn't your spacesuit fit? Why not? Oh dear, who told you to do it *that* way . . . sir?"

"Now keep that helmet buttoned tight until after the launch, Ms. . . . and have a good trip!"

Marianne was too shrewd not to see the boredom and alarm that alternately lurked just beneath the smiling faces, and it made her uneasy. But unless she was willing to make a scene it was too late, for suddenly she and Mays were left alone, strapped into the cramped cabin of Moon Cruiser Number Four, lying side by side in standard suits that stank of a thousand users before them. They faced a videoplate screen wide enough to virtually fill the field of view. The console below it was so simple it looked fake. There were no instruments on this ship except those needed to monitor volume and frequency, no controls except those needed to change channels and adjust sound and picture quality.

At the moment, the wide screen videoplate was displaying the view from the capsule of the launcher's marshalling yard. It was about as attractive as a subway station in mid-20th-century Boston.

"Somehow this wasn't how I pictured the business of interplanetary investigative reporting, Randolph," said Marianne. Her thin voice through the commlink sounded weary, on the verge of discouragement.

"No one could *possibly* understand the background of the events on Amalthea without a first-hand *look* at the Jovian system," Mays replied. For all the effort in his delivery, he didn't sound completely convincing.

"I must be getting to know you too well," Marianne murmured. "I could swear there's something you're not telling me."

The capsule lurched violently, and he was saved from the necessity of a reply. Somewhere machinery had begun to hum, jostling their capsule forward onto magnetic tracks. They were moving through the switchyard to join a string of other capsules, lined up for launch. Most carried cargo destined for transfer to ships in orbit, while others were going up empty, for more cargo came down to the surface of Ganymede than left it. Perhaps once a week, a couple of Moon Cruisers held tourists like themselves.

"One minute to launch," said the soothing androgynous voice on the speaker system. "Please lie back and relax. Have a good trip."

The image on the videoplate showed the capsule nearing the end of the electromagnetic cannon that would shortly fire them into space. Except for entertainment programs prerecorded on chip, only one other view could be accessed by the passengers, and that was a schematic of the planned trajectory.

Tour itineraries varied constantly with the positions of the Galilean moons. Often no tours were possible, especially when Io was inaccessible, for Io, with its Technicolor landscape and its sulfur plumes a hundred kilometers high, was the moon tourists really wanted to see.

When the little Moon Cruisers were running, an average circuit might last sixty hours or so, some two and a half days. What the tour operators didn't emphasize was how very few minutes of this time would be spent in the near vicinity of any celestial body. The video player was stocked with an exciting selection of programs for all tastes, and the food and liquor cabinets were equally lavish. The personal hygiene facility at the back of the capsule offered the ultimate in robomassage. Or a passenger could select sleep mode, and with the aid of precisely measured drug injections, skip the boring parts of the trip.

"Thirty seconds to launch," said the voice. "Please lie back and relax. Have a good trip."

Just as the video showed them about to enter the breech of the launcher, Mays reached up and tapped the plate's selector switch.

"Hey," Marianne protested. "The launch is the last exciting thing that's going to happen to us for eighteen hours. We'll have plenty of time to look at the map later."

"That is not *us* on the screen, you know," said Mays. "It's *prerecorded*." Mays was right. Where things could actually go wrong—however rarely—the tour operators thought it best to let the passengers see only a stage show, a shiny new capsule undergoing a perfect launch.

"I want to see the launch, not look at some stupid map," she said heatedly. "Even if it's only fake-live, at least it's educational."

"As you *wish*." He flipped the channel back. On-screen, the idealized launch capsule that might have been theirs, but wasn't, was almost into the breech; electromagnetic coils were poised to seize it and hurl it forward. "Do you *mind* if I monitor the trajectory *after* we clear the rails? The map at least is generated in *real* time."

"Whatever you wish, Randol . . ."

Their conversation was interrupted by the robot voice. "Ten seconds to launch. Please lie back and relax. Have a good trip. Nine seconds, eight, seven . . . just lie back and relax completely, your tour is about to begin . . . three, two, one."

The acceleration didn't hit like a fist, it came like a feather pillow laid across their tummies—a feather pillow that magically increased in weight, becoming first a sack of flour, then a sack of cement, then an ingot of cast iron. . . .

"Only thirty more seconds until our launch is completed. Just relax."

Inside the capsule, the passengers lay smothered

under ten gravities of acceleration. A row of diodes on their control panel showed all green, but they would have been all green even in a dire emergency; the little green lights were window-dressing, intended to reassure passengers who were utterly helpless to affect their fate.

On the videoplate, the perfect prerecorded launch proceeded. The capsule silently accelerated at a hundred meters more per second each second that ticked away, until it was moving far faster than a high-powered rifle bullet.

The coils of the launcher smeared into invisibility. Only the longitudinal rail that supported the coils could be seen, a single impossibly straight ribbon of shining metal vanishing somewhere above the distant horizon, into the stars.

They were weightless.

"Acceleration is complete," the voice of the capsule reassured them. "Only five more seconds until our launch sequence is over. Just continue to relax."

Along the final few kilometers of the electric raceway the capsule drifted weightless at blurring speed, subjected to fine magnetic adjustments in aim and velocity—here each individual capsule had its trajectory tailored to fit its particular destination, whether near-Ganymede parking orbit or distant moonscape fly-by.

Meanwhile the frozen surface of Ganymede curved away beneath the track, which in order to maintain its artificial Euclidian straightness now rose above the ice on spindly struts.

In an eyeblink it was over; the long launcher rail was behind them, and the ice mountains of Ganymede were falling rapidly away. The screen was filled with stars.

"All right with you?" said Mays, not really asking her permission, as he tapped the channel over to "Itinerary."

On the wide screen the scale of the graphic was set so as to fill the plate with the icy disk of Ganymede; a pale green line parallel to the equator extended from the far right side upward, and along it a bright blue line crept imperceptibly. The green line was their planned route; the blue line was their actual track, as monitored by ground-based radar and navigation satellites. The two lines currently followed an identical trajectory for as far as they extended, and unless something went terribly wrong, they would stay that way throughout the trip.

Mays adjusted the scale. The disk of Ganymede zoomed down to a tiny speck in the lower right portion of a screen filled with stars. The larger disk of Jupiter, realistically patterned with cloud bands, now dominated the center of the screen. Arranged around it in concentric rings were the orbits of Amalthea, Io, Europa, and Ganymede itself. Callisto lay farther out, offscreen. It was the poor sister of the Galilean moons, thought to be too like Ganymede to be worth a special trip; only when the moons were arranged so that the laws of celestial mechanics decreed it easier and quicker for a capsule to fly past Callisto than not were tourists able to judge Callisto's charms for themselves.

The pale green line was a graceful loop of string that swooped inward past Io, curved steeply around Jupiter, came near Europa on its way back, and finally rejoined the orbit of Ganymede a third of the way farther along in its circuit. Amalthea was not on the itinerary; its orbit lay well inside the capsule's closest approach to Jupiter.

Given the capsule's energetic initial acceleration from Ganymede, most of the ride was coasting. But at certain key junctions, a nudge from the capsule's strap-on rocket was necessary to get the roller coaster all the way around the curve.

Mays contemplated the graphics on the videoplate, which at this scale changed too slowly to be perceived. The orange light of the false Jupiter was reflected in the faceplate of his spacesuit and lit a warm gleam in his eye.

Marianne yawned. "Maybe I'll take the sleeper. Wake me when we get to Io."

His reply was unnaturally delayed. "Delighted, my dear," he murmured at last.

Something in the tone of his voice attracted her glance. "What are you scheming, Randolph?" she asked lazily, but the hypnotic was already running in her bloodstream, and she could not stay awake to hear his answer—

—which at any rate he did not give.

15

The columns of white vapor that blew out of the crevices in the ice gave an illusion of great force, but there was nothing to them, only widely spaced water molecules moving at great velocity under virtually no pressure. These most tenuous of winds had blown the huge alien antennas clear off into space; as the ice had dissolved from beneath their roots, the massive structures had drifted free and wafted away as lightly as if they'd been dandelion seeds on a summer breeze. With them went the secret of their communication with the stars—and with the core of their own moon.

Blake and Forster lay side by side in the Europan sub, Blake in the command pilot's couch, skimming across the lacy ice. Hawkins and McNeil guided the sub by the tips of its wings. The pearly mist was so thick that light from their helmet lamps bounced back into their faces from a meter or two away.

Without a thread to guide them, they could have floundered for hours; they had to feel their way to the entrance shaft along the communications cables that hung like garlands in the mist. They found the opening of the shaft, a wider artificial blowhole in the featureless fog and ice, and the Old Mole tethered nearby, stationed there in case the shaft needed re-opening against the tendency of the boiling water down below to freeze over again.

"We're ready to go in," Blake said over the commlink.

"All right, then," came back Walsh's voice.

The launch was pure simplicity. Blake curled the submarine's flexible wings around its body until the craft was smaller than the diameter of the shaft in the ice. Hawkins and McNeil positioned it above the opening and gently shoved it into the pressureless blowhole with the force of their suit-maneuvering systems.

The sub dived blind into the impenetrable fog. A hundred meters down, the surface of the water came up suddenly, a vigorously boiling surface over which a steaming skin of ice constantly froze and broke apart and reformed.

Triggered by radar to ignite upon impact, the submarine's rockets fired a brief burst to drive the buoyant craft below the surface that otherwise would have rejected it. The rockets continued firing, blowing out a stream of super-hot bubbles, until the free-swimming craft's wings could unfurl and grab water. With strong strokes, the submarine swam swiftly down into the deep. Then it turned on its back and sought the undersurface of the ice. The water was murky with life—swarming, concentrated life.

"Hungry little devils." Forster laughed, the happiest sound he'd made in months. "They're exactly like krill. Swarms and swarms of them." His bright eye had fixed upon one among the myriad swarming creatures fumbling against the polyglas, and he followed it closely as it wriggled helplessly for a moment before orienting itself and darting away.

"Are they feeding?" Walsh's voice came to them over the sonarlink.

"Yes, most of them," Blake answered. "They're

feeding on the underside of the ice, on mats of purple stuff. An Earth biologist would call it algae . . . maybe we should call it exo-algae. And miniature medusas, clouds of them, are feeding on *them*.''

''We'll have to let the exo-biologists sort it all out,'' Forster said. ''I'll get a few samples, Blake. But don't let me take too long about it.''

''If you didn't know we were inside one of Jupiter's moons,'' Blake said into the comm, ''you'd think we were in the Arctic Ocean. And that it's springtime.''

Forster and Blake were lying prone in the Europan submarine, nominally a two-person craft with just enough room for a third occupant to squeeze into the passage behind them. The Manta, they had nicknamed it, on the principle that if an old ice mole deserved a name, so did an old submarine—doing what the Old Mole couldn't do, for the ice miner had served its main purpose as soon as it had cut its way into Amalthea's interior.

The Manta was swimming upside down with respect to Amalthea's center, its ventral surfaces skimming along only a meter from the rind of ice. The teeming biota of Amalthea's ''arctic'' seas—or at least a good and lively sample of it—was spread before them, brightly illuminated by the sub's spotlights, separated from them only by the thin clear polyglas of the sub's bubble. The white light was quickly diffused in water so thick with living particles—all of them eating or being eaten—that it resembled a thin broth. The darting, teeming schools of transparent krill were a shifting veil of rainbows in the beams of the floodlights.

The men in the sub used magnifying optics to examine the creatures on something closer to their own scale. The medusas were like many of the myriad species of jellyfish that swarm through all the seas of Earth, pulsing with strips of colored light. The creatures Forster called ''krill'' were shrimp-like, multi-legged little beings with flat tails and hard transparent shells which left their pulsing circulatory systems visible. Whenever the submarine's lights were directed toward them they swam frantically away—behavior that was easy enough to understand, given that a boiling "sun" was visible as a hot point of light many kilometers down in the murky depths and that the foodstuff of the krill lay in the opposite direction.

"What was that?" Blake said suddenly.

"*Ventris*, we have new visitors," said Forster. "Something bigger than anything we've seen yet."

"Looked like a squid," said Blake. "There's another . . . a bunch of them. I'm rolling the Manta."

The submarine flapped its wings and made a lazy half roll in the soupy water. The dark waters came alive with flickering, glowing life. Uncountable multi-tentacled, torpedo-shaped creatures danced in synchrony beneath them, none of them bigger than a human hand, but packed together in an immense school that darted and turned like a single organism. Each translucent, silvery animal was bright with turquoise beads of bioluminescence; together they formed a blue banner in the dark.

"They're diving again," Blake said.

"We'll follow them, *Ventris*," Forster said into the sonarlink. "I'll worry about specimens later."

Blake pushed the Manta's diving controls forward and the sub put its transparent nose down. Flexible wings rippled, driving the craft deeper into darkness.

The Manta was a well-used sub, not as old as the Old Mole but based on vintage technology. Its passengers rested in an Earth-normal pressure regime of mixed oxygen and nitrogen. The sub carried liquid nitrogen in pressurized tanks and got its oxygen from the water, but while its oxygen-exchange mechanisms—its "gills"—were efficient enough at constant depths, the craft needed time to adjust internal working pressures to constantly changing external pressures.

And the pressures on little Amalthea, while they didn't change as rapidly as they did on big Europa (or on bigger Earth), nevertheless mounted swiftly toward impressive numbers. At the surface, a person in a spacesuit weighed a gram or two, and the pressure was zero, a near-perfect vacuum. At the moon's core the same person would weigh nothing at all—but the pressure of the overlying column of water would have increased to several hundred thousand kilograms per square centimeter.

Blake, frustrated, couldn't keep up with the rapidly descending school of exo-squid. The Manta's alarm hooter went off before he'd descended four kilometers: *Do not attempt to exceed the present depth until the gill manifold has been recharged,* the sub's pleasant but firm robot voice instructed him.

Blake let the Manta level itself. They could do nothing but wait while the artificial enzyme mixture in the sub's gill manifold was enriched. Outside the craft swam a menagerie of weird creatures, resembling several new species of luridly colored medusas and jellyfish and glassy ctenophores. A fish with a mouth bigger than its stomach drifted past, peering hungrily in at them with eyes as big as golf balls.

"They're coming back," Forster said.

"Sir?" Blake was paying attention to the instruments, not to the view through the bubble.

"Unfortunately we have a poor image up here," said Walsh on the sonarlink. "Can you tell us what you are observing?"

"The squid. It's almost as if they're waiting for us," Forster said. "The way they dance, you'd think they were laughing at us."

"That's *your* mood talking, sir," said Blake, smiling.

"Perhaps we're thinking alike."

Blake gave the professor a strange look. "You and them?"

Forster didn't elaborate.

Blake watched the rippling sheet of blue light half a kilometer below them, undulating as if in a lazy current, a sheet made of a thousand little vector-arrows, a thousand tentacled projectiles.

You may proceed to depth, said the sub's voice, and a tone sounded, indicating it was safe to descend. Blake pushed the controls forward. Instantly the school of fiery creatures peeled away, diving toward the bright nebulosity that lay at Amalthea's center.

The water was less clouded with nutrients here, but hazy with rising bubbles. The Manta was diving against a lazy upward flow of bubbles.

"Outside temperature's going up fast," Blake said.

The core object, though still at a great distance, was more than a blur of light; it was a pulsing white sphere, too bright to look upon directly, a miniature sun in watery black space.

The hooter sounded again. The pressure was approaching a tonne per square centimeter. *Do not attempt to exceed the present depth until . . .*

"Yeah, yeah," Blake grumbled, taking his hands away from the controls. They waited longer this time, while the oxygen from the sub's gills dissolved in the large volume of fluid in its circulatory system.

"I say, they're doing it again," Forster exclaimed. Again the school of squid appeared to be waiting for them, wheeling and darting at a constant depth almost a kilometer below. Forster's voice was as excited as a boy's. "Do you think they're trying to communicate?"

"Not much sign of that," said Blake, playing the skeptic.

You may proceed to depth, said the sub. The tone sounded, and they dived.

The water around them was thick with bubbles now, microscopic spheres streaming past in the millions, and big wobbling spheroids that looked alive. The school of squid swam away below, sliding off to the right as it dived.

"Those bubbles are *hot*," said Blake.

"They're full of steam," the professor said. "Rising in columns. The squid are avoiding this one—we'd better do the same before our gills cook."

The Manta flapped its wide wings and slid off to the right, following the invisible wake of the glowing squid. Suddenly they were in still, cool water.

Beneath them, the hot core had grown to the apparent size of the sun seen from Earth—too bright to look at directly, without the viewport adjusted to filter the light. Streams of bright bubbles were flowing slowly away from Amalthea's white core in serpentine columns, radiating symmetrically away from the region of maximum pressure, reaching steadily upward in every direction toward the moon's surface.

"I'll bet there's a geyser at the top of every one of those," said Blake.

"Bet not taken," said the professor, who had noted the regular geometry of the bubble streams. "I'd say you're right."

Amber lights glowed on the panel beneath the spherical window. In a reasonable voice the sub said, *Please exercise caution. You are approaching the absolute pressure limit.*

The inner polyglas hull of the Manta, in which they rode in comfortable Earth-normal conditions, was nearing the point where it would implode from the crushing pressure of the water.

"This is about as close as we're going to get," said Blake.

"We'll break off now," Forster ordered. "We'll

get what we can in the way of images. On the way up, stop long enough to let me take water samples every five hundred meters."

"Right," said Blake. His hands flexed on the controls—

—but the professor reached to touch him, his dry fingers lying gently on Blake's, commanding him to be still. "A moment more. Just a moment."

Blake waited patiently, trying to imagine what was going through Forster's mind. The professor had come tantalizingly near the object of his decades-long search, but still it kept its distance, if only for a little while longer.

Forster listened to the sounds that came through the hull, broadcast on the sub's sonar: the squeaky fizz of billions of pinpoint bubbles boiling off the hot core, the liquid slither and plash of bigger bubbles colliding and joining together. Almost overwhelming these inanimate sounds were the skirring and chittering of masses of animal life in this spaceborne aquarium, this vast dark globe of water rich in the nutrients of a terrestrial planet's oceans.

There were patterns in the cries of life, mindless patterns of busy noise that marked feeding and migration and reproduction—and bolder patterns as well?

The school of squid still waited below, swirling and diving and soaring and darting; the thousand wriggling creatures sang as they swam, in rhythmic birdlike chorus. Beneath the soprano choir a deep bass boomed with studied deliberation, like the slow ringing of a temple bell in the tropical night.

As Forster listened, he imagined that he knew what the booming was . . . that the core itself was calling him.

16

> Here it came: a hemisphere bulging
> with mountains of orange sulfur,
> flooded with red sulfur lava, wind-
> swept with yellow sulfur dust, pitted
> with burned black sulfur cinders,
> drifted with white sulfur frost . . .

The first humans to see Io, in reconstructed video data sent back by *Voyager 1*, had called it a "pizza pie." What would it have been called if those first observers had lived not on the outskirts of Los Angeles but in Moscow or Sao Paolo or Delhi?

Or seen it as Randolph Mays and Marianne Mitchell were seeing it now . . . ? The videoplate of their tin can capsule showed the fast-approaching moon in real time, at the same angular spread as if they'd been looking out the hatch with their own eyes. Io did not look much like a pizza pie to Marianne. It looked like hell frozen over; not counting the insides of various spaceships, it was the ugliest thing she had seen in her travels yet. But Io's ugliness was so bold and wild, its elemental forces so immodestly displayed, that she found it almost arousing.

She was glad she'd let Randolph bully her into this—literally canned!—tourist adventure. She smiled and let her eyes wander from the ruddy moon. Her gaze lingered fondly on his craggy looks.

He seemed lost in thought, his own eyes not focused on the landscape of Io but somewhere infinitely far beyond.

A voice she had learned to regard as background noise interrupted her thoughts: "Four active volcanos are visible from the current range and position of your Moon Cruiser, with plumes ranging from thirty to over two hundred kilometers in altitude. . . ."

Mays managed to keep his inner concentration even when the robot voice of the capsule chimed in with one of its periodic sightseeing lectures. He was like a Zen monk, sitting calmly, thinking nothing, knowing nothing but the incoming and outgoing of his breath.

". . . the most easily visible in the lower right quadrant of your screen, near the terminator. Observe the umbrella-shaped plume of material, ejected from the vent at a velocity approaching one kilometer per second, more than a third of Io's escape velocity. If you wish to see the larger globe of crystallized gases surrounding the volcano's inner solid plume, tune your videoplate to the ultraviolet spectrum. . . ."

Now their capsule was approaching Io so fast that their movement toward it was perceptible. What had been a detailed and fascinating but still-distant landscape took on a new dimension; Marianne was reminded of her visit to the Grand Canyon on Earth, standing at an overlook, admiring distant vistas of buttes and mesas, when suddenly the gravel beneath her foot slipped and carried her a few inches toward the edge. . . .

She was seized with terror. "Randolph, we're falling!"

"Mm, what's that, dear?"

"Something's wrong! We're falling right into it . . . into that volcano!"

Mays suppressed a smile. "If for a moment you

can *tear* your eyes away from our impending doom, let me switch to the schematic."

Idealized graphics replaced the more immediate reality on the screen. He tapped the controls, adjusting the scale to include the surface of Io.

The green line of their planned trajectory brought them to within three hundred kilometers of the surface of Io. At this scale the blue line of their actual track could have deviated from the green line by no more than the width of a pixel or two, for it was still identical.

Their velocity was impressive, however—the blue line crept along the green at several millimeters per second. And still Marianne's heart was pounding; she couldn't get her breath.

"We're falling, you *might* say," Mays conceded. "But we're falling past the volcano, not into it. We're falling *past* the surface of the moon. And then, of course, we'll be falling toward Jupiter." He enlarged the scale of the graphic swiftly—the familiar green ellipsoid was still there where it had been, looping around and eventually back toward Ganymede. "With any luck, we'll miss *it*, too." He smiled at her, and it was a smile with enough warmth in it to be what she needed, truly comforting.

Marianne studied the graphic as if her life depended on it. Her pulse slowed; she could feel the tension draining away. "I'm sorry, Randolph," she said weakly.

"No need to apologize. Such a rapidly *changing* perspective is frightening indeed."

"It's just that . . . it's clear enough when it's explained to me, but I feel . . . I think I should have done my homework."

"Indeed, *intuitive* physics is usually wrong"—he emitted his history professor's throaty chuckle—"as Aristotle repeatedly demonstrated."

She didn't think it was all that funny, but she

forced herself to smile. "We can turn the picture back on now. I'll try to overcome my . . . intuition."

She switched back to realtime. The picture was strikingly different. Gripped by Io's gravity, they were falling now at 60,000 kilometers per hour, an astonishing speed this close to a fixed surface. Her facial muscles tightened, but she held her smile and made herself watch.

The volcano's copious outpouring was as dark and as fluid as blood, a translucent mound of soft red spreading outward from the dark vent at its center in a symmetry that was almost voluptuous. Their capsule was a missile homing on the center of the plume's creased pillow, which swelled as if to take them in. All around them rose soft mountains the color of flesh.

Then everything curved away, dropped away.

The voice of the capsule said, "Your Moon Cruiser's videoplate field of view is no longer selecting the surface of Io. If you wish to continue viewing Io, you may easily adjust your viewpoint by selecting 'autotrack' on your video console."

"No thank you," Marianne said softly.

"It's all going into memory," Mays said. "We can play it back later if you'd like. When we're well away."

"Randolph," she said, in a voice that was low, almost angry, "can't we get out of these stupid suits? I want you to hold me." She didn't wait for his answer before slapping at the clasps of her harness to free herself from her acceleration couch.

He said nothing, but he followed her example. By the time he'd released his harness she was out of her suit; she helped him get out of his, kneeling on top of him in his couch, as weightless as he was.

She helped him catch up; then she continued with the rest of her clothes. Before long they were both tumbling naked in the feeble light of the screen, the dark and supple young woman, the hard-muscled, odd-angled, definitely older man.

In her urgency she paid no attention to the faint rumble of the capsule's maneuvering system. Since she had done no homework, and currently had no interest in schematics, she had no way of knowing that the trajectory program had scheduled no course adjustment for this moment.

"It's happening," said Sparta. Ever since Mays and Marianne had launched for Io, Sparta had haunted the firefly darkness of the AJE, the Space Board's Automated Jupiter Environment traffic control center, whose green screens and trembling sensors tracked every craft in Jupiter space.

"*What* is happening, Inspector?" demanded a young German controller, her white-blond crew cut as square and shiny as the epaulets on her blue uniform. With audible contempt the controller said, "No alteration in the trajectory of the *tourist* canister is visible."

Not to you, thought Sparta, but she said only, "While you're watching and waiting, I'm putting our cutter on alert."

Five minutes later the controller finally noticed a tiny discrepancy in the Moon Cruiser's course, as yet within the limits of uncertainty of the tracking system; meanwhile Sparta took a call on her personal link.

"Awkward moment, Ellen," the commander growled at her.

"Sorry, sir," she said cheerfully. "Catch you in the john?"

"Caught me as I was recording a smuggling operation going down at Von Frisch's place. Now I'll have to leave it to the locals."

"All the better for Space Board public relations. I need your chop for the cutter to get me to Amal-

INFOPAK
TECHNICAL
BLUEPRINTS

On the following pages are computer-generated diagrams representing some of the structures and engineering found in *Venus Prime*:

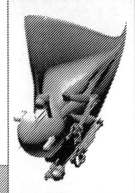

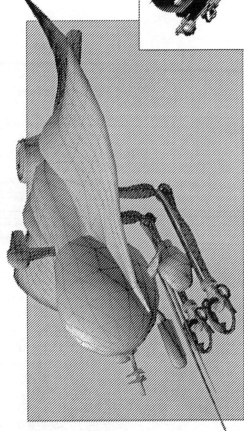

MANTA

EUROPAN
SUB

AMALTHEA
EXPEDITION

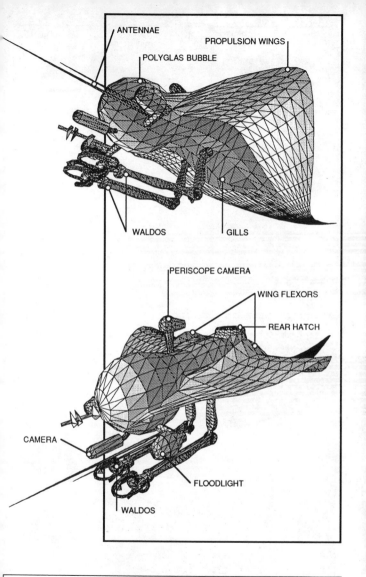

ANTENNAE

PROPULSION WINGS

POLYGLAS BUBBLE

WALDOS

GILLS

PERISCOPE CAMERA

WING FLEXORS

REAR HATCH

CAMERA

FLOODLIGHT

WALDOS

EUROPAN SUB -- MANTA

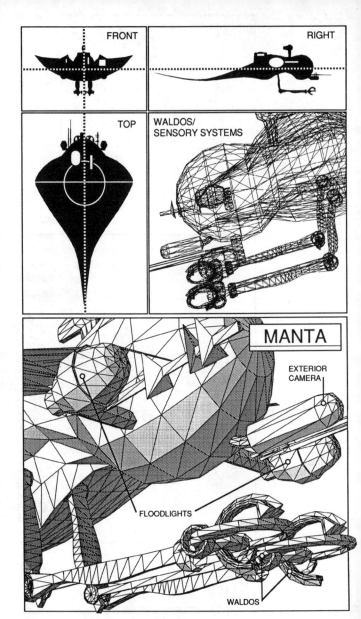

FRONT

RIGHT

TOP

WALDOS/
SENSORY SYSTEMS

MANTA

EXTERIOR
CAMERA

FLOODLIGHTS

WALDOS

4

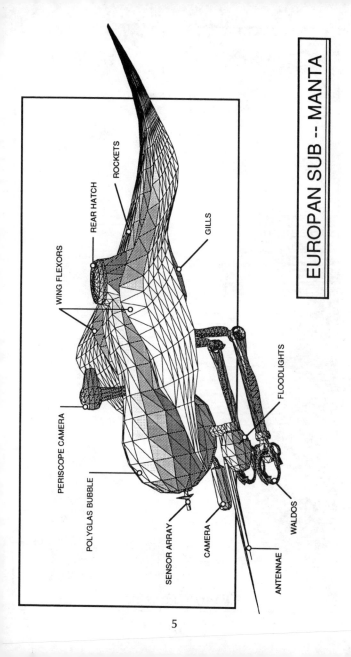

EUROPAN SUB -- MANTA

ROCKETS

REAR HATCH

GILLS

WING FLEXORS

PERISCOPE CAMERA

POLYGLAS BUBBLE

FLOODLIGHTS

SENSOR ARRAY

CAMERA

WALDOS

ANTENNAE

5

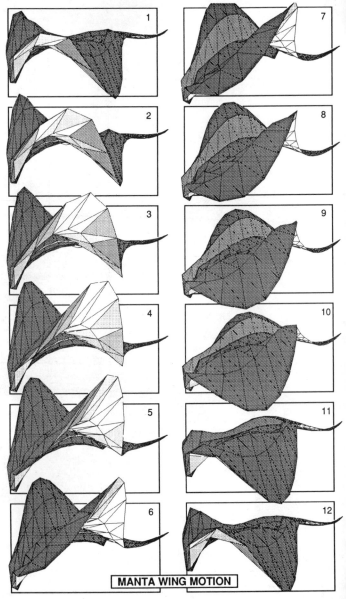

MANTA WING MOTION

6

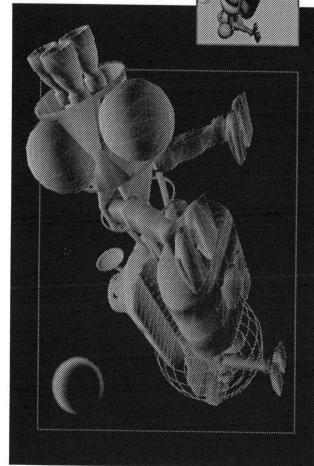

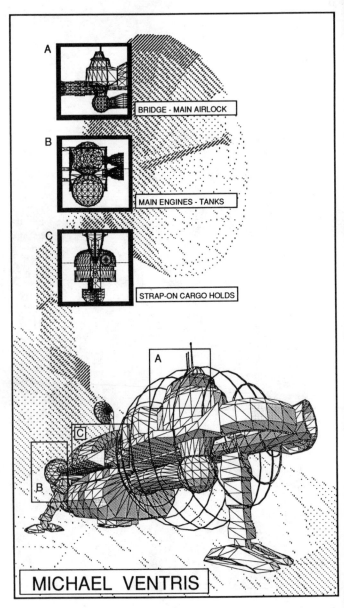

A BRIDGE - MAIN AIRLOCK

B MAIN ENGINES - TANKS

C STRAP-ON CARGO HOLDS

MICHAEL VENTRIS

8

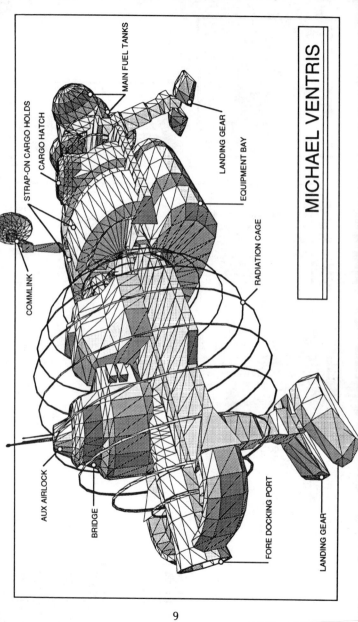

MICHAEL VENTRIS

MAIN FUEL TANKS

STRAP-ON CARGO HOLDS

CARGO HATCH

LANDING GEAR

EQUIPMENT BAY

COMMLINK

RADIATION CAGE

AUX AIRLOCK

BRIDGE

FORE DOCKING PORT

LANDING GEAR

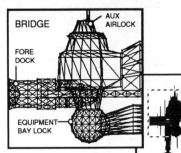

BRIDGE

AUX AIRLOCK

FORE DOCK

EQUIPMENT BAY LOCK

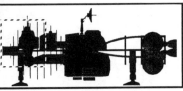

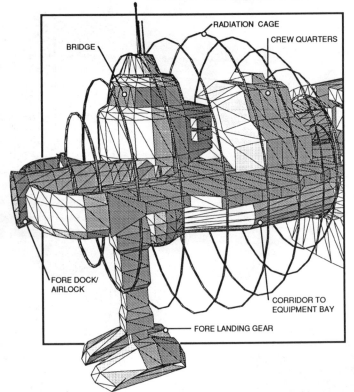

RADIATION CAGE

CREW QUARTERS

BRIDGE

FORE DOCK/ AIRLOCK

CORRIDOR TO EQUIPMENT BAY

FORE LANDING GEAR

MICHAEL VENTRIS

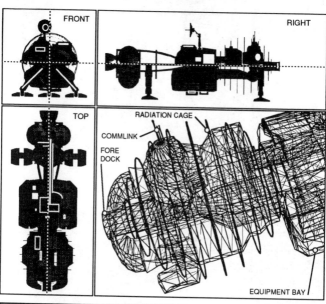

FRONT

RIGHT

TOP

RADIATION CAGE

COMMLINK

FORE
DOCK

EQUIPMENT BAY

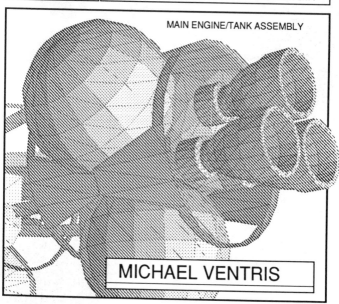

MAIN ENGINE/TANK ASSEMBLY

MICHAEL VENTRIS

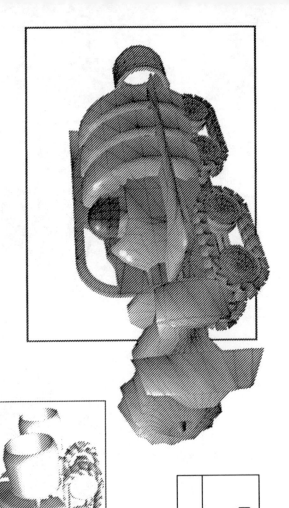

ICE MOLE

AMALTHEA
EXPEDITION

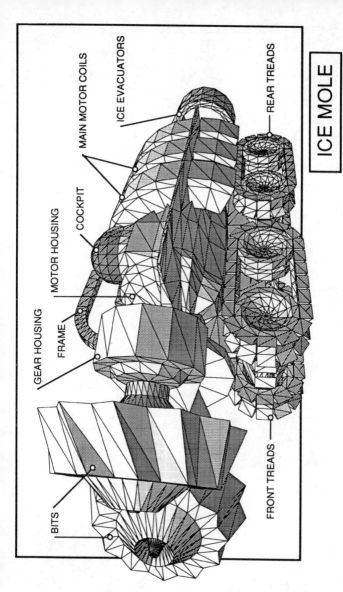

ICE MOLE

MAIN MOTOR COILS

ICE EVACUATORS

REAR TREADS

COCKPIT

MOTOR HOUSING

FRAME

GEAR HOUSING

FRONT TREADS

BITS

13

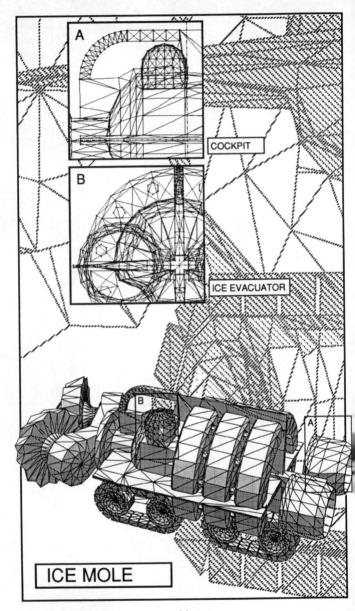

A

COCKPIT

B

ICE EVACUATOR

B

A

ICE MOLE

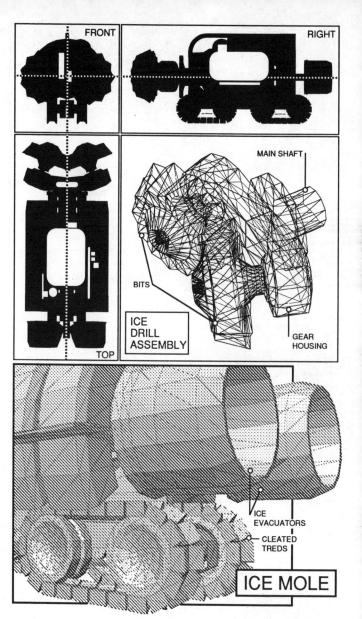

FRONT

RIGHT

MAIN SHAFT

BITS

ICE
DRILL
ASSEMBLY

GEAR
HOUSING

TOP

ICE
EVACUATORS

CLEATED
TREDS

ICE MOLE

15

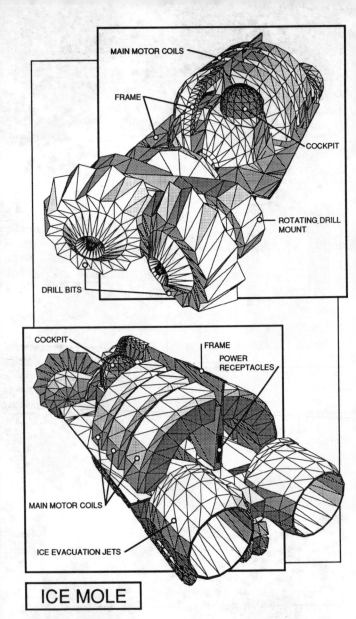

MAIN MOTOR COILS

FRAME

COCKPIT

ROTATING DRILL MOUNT

DRILL BITS

COCKPIT

FRAME

POWER RECEPTACLES

MAIN MOTOR COILS

ICE EVACUATION JETS

ICE MOLE

thea, ASAP. I've already got the crew hopping and a shuttle standing by to get me up there."

"All right, I'll confirm your arrangements. Mind telling me what's happening anyway? Case anyone I answer to wants to know?"

"Looks like Mays could be making a move."

"What? Never mind, I'll be with you in half an hour."

"Better that you stay on Ganymede, sir. Cover our rear."

He laughed. "All I'm good for in my old age." He sounded uncharacteristically weary.

"Cheer up, boss. The war's not over yet."

In the Moon Cruiser, time passed unnoticed.

"You're not *sleeping*," Marianne whispered fiercely.

Mays opened his eyes. "On the *contrary*, dear," he said, only slightly less energetically than usual. "You invigorate me."

"And certainly you don't think I'm *done* with you yet."

"Oh I certainly . . . hope not." He hesitated. "But I'm selfish. I like to *mix* my pleasures."

"Sounds interesting." Her words were halfway between a purr and a growl.

"Yes. I mean, we wouldn't want to miss our *view* of Europa—we'll be approaching it within the hour"—he hurried on as he saw the cool shock on her face—"and I do want to *savor* you at leisure."

Her expression softened again. He wasn't pushing her away, but she realized she really would have to make some allowance for his . . . maturity. "But do we have to put our clothes back on? Is there any reason we have to wear those smelly things in this perfectly cozy little steel container?"

He looked at her in warm Jupiter-light from the viewscreen, at her grainless skin and supple curves and glossy black hair floating weightless, and then at his own body, nobbed and irregularly textured. "There is no reason for *you* to do so, but unfortunately my appearance . . ."

"I want to look at you."

"*I* don't want to look at me. I gangle. I am too *long-limbed* to avoid seeing at least some part of myself every time I move." He plucked his floating trousers from the air and began to struggle into them.

Marianne watched a moment, then sighed expressively and reached for her jumpsuit. "I guess I have to get dressed too. I refuse to be held at a disadvantage. Even a symbolic one."

"Wait 'til after Europa, dear."

Her ardor had cooled, and she said nothing more until she was fully dressed. For his part, Mays seemed once more lost in thought. Marianne floated toward her acceleration couch, not eager to strap herself in again, and looked at the huge curve of Jupiter against the field of stars on the videoplate.

She studied it more closely, and a tiny crease formed in her brow. "Randolph, you said Europa in an hour. Shouldn't it be visible on the screen?"

"Why yes, certainly . . ." He flinched as he studied the screen. Jupiter was there, but none of its moons were evident. Without a word, he switched the image to the flight-path schematic.

"My God, this *can't* be right."

Since shortly after they had left Io, the blue line of their path through space had been steadily diverging from the green line planned for them. The angle was small, but their velocity was large—and growing larger. They were no longer headed away from Jupiter, outward to Europa, but instead were spiraling lazily inward toward the huge planet.

"There was no *warning!* How could there be no *warning!*" Mays's voice was rich with outrage.

The capsule's robot voice chose the moment to speak up. "Please relax and prepare for the next thrilling episode in your Jovian excursion. Your Moon Cruiser is about to fly past the world of buried oceans—Europa!''

Marianne was staring at the schematic. ''Randolph, we're falling right into Jupiter.''

''We've got lots of time before *that* happens,'' Mays said. ''And it needn't, if I can get to this machine's control circuitry. This is all probably a pretty *simple* thing. But . . .'' His voice faded out abruptly, as if he'd been about to say more than he should have.

''Tell me what you were going to say,'' she said. She looked at him steadily, full of courage.

''Well, we're *already* in the radiation belt. Even if I can *correct* our course, we will . . . absorb a very large dose.''

''We may die,'' she said.

He said nothing. He was thinking of other things.

''Don't give out on me, Randolph,'' she commanded. ''I don't intend to die until I have to. You either—I won't let you.''

17

"Manta, come in please."

The Manta had disappeared from the bright screens on the flight deck of the *Michael Ventris*. The sonar channels gave out nothing but the deep throbbing of the core, underscoring the watery sounds the crew had grown used to.

"Professor Forster. Blake. Please respond." When there was no reply, Josepha Walsh turned to the others and said, almost casually, "We've lost them in the thermal turbulence. Not unexpected." The tension in her voice was barely a notch above business-as-usual.

Tony Groves was sitting in at McNeil's engineering console; McNeil and Hawkins had come onto the flight deck still in their spacesuits, helmets loose, to follow the progress of the Manta on the high resolution screens. They matched the captain's mood—alert, serious, but not alarmed. They'd heard Blake's and the professor's descriptions as they dove, seen the fitfully transmitted images from the old sub, read the sonar data. They knew the core was shielded from their sonar probing, and that at any rate communication with the Manta might be difficult in the vicinity of its boiling surface. There seemed no good reason to fear mishap.

"At any rate, the last message was they were

coming up. Angus, you and Bill might as well head for the lock; it can't be long before . . ."

A sudden loud wailing from the radiolink interrupted her.

We are receiving an emergency signal. A space vessel is in distress, the ship's urgent, dispassionate computer voice announced. *Repeat. We are receiving an emergency signal. A space vessel is in distress.*

"Acknowledged," Jo Walsh told the computer. "Vector coordinates on graphics, please."

The big video screen switched to a map of near space. The distressed craft was seen creeping in from screen left, on a projected course that was bringing it into the lee of Amalthea—where, it appeared, it was on a collision course with the moon.

"I'd give it three hours to get here," said Groves.

"And who the hell would that be?" demanded McNeil. "Nobody could have got this close without sector I.D."

"Computer, can you identify the distressed vessel?" Walsh asked calmly.

The vessel is an automated tour capsule, registry AMT 476, Rising Moon Enterprises, Ganymede Base, presently off its pre-set course . . .

"You don't say," Groves muttered.

The vessel does not respond to attempted radio contact, said the computer.

"Silly question perhaps, but are we sure it's occupied?" Blake demanded.

"Computer, can you confirm that the capsule is occupied?"

According to manifest the vessel is occupied by two passengers: Mitchell, Marianne; Mays, Randolph.

McNeil looked at Groves and before he could help himself, he laughed a half-embarrassed laugh. Groves nodded knowingly.

Bill Hawkins looked at him in shocked disapproval. "They've been in the radiation belt for hours! In a minimally shielded . . . canister. We'll be lucky to reach them alive!"

"My apologies," McNeil said. "But Mays—what an extraordinary man! What gall!"

"What the hell are you going on about, McNeil?" Hawkins yelled at him.

"Later, gentlemen," said Walsh. "We'll have to see to them."

"What do you want to do, Jo?" asked Groves.

"You guys jettison the hold, along with everything loose. I'll need you with me, Tony, to run the trajectories."

"All right, but what then?"

"Stripped, this ship's got the delta-vees to cut a low orbit around Jupiter, match orbits with the capsule, take them aboard. Reach them in under three hours, do another go around, get back into the shadow in maybe another four, with maneuvers—before we take too many rads."

"We've got a duty to a vessel in distress—but we've got a duty to the mission as well," said McNeil reluctantly. "If we use all that fuel to rescue them, we'll be stranding ourselves here."

"What the hell are you talking . . . ?" Hawkins interjected again, his clear English skin turning bright red.

"No excuse, Angus," said Walsh, cutting Hawkins off firmly. "The Space Board will take us off. Before then, a few hours in radiological clean-up should do for us."

"For us, maybe," said McNeil, persisting. "What about them?"

Groves said, "He has a point. Add three hours to their exposure, even partially shielded, and they'll be pushing the limit. We've got the delta-vees to do what you suggest, Captain," Groves added quietly, "but not enough time."

"We're wasting what time we've got, talking,"

Walsh said. She ran her hand through her brush-cut red hair; others had long ago learned to read this unconscious gesture as her way of displacing anxiety when she needed to concentrate. "We do it my way unless you've got a better idea."

"One idea, anyway," said Groves. "That capsule is incoming with about three hundred meters per second delta with respect to Amalthea. If it's as well-aimed as it appears to be . . ."

"Yes?"

"Let it crash."

"*What!*" Hawkins was quick to react. "Let them *die* . . . ?"

"Oh, do be quiet, Hawkins," Walsh snapped at him. Like the others, she had responded to the navigator's suggestion with thoughtful silence.

"Listen, Walsh . . . Captain Walsh . . . I insist . . ."

"Hawkins, we're not going to let them die. Now either keep quiet or leave the flight deck."

Hawkins finally perceived that the others knew something he didn't and wanted silence in which to think about it. He shrank back into a corner.

"The sublimed ice is about ten meters deep," said McNeil. "That will take up some energy."

"Yes, that's a plus. Given the snow density—what's your guess, maybe point four gee-cee?—and their inertia"—Groves was bent over the navigator's board, tapping keys—"they should experience instantaneous deceleration of . . . oh, about forty gees. We'll have to look up the specs, but it's my impression those Moon Cruisers are built to maintain structural integrity well beyond that."

"And the people inside?" Walsh asked.

"Tied in properly . . . they can survive it."

"Assuming they're eyeballs-in," McNeil added. The engineer seemed almost diffident. "Should they have the unfortunate luck to come in upside down . . ." He left the rest unsaid.

"Right," said Walsh. "We'd better have a look through the telescope."

Groves addressed himself to the console, releasing the optical telescope from its tracking function, re-orienting it according to the computer's coordinates for the incoming capsule. The fuzzy image of the gray tubular capsule with its belt of fuel tanks and its single little rocket motor came up on the big videoplate; at this distance it appeared to be motionless against the limb of Jupiter.

The people on the flight deck studied the image in silence.

"Remarkable," said Jo Walsh.

"Now is that luck? Or is that luck?" asked McNeil.

"I think the answer is no both times," Groves said dryly.

Hawkins could stand it no more and broke his silence. "What *is* everyone clucking about?"

McNeil explained. The apparently disabled capsule was oriented so that its rocket engine was perfectly aligned to brake its fall onto Amalthea. Even without the help of a retrorocket, the capsule was in the ideal attitude for a crash landing.

"This looks less like an accident than it did two minutes ago," Jo Walsh said.

"Talk about party crashers; this Mays fellow takes the cake," Groves said.

"You mean they *planned* to land here?" Hawkins said, wiping his blond hair, slick with perspiration, away from his staring eyes.

"Not that it makes much of a practical difference," said McNeil jovially. "Whether they understand it or not, they'll have taken damn near a lethal dose of rads by the time they arrive—we've no choice but to take them under our wing."

"All right, Tony, you've got your way," said Walsh. "We'll let them hit and pick up the pieces later."

"Let's just hope they don't hit on top of us," Groves said brightly, ever the pixie.

"Now that really would be pushing coincidence into the realm of the supernatural, wouldn't it?" But Walsh's riposte landed more heavily than she'd intended—no one laughed.

Three hours passed. The timing was lousy: the disabled capsule was incoming on the sidescreen, the Manta was upcoming on the main screen. But Walsh was a cool head who'd handled many a more complex emergency.

She figured Professor Forster and Blake Redfield could fend for themselves. Hawkins and McNeil were already suited up, standing by to rescue the passengers in the capsule when it hit. Groves stayed with her on the flight deck to help her keep track of everything and everybody.

The capsule arrived first.

Silent right to the end, too fast to follow by eye, it arrived in a flash of orange light and a hemispherical cloud of vapor.

"Ouch," said Tony Groves. Walsh just gave him a look, which they both knew meant, *let's hope you didn't screw up the calculations.*

Within seconds, Hawkins and McNeil were out the *Ventris*'s airlock and jetting over the misty landscape toward the impact site.

"God, they hit fast. Did you see rocket flare?" Hawkins asked, his throat tight. "You think they had time to brake?"

"Too quick for my eyes," McNeil replied. He was reluctant to say that there had been no retrorocket flare. "They could have been lucky. People have survived peak gees of sixty, seventy, even more." Survived, if you could call it that . . .

The point of impact wasn't hard to find even by eye, for the crash had blown a huge hole in the mist and, like a giant smoke ring, a rolling donut-shaped cloud of weightless vapor held its shape and position over a shallow crater in the ice. In the exact center of the wide bowl, wreathed in steam, was the capsule, rapidly cooling but still glowing from impact.

"Are you all right in there?" Hawkins was shouting into his suitcomm, as if they could somehow hear him better the closer he got and the louder he yelled. "Marianne, can you hear me? Mays?" He flew like an arrow toward the upright capsule.

"Careful, don't touch it until the temperature's manageable," said McNeil. "You'll burn your gloves off."

"Wha . . . oh." Hawkins drew back just in time. "They could be dying in there!"

"Get hold of yourself, Bill. If you blow the hatch and they haven't got suit pressure, you'll finish them."

In his frustration, Hawkins hovered beside the steaming capsule and banged on its hatch with the butt of the heavy laser drill he'd brought along. The suitcomm brought them no sign of life inside.

Walsh's voice sounded in their helmets. "What's the situation there, Angus?"

"The capsule seems to be intact, but we haven't established contact with the people inside."

"What do we do?" Bill Hawkins cried in anguish.

"Dump the rocket and tanks and bring the whole thing back to the *Ventris* and shove it into the equipment bay," Walsh ordered.

By now the Moon Cruiser had cooled to black and the mist was rising. McNeil showed Hawkins how to trip the latches that fastened the strap-on fuel tanks and rocket motor to the capsule; they kept their distance as the explosive bolts blew the propulsion rig loose.

Even with their suit maneuvering rockets on full

it took several seconds before the two men could get the big canister to move. Their helmet beams sent odd shafts through the fog as McNeil and Hawkins grappled with it; finally it rose reluctantly from the steaming fumarole it had blasted in the middle of the ice.

The strange flying assemblage, two white-suited astronauts holding a burned and blackened wreck between them, came through the mist like something from a ruined Baroque ceiling, a mockery of apotheosis. The lights of the far-off *Ventris* beckoned them through the white limbo.

The big ship's equipment bay doors were split wide open. With the Manta still somewhere underwater and the Old Mole parked out on the ice, there was more than enough room inside for the battered Moon Cruiser. Groves had left the bridge and was on hand to help the others wrestle the capsule into the hold. Motors spun in dead silence and the clamshell hold slowly resealed itself. Valves popped and air poured into the hold, imperceptibly at first, then with a whisper, then in a hissing crescendo.

The men tore their face plates open.

"Inside, inside. Get a reaction wrench on those."

"Watch out, those are explosive bolts—"

"Careful, Hawkins!"

"—let me disarm them before you blow my head off."

The Moon Cruiser's hatch pulled away. Hawkins got his head inside first. He found two bodies, completely limp. Inside their helmets, their faces were black and their staring eyes were full of blood.

18

Angus McNeil, designated ship's doctor, found himself rigging two life-support systems in the ship's tiny gym, which doubled as the clinic. Bill Hawkins, still wearing his sweat-stinking spacesuit, glued himself to a monitor screen in the wardroom, watching McNeil work, until Jo Walsh finally talked him into getting out of his suit and into fresh clothes.

Tony Groves was staying out of Hawkins's way. Hawkins blamed Groves for what had happened—*he'd* persuaded the captain to let them crash—and for that matter, Groves blamed himself.

Force against duration, that was the critical curve, and Groves thought he'd blown it. The fluffy sublimed stuff on the moon's surface hadn't been deep enough; the underlying ice had been too hard; the capsule had stopped too fast. Worst of all, the retrorocket hadn't fired. The cynical faith that Groves and McNeil had expressed—that Mays had planned it all, that he knew exactly what he was doing—had apparently been misplaced.

Hawkins, meanwhile, was driving himself into ecstasies of despair. Unable to help or even get close to the clinic, given the cramped quarters, he was calling up the entries under "kinetic trauma" from the wardroom's library, trying to make himself an expert.

Case histories, garnered from accident reports in over a century's worth of space travel, made grim reading: "Onset of 8,500 gees per second averaged to 96 gees in an exposure lasting 0.192 seconds was fatal within 4 hours with massive gross pathology. . . . The 8,500-gee per second rise time to 96 peak is 0.011 second, corresponding to 23 Hertz, which excites whole-body resonance. . . . Orientation of impact force applied to the body relates to axes of internal organ displacements, hydraulic pressure pulsation in blood vessels, and interaction of head, thorax and pelvic masses between spinal couplings. . . ."

Mays had gotten the worst of it, with a broken neck and lower spine and a severed spinal cord. Marianne, lighter, younger—and shorter—therefore less massive and more flexible, had broken no bones. But her internal organs had suffered as Mays's had, having been subjected to "whole-body resonance."

Hawkins couldn't bring himself to care if Mays died. But Marianne's death would desolate him, and for that he would blame himself.

The Manta was coming up from below. Once clear of the boiling core and its turbulence, with communication between the Ventris and the Manta restored, Blake and the professor had been able to monitor events overhead.

The submarine rose from the seething surface of Amalthea and made its way unaided through the cloying mists of the vacuum, using short bursts of its auxiliary rockets, to the hold of the Ventris. They managed to dock the awkward little makeshift spacecraft—which had never been intended to be one for more than a few seconds at a time—without incident. Through the mists, the copper sky above the *Ventris* held a bright new object, a Space Board cutter keeping station in Amalthea's wake.

Blake and Forster got through the equipment bay airlock in time to hear the announcement from the ship's computer over the intercom: *CWSS 9, Board of Space Control, now holding in orbit. Inspector Ellen Troy requests permission to board Ventris.*

Up on the flight deck, Jo Walsh said, "Permission granted. Advise Inspector Troy to use the main airlock."

I'm already here, Sparta's voice on her suitcomm came over the cabin speakers. *Outside your door. Any problem coming inside?*

"Come aboard," said Walsh.

Blake and the professor climbed onto the flight deck as Sparta came through the overhead hatch, helmet in hand. "What's the condition of the casualties?" she asked.

"Not good, Inspector," said Walsh. "Your timing is excellent, though"—suspiciously excellent, she didn't bother to add. "We need to get them aboard that cutter of yours and into first-rate medical facilities."

"Sorry, too late," said Sparta.

"What do you mean, too late?" Walsh glared at her.

"Cutter's on its way home." Sparta nodded toward the navigation flatscreen. At that moment the blip of the cutter brightened and the screen displayed the fast-rising trajectory of the departing ship.

"What's this all about?" Forster demanded.

"The quarantine of Amalthea is officially ended," Sparta said to Forster. "We're on our own here, Professor. I urgently need to have a word with you in private."

Walsh interrupted him before he could reply. "I don't know what the politics of this are, but I guess they must be pretty important," said Walsh, who'd put in tens of thousands of hours on the flight decks of Space Board cutters. "I hope you're prepared to accept responsibility for the deaths of those two people, Inspector. You've sent away their only good chance to survive."

Sparta faced her old acquaintance, who managed to contain her anger only because her discipline was greater than her pride. "I do take responsibility, Jo. If there's anything I can do to prevent it, they won't die."

Inside the makeshift clinic there was barely enough room for both crash victims. Loose straps kept them from floating away from their pallets in the near-zero gravity, although they would not have gotten far, entangled in webs of tubes and wires that monitored heart rhythms, brain rhythms, lung function, circulatory system, nervous system, digestion, chemical and hormonal balances. . . .

On top of damage from torn tissues, broken bones, and displaced internal organs, Mays and Mitchell were suffering from the effects of ionizing radiation absorbed in a lightly shielded capsule during more than eight hours inside Jupiter's radiation belt. That damage posed more of a problem than fractured bones, ruptured flesh, or severed nerves.

Through tubes of microscopic diameter, prepackaged molecules entered their bodies to course like emergency vehicles through their bloodstream. Some were natural biochemicals, others were tiny artificial structures, "tailored nanocytes," that worked not by snipping and pinching and whirring, not like Lilliputian machines, but by lightning catalysis, the complexification and decomplexification of interlocking molecules. Frayed muscles and ligaments and organ flesh, torn nerve fibers, fractured bones were sought out; damaged bits were gobbled away and digested, the waste products

scavenged for their constituent molecules; replace-
ments were constructed on site from the sea of bal-
anced nutrients in which they swam by incalculable
swarms of natural and artificial proteins and nucleic acids. . . .

Sparta joined them in the clinic and stayed there
the whole time, with the PIN spines beneath her
fingers extended and inserted into the ports of the
machine monitors. Beneath her forehead, the dense
tissue of her soul's eye reviewed the analyses, partly
smelling the complex equations that presented
themselves for her mental inspection, partly *seeing*
them written out on the screen of her consciousness. From time to time, several times a second, she
made subtle adjustments to the chemical recipe.

Six hours passed—less than half a circuit of Jupiter, for Amalthea was less massive now and had
gradually moved itself into a higher, slower orbit.

Life-signs monitors went to yellow: the patients
were out of danger. They'd be tired and sore when
they woke up, and it would take some getting used
to the stiffness of their repaired flesh, but in every
measurable respect they were well on their way to
good health. Sparta had known it before the monitors announced it. She had already gone to the
cabin they'd assigned her and was sound asleep,
unconscious from exhaustion.

Blake was there when she woke up. It was his
cabin too.

She was still wearing the velvety black tunic and
pants she'd favored since their reunion on Ganymede. In Blake's eyes she'd always looked sexy,
wearing her usual shiny don't-touch-me suit or
even in a spacesuit, a bag of canvas and metal, but
these days she was starting to dress like she didn't
mind people thinking so. It was less a surprise than
it might have been when she smiled wearily and
began taking off her crushed and slept-in clothes.

"What's it about . . . Linda?"

Naked now, she sat on the bunk facing him, folding her bare legs into lotus position. "It's about the Knowledge, and what it really means." She easily resumed the conversation they'd begun on Ganymede as if no time had passed.

He nodded. "I knew it was something like that."

"I was never initiated, you know. I was never Free Spirit *or* Salamander. It's only from your initiation that I know whatever details I do."

"I always thought the main thing to know about that was that they really would have let me die— and anybody else who couldn't get through it."

"They were looking for supermen," she said. "But there must have been more to it than pride. Back at the Lodge I spent hours quizzing my father and the commander and the kids on the staff, finding out what they knew of Free Spirit practices, what they had learned of the Knowledge, how they interpreted what they knew. I tried to see if it fit with my own understanding of the Knowledge. I was never taught, you know; they programmed it right into the neurons."

"That's what they were trying to wipe out?"

She nodded. "I learned a lot this year, some from other people but most from self-guided deep probes of my own memory. But the most insistent image came from me: a vivid experience I had when I was . . . crazy. There was a moment in the darkness in the crypt under Kingman's place, St. Joseph's Hall— when I looked into the pit—under the ceiling map of Crux. There was a head of Medusa on the stone that covered it."

"The Goddess as Death. You told me."

"In a dream I had, my name was Circe. She was Death, too."

"You still see yourself that way?" he asked carefully.

"We're many things, Blake, both of us. In the pit,

there were scrolls and the chip of Falcon's reconstruction and a bronze image of the Thunderer, but what I see whenever I think of that moment are the two little skeletons, so delicate—so yellow and old. Infants, identical in size. I knew immediately that they must have been twins. And I knew what they symbolized. Like the king and queen of the alchemists, they were the Heavenly Twins—and the Heavenly Parents—Gold and Silver, the male Sun and the female Moon.''

"Yes, that's what Salamander say," Blake said.

She smiled. "I warned you it was a long story."

"You're getting to the part I love. The old-book part."

"All right. The point is that for thousands of years there's been a cult of Knowledge, using lots of different names to hide its existence. Free Spirit is a pretty recent one, from the 12th or 13th century. And for all those centuries they've been busy putting out *false* knowledge, to screen their precious truth."

Blake couldn't restrain himself. "Egyptian, Mesopotamian, Greek mythology, it's loaded with hints. It's there right in Herodotus, those tales of the Persian Magi—they were the historical adepts of the Knowledge. And Hermes Trismegistus, those books that were supposedly priestly revelations of the ancient Egyptians but were really Hellenistic fictions concocted by worshippers of the Pancreator to put people off the track. Weren't they marvelous fantasies though, wonderfully vague and suggestive? Some people still believe that stuff today! And the so-called great religions . . . Don't get me started."

She smiled. "I'll try not to."

"In the beginning was the Word, and the Word was a lie," he said vehemently. "The original Free Spirit heresy itself—poor people thumbing their noses at the church and getting crucified—but those were just the shock troops. Half the *prophetae* by night were cardinals and bishops by day." He paused and saw her smiling at him. He laughed and shook his head. "Sorry. You're supposed to be telling it."

"You probably know more details than I do. It was alchemy that intrigued me—all those undecipherable alchemical texts going all the way back to Roman times, senseless either as theory or as practice . . . But finally I realized it was as if they were refracting real traditions, horrible traditions, through a distorting lens." She began to recite then, her voice taking on a raspy, menacing monotone:

> *"Hail beautiful lamp of heaven,*
> *shining light of the world. Here*
> *thou art united with the moon, here*
> *ariseth the bond of Mars, and the*
> *conjunction with Mercury. . . . When*
> *these three shall have dissolved not*
> *into rain water but into mercurial*
> *water, into this our blessed gum*
> *which dissolves of itself and is*
> *named the Sperm of the Philosophers.*
> *Now he makes haste to bind and*
> *betroth himself to the virgin bride . . .*
> and so on."

"You've figured out what that means?" Blake asked.

"The worst of it, anyway. The cult has been building temple planetariums since Neolithic times—in the alchemical writings the temples are disguised as the *alembic*, the sealed reaction vessel—and to dedicate the foundations, the adepts of the Knowledge would kill and eat a pair of male and female infants, fraternal twins . . . children of cult members, if they could get them. The twins were surrogates for the spiritual leader."

"They would have eaten *him* instead?"

"Or her," Sparta replied. "In the end, there was supposed to be only one such person, who would unite in his or her body the male and female principles; it was the task of the highest circle to bring this sacred and magical creature into being. In every age the Free Spirit has tried, using the most advanced crafts of their own times, to create the perfect human being."

"The Emperor of the Last Days," said Blake.

"Yes, and you were the first to tell me about the Emperor of the Last Days—that when the Pancreator returned from the farthest reaches of heaven, from the home star in Crux, the Emperor was expected to sacrifice himself—or herself, if she was the Empress—for the sake of the *prophetae*."

"Yeah, the Pancreator is some benefactor," Blake said. "Like the god of the Bible. A Jealous God, who demands death as a down payment."

Sparta said, "The ancient symbol of the Emperor, this sacred and perfected personality, was the snake devouring itself—with the legend 'If you have not All, All is Nothing.' "

"All will be well," Blake murmured.

"They distorted what had once been a reassurance into something sinister. I think the practice of twin sacrifice didn't stop until the 18th century—when modern science finally started to make an impression on the cult—and it is still echoed in the ritual meals of the knights and elders. The self-sacrifice of the Emperor or Empress, however, is not supposed to be symbolic. . . ."

"But we haven't heard a peep from the Free Spirit since we squashed the *Kon-Tiki* mutiny," Blake said. "We cut the head off that particular snake."

"They failed because they misinterpreted the Knowledge. When they tried to make *me* into the Empress, they made plenty of mistakes. I've corrected them."

He studied her, suddenly unnerved. "What you showed me . . . ?"

"I have no intention of sacrificing myself. But Blake, to my own surprise—reviewing everything I've been taught and what I've learned since—I find that I've recovered my belief in the Pancreator. The Pancreator is real. And I think we will soon meet . . . her, or him, or it."

"That's superstition," he said quietly, growing increasingly uneasy. "We all think we're going to find remnants of Culture X—it's an open secret by now. The Pancreator is a myth."

"I have no truck with the Free Spirit. Don't worry. But I am still the Empress." Her smile had an edge, and her eyes gleamed like sapphires. "And you are my twin."

Forster assembled the others in the wardroom.

"Angus, will you please tell us what you found inside the capsule?"

The engineer's face was as stern as a cop's at an inquest. "Both the communication and ranging systems were deliberately put out of commission. Someone with a good knowledge of celestial navigation reprogrammed the capsule's guidance computer to depart from the planned trajectory during close approach to Io . . ."

"What are you saying, McNeil?" Hawkins interrupted. "That they tried to kill themselves?"

". . . specifically in order to rendezvous with Amalthea," McNeil continued, acknowledging Hawkins's interruption with a single slow shake of his head. "With the intention of making a *soft* landing. That part of the rewrite seems to have been a bit miscalculated. On the basis of Doppler input, the main engine did in fact retrofire—unfortunately, a few seconds late to do them any good. They'd already hit the ice."

Jo Walsh grunted, a sound of reluctant satisfaction. "You were right, Tony."

"Wish I could take comfort in that, but I can't," Groves said. "It was a hard, hard landing."

"If they were dead now, you'd be calling it more than a hard landing," Hawkins said angrily.

"No more interruptions," Forster said sternly, fixing Hawkins with a hot and bristling stare. "Everyone will have a chance to speak. For my part, it's my opinion that Tony's initial analysis of the situation was accurate. Mays planned the thing carefully. And even without main-engine retrofire, he and his"—Forster's glance flickered back to the distraught Hawkins—"no doubt innocent companion survived."

Hawkins's face was a study in conflict.

Forster went on hastily. "Josepha, make sure we have complete records, safely stored, of everything that has occurred. Especially everything that Angus found. Check the monitoring functions regularly."

"Sir." Walsh was too cool to show surprise. Everything that had happened *was* recorded; Board of Space Control regulations required it, and the ship's automated systems virtually prevented anyone from disobeying. Forster evidently expected sabotage.

"It's my opinion that if Mays's plan had succeeded, he would have reprogrammed his computer—or perhaps destroyed it, if necessary—and claimed that the crash had been caused by malfunction. He is here for one reason, and that is to spy upon us." For a moment the professor withdrew into his own thoughts. Then he said, "All right. Let me have your comments."

"They're going to wake up within the hour, Professor," said Groves. "They'll be hungry and curious and eager to get rid of those tubes and wires and straps. How do you want us to handle the moment when it arrives?"

"We have an impossible job to do, and only a few days in which to do it," Forster said. "I can think of no way that Sir Randolph Mays, once he is awake and mobile, can be prevented from learning what we learn, almost as fast as we learn it."

"I suppose we can't keep them tied up?" McNeil said hopefully.

"Out of the question. I want this clearly understood: no one among us is to behave other than according to the highest dictates of ethics and space law." He cleared his throat. "We'll just have to find a way to keep him and his young friend busy."

PART
4

INTO THE HEART
OF THE DEEP

19

Amalthea was contracting faster now, shedding proportionally more mass as its surface area decreased. The smaller it got, the faster it got smaller.

The oceans of the little moon would have simply boiled away beneath the *Michael Ventris* if Forster had been willing to wait. But there were too many questions that could never be answered if that extraordinary biosphere were allowed to evaporate into space unobserved. Besides, the professor was an impatient man.

Sparta was at the controls of the diving Manta when they reentered the teeming sea.

"There they are already," Forster said, surprised. "The animals we met before."

"They've been waiting for you," Sparta said. "I'll bet they weren't happy when you and Blake turned back."

A school of luminescent "squid" was arrayed in glittering splendor below them, a whole sheet of creatures rippling all together as one, almost as if with pleasure.

Forster raised a bushy eyebrow in her direction. "You seem rather certain of that."

"She's right, sir," Blake said, hunched over in the cramped space behind them. "Listen on the hydrophone."

Taking Blake's cue, Sparta adjusted the volume of the external phones until the eerie cries of underwater life engulfed them.

"I'm listening. I'm not a biologist. Could be any school of fish. . . ." Forster's eager brows twitched. "A strong pattern, though, stronger than before. Not regular, actually, but with important elements repeated. A signal, you think?"

"Encoded in squeaks and whistles," Sparta said.

"And possibly saying the same thing," Blake said. "The same as Jupiter's medusas, I mean."

"Yes, sir," said Sparta. "Saying the same thing."

" 'They have arrived.' " Forster mulled that over for a moment. "I won't ask you how you know this, Troy . . ."

"Your analysis will confirm it. When you have time to get to the recordings we've made."

"Things are happening too fast for *that* to happen—not until we've left here." He looked at her. "You didn't tell me everything. You've known all along what we're here to find, haven't you?"

She nodded.

"And today we *will* find it," he said, triumphant.

She said nothing, paying attention only to her driving. With powerful beats of its wings the Manta followed the glowing squadrons toward the bright heart of Amalthea. As before, the sub was forced to stop to adjust for depth, but because Amalthea was smaller now, the distance from the surface to the core was well within its absolute pressure limit.

Soon they approached the core.

The core was everywhere bright but not everywhere hot. As they swam closer they saw that the multiple streams of bubbles that radiated in every direction were being generated by complex structures, glowing white towers a kilometer or more high, studding a perfectly mirrored ellipsoid. The light from the near-molten towers—for even through dozens of kilometers of water they blazed brighter than the filaments of an incandescent bulb—was reflected in the curving mirror surface; it was these reflections, as well as their sources, that from a great distance had given the impression of a single glowing object.

"You know what we've found, don't you, Troy?"

"I do."

"*I* don't," said Blake.

"A spacecraft," Forster said. "A billion-year-old spacecraft. It brought Culture X from their star to ours. They parked it here, in the radiation belts of Jupiter, the most dangerous part of the solar system outside the envelope of the sun itself. And they encased it in a rind of ice thick enough to shield it for as long as it took. They seeded the clouds of Jupiter with life; generations upon generations kept passive watch, for *us*—never evolving, the cloud ecosystem was too simple for that, but neither was it ever subject to the catastrophic changes of a geologically active planet—until *Kon-Tiki* revealed that *we* had evolved ourselves, to a planet-faring species. That *we* had arrived." He paused, and upon his young-old face there came an almost mystic rapture. "And now the world-ship awakes, and sheds its icy shell."

Sparta, privately amused at his rhetoric but careful of his mood, said quietly, "What do you suppose will happen next?"

Forster gave her a bright shrewd eye. "There are many options, aren't there? Perhaps *they* will come forth to greet us. Perhaps *they* will simply say goodbye, having done whatever they came to do. Perhaps they are all dead."

"Or perhaps they will bring paradise on Earth," Blake said ironically.

"That's what that cult of yours teaches, I suppose?"

"It was never my cult," he said. "Nor hers."

They fell silent, as the searing core loomed beneath them, growing larger until it filled the field of view. Small by comparison to the bulk that had once surrounded it, the core of Amalthea was still enormous, bigger by far than most asteroids—three times as big as Phobos, the inner moon of Mars. Since their first soundings they had known they were not dealing with a natural object, but the sight of an artifact thirty kilometers in diameter was enough to make even Sparta, who was inured to wonders, grow contemplative.

With her infrared vision Sparta easily read the hot and cold convection currents that flowed over the shining expanse of the ellipsoid, a vista of strong currents and roiling turbulence. Heated to boiling, the columns of water that ascended from the glowing manifolds were marked by whole galaxies of microscopic bubbles, to her vision as bright as quasars. Colder, clearer water descended like purple night around them, feeding the intakes at the bases of the towers.

She steered the Manta away from the heat, letting the relatively cooler water carry the sub downward. Even without her temperature-sensitive vision to guide her, she could have chosen the safe path merely by following the diving school of squid.

There were many such schools near the core, swooping and wheeling about the bases of the great towers, seeming to dart in and out of the mouths of the fiery boilers without harm to themselves.

"I'd like to know what the heat source is," said Forster. He had to shout over the boom and roar of the boilers, which made the little submarine quiver. "Looks nuclear."

"Not these structures," Blake said. "The instruments show no neutrons. No gamma rays. Whatever the heat source locally, it's not fission or fusion."

"We'll have time for that later. Right now I want to find a way in."

They were still following the squid. "Perhaps our friends will help us," Sparta said.

The sub came down to within a few meters of the gleaming surface. It showed no sign of plates or rivets, no hint of a seam or even an irregularity. It was perfect. They flew over it with stately wing-flaps as if over a landscape plated with a film of diamond. The horizon was curved as gently as a moon's, and the black-water sky was spangled with living, darting stars.

"What if we *can't* get in?" said Blake.

Forster's reply was uncharacteristically tentative. "Difficult to imagine anything more . . . *tantalizing* than to be locked out of the greatest archaeological find in all history."

Sparta was silent, almost contemplative, as if nothing that happened could upset or surprise her.

The objective of the school of glittering squid seemed to be a broad, low dome at least a kilometer in circumference. Soon they were over it; far off on the diamond plains stood the great bright towers, evenly spaced in rows around then, catching them in a reticule of shimmering reflection.

Now the school of squid spiraled above them like bright-colored autumn leaves caught up in a whirlwind, soaring into the sky and falling, only to be swept aloft again in the swirling dance. The Manta flapped its way to the middle of the spiral of ascending transparent animals. There below them in the center of the otherwise flawless dome the three submariners saw the first interruption in Amalthea's perfect surface, a circular hole some two meters across.

"Too small to get in," said Forster, crestfallen.

Sparta let the Manta settle toward the dark opening, probing it with the sub's lights. Inside were other bright structures, a tunnel-like opening whose walls were fretted and filigreed in bright metal.

"This doesn't look artificial," Forster said, with increasing pessimism.

"Could be a meteor strike," Blake said brightly, leaning forward to peer between their heads at the opening below.

"Mighty lucky hit," said Sparta. "Awfully round hole, wouldn't you say?"

"Big meteors always produce circular holes, unless they strike very glancing blows." It was as if Blake wanted to convince them of the worst.

"I doubt that a meteor would make a round hole in this material," Sparta said, "This is the same stuff as the Martian plaque."

"But look at the edges," Blake persisted. "You can see there's been an explosion of some kind."

"I don't think so. That etching looks too intricate to have been done by an explosion."

Forster cleared his throat with a growl. "What do *you* think it is, Troy?"

"I think they left the door open for us."

"*They?* This is a machine," Forster exclaimed hoarsely. "A billion-year-old machine."

She nodded. "A very smart one."

"You think it's programmed to let us in?" He was transparent; he wanted her to tell him what he wanted to believe.

She nodded again, obliging him at least partly. If he wanted her to say that *they* were still inside, however, she would have to disappoint him.

Sparta studied the interior of the round hole and its scalloped and serrated surfaces; she fixed it in memory and then, for an imperceptible moment—

—she fell into a trance, into a mathematical space of unpicturable dimensions where no real-world sensations penetrated—only the chittering squeaks of the squid, still echoing inside her head. Her soul's eye performed the analysis and the computation and suddenly she saw how the thing worked. Her eyes flickered—

—and she was back in the strangely lit underwater world—partly bright, partly dark, partly cold, partly hot. The Manta bobbed sensuously in the dark water. Without bothering to explain herself to Blake or the professor, Sparta manipulated the Manta's waldos, brushing its sensitive titanium fingers along the complex inner surface of the cylindrical hole, brushing and stroking the textures that could as easily have been melted slag or fine jewelry by their appearance but were really something as straightforward and purposeful as a mathematical constant, like the written-out expansion of pi.

"Something's happening," said the professor.

"I don't see anything," Blake said. "Or hear anything."

"I feel it—I mean, somehow I *sense* it." Forster's eyes widened. "Look there, what's that?"

The low dome over which they hovered seemed somehow less adamantine, less perfect in its reflection of boiling incandescent towers.

"It's brighter here," he said excitedly.

"Really?" Sparta's voice was teasing.

"The ground—I mean the hull, or whatever it is—it's glowing."

"The instruments don't show any increase in temperature," said Blake.

"I didn't say . . . look at that!" Forster scooted himself forward and practically shoved his nose against the Manta's polyglas window. "I can see right through it!"

For indeed the low dome had begun to glow, like an immense light fixture on a very slow rheostat; the whole surface of the bulge in the diamond moon was a rosy pink, as of a soft neon sign. But it swiftly grew brighter, and suddenly what had appeared to be a solid—an opaque, polished metal surface—had become as transparent as lead crystal.

For the first time in several minutes, Jo Walsh's voice came to them over the sonarlink. "We're seeing a change in the seismic profile of the core, Professor."

"What change?" Forster asked.

"Computer can't make sense of it. But the core's no longer opaque to sound. It's uncertain we have the appropriate programs to interpret what we're seeing. . . ."

"Just record. We'll analyze later."

"As you say, sir."

Forster and Blake and Sparta were staring in wonder, straight through the perfectly clear kilometer-wide dome into a glowing open space, far bigger than Earth's biggest cathedral.

"It's an airlock," said Forster. "Big enough for whole spaceships."

"Not an airlock, I think," said Sparta.

"What? Oh, of course . . . what's inside isn't air."

"How do you suppose they open the hatch?" Blake asked.

As if on cue, the crystal dome beneath them began to melt visibly away. First the lock mechanism immediately below them—which had retained its shape although it had grown as fragile-looking as a spun-sugar sculpture—visibly quivered and dissolved. From the place where it had been, a gossamer gyre peeled off, Fibonacci-like; it was as if the material of the hull had grown thinner, losing layer after layer, faster and faster, down to the final layer of molecules—and then even these had been stripped away.

There was a great inpouring of water. Caught in the turbulence, the Manta tumbled inside, into the liquid arena.

A moment later it was all over: the gossamer window reformed overhead, layers of invisibly tiny molecular tiles relaid themselves in reverse order, and—even faster than it had become transparent—the great dome was once more opaque. The last sight that the three in the Manta saw through it, as the submarine tumbled inside in the eddies, was a bright school of squid flashing away in every direction, like a shower of meteors.

Sparta took a moment to stabilize the rolling submarine, orienting the weightless craft with its belly toward the center of Amalthea, the "floor," and its roof toward the center of the dome, the "ceiling."

Eerie silence closed on them. The clattering rush and roar of the boiler towers outside had vanished, along with the subsonic phasing that had sounded so like a giant heartbeat. All the sub's hydrophones picked up was the rhythmic watery fizz of its own respiration.

"Jo, do you read us?" Sparta said into the sonarlink.

She was neither surprised nor concerned when there was no answer. She glanced at Forster, whose shiny face registered excitement but no fear.

"Whatever's damping the seismic signature of this thing is back in place," Blake said.

"As long as we're in here we won't have any communication with the surface," said Sparta.

"I expected as much," said Forster. "Walsh and the rest will know what's happened. We'll keep to our prearranged schedule."

Sparta didn't think the crew would realize what had happened, but she knew they were disciplined enough not to depart from the mission plan. She glanced at the console. "Outside pressure is dropping rapidly."

"Good trick," said Blake.

Forster was surprised. "Must be some rather large pumps at work. But it's perfectly silent."

"Rather small pumps, I think," Sparta said. "Molecular pumps, like a biological cell's, all over the surface of the lock."

They were a tiny speck adrift in the center of a huge bowl, smaller than a guppy in a fish tank. A pale blue light, like that a dozen meters below the surface of the tropical seas of Earth, came from the softly glowing walls and floor of the chamber itself. On the roof of the dome, a random scatter of blue-white pinpricks shone more brightly.

While the spectrum did not extend either to the infrared or the ultraviolet, the ubiquitous glow was bright enough to allow Sparta to make out the graceful architecture of the vault. The space was sparsely filled, the shell lavishly decorated with Gaudi-like, apparently melting pilasters and sagging arches, all fretted about with a network of fractal piping, as intricate as the branching alveoli of a mammalian lung.

Blake could see it almost as well as she, and—"Something about this place"—he noticed what she did, although he could not pin down his impression—"looks very . . . familiar."

To Sparta—allowing only for severe foreshortening—it was a familiar pattern indeed. "You saw the holos of the Free Spirit temple under Kingman's place?"

"Yes."

"Put that in a graphics program and flatten the Z axis about four hundred percent."

The crypt beneath Kingman's English manor was built in the high-flying Perpendicular style of the 14th century, while this space bulged outward more extravagantly than the central domes of the Blue Mosque. Yet the architectural elements—the graceful arches, the eight-fold symmetry, the interlocking ribs, the radiating foliate patterns from the central boss overhead—made for a sort of squashed High Gothic.

Forster craned his head to look up through the Manta's bubble. "And those white lights overhead? Almost like stars."

"Crux," she said. "Perhaps they were sentimental. The center of the hatch, where we came in, marks the position of their home star."

"And directly beneath it, the inner sanctum," said Blake.

"Yes." She nodded at Forster. "Directly beneath, sir, is the way in."

She steered the Manta down into the blue water. The floor beneath was as intricate as a coral reef, encrusted with multi-armed and multi-tentacled creatures. Directly below lay a forest of frozen metallic tentacles, baroquely curled and bent, like the arms of a basket starfish. In the center of the array, where the sea star's mouth would be, there was a dark opening. Sparta plunged the tiny Manta toward it.

Moments later they were in black water.

Sparta played the searchlights on the roof above; the ovals of light danced away into the distance until they were too diffuse to be visible. The Manta hovered in the midst of a space so vast and dark its light beams reached nothing below it.

"I feel like a spider suspended beneath the dome of St. Peter's," said Forster, peering around him in the gloom.

"I didn't know you were a religious man, Professor." Sparta's cool tone did not betray her amusement.

"Oh, well . . . it's a very large construction, that's all I meant."

"Surely this is exactly what you expected to find? The ship that brought Culture X to our solar system."

"Yes, certainly. I've even argued it in papers that no one seems to have read—or if they did, they thought they were doing me a favor by pretending I hadn't committed the indiscretion."

"I recall one in *Nature* in '74," Blake said. "It got some attention."

"You were hardly old enough to read in '74," said Forster.

"I came across it in files later," Blake said.

Forster admitted he was flattered. "It *was* rather a good statement of the thesis, wasn't it? Suppose a civilization wanted to cross interstellar space—how would it attack the problem? I argued that it would build a mobile planetoid—a world-ship I called it—taking perhaps centuries over the task."

"At least centuries, I should think." Sparta's tone of voice subtly encouraged him to keep talking as she nosed the Manta lower into the water below them—crystal clear and utterly devoid of light.

"Since the ship would have to be a self-contained world which could support its inhabitants for generations it would need to be as large as . . . as *this*. I wonder how many suns they visited before they found ours and knew that their search was ended?"

"So you guessed all this before we started," Blake said.

"Oh, not all of it."

"No?" Sparta glanced at him curiously.

"I never thought they would be sea creatures," said Forster, his soft voice full of wonder. "Even with all we've encountered, the ice and the temporary sea outside—full of life—it never occurred to me that they would *live* in water. When we came into the inner lock, my first thought was that the vessel had sprung a leak, that all of them were dead and that the melting ice had filled their world-ship with water."

"What changed your mind?"

"You knew it right away," he said sharply. "The pressure and temperature in here are like the shallowest seas of Earth."

"Yes. And like the seas that once covered Mars and Venus," said Sparta.

"The *salt-worlds*, that's what the Martian plaque calls them. We knew that must mean ocean worlds, but we didn't know how important oceans were to them. Oceans with just the right mix of nutrients to sustain their own kind."

Something loomed out of the darkness below them, a vast and lacy strutwork of crystalline vaulting. Farther down, according to the Manta's sonar, there was another smooth shell.

"If I had to guess, I'd say we were inside a hangar," Blake said. "They must have had smaller ships that could take them down to the planets.

"I wonder if we'll ever find one of those," Forster said. "Or did they return here a billion years ago?"

"If this is a hangar, it's empty except for us," said Sparta.

"Yes. Too bad."

"Why too bad, sir?" Blake asked.

"Their wonderful machinery performed on cue. Their myriad animals woke from frozen sleep and did what in their genes they'd been programmed to do. But apparently a few too many million years have passed. On the outside, everything is alive and working. Here in the interior, all is dark and empty."

Sparta and Blake said nothing, and Forster fell silent, not caring to say more. The Manta glided lazily through the dark water, its blue-white beams picking out structural elements as delicate as fronds of kelp or branches of coral. On every side dark passageways beckoned them to enter labyrinthine corridors; there were too many entrances to make any choice obvious or easy.

"We should start back before we worry the others," Sparta said.

Forster nodded, still brooding.

She was moved to comfort him. "Just think what you'll find."

"Yes, but really, it's almost *too* big," he said wearily. "Not to mention filled with water."

"Don't worry, we'll put everyone to work," she said.

"How?" He stirred. "I'm not sure I understand."

"We'll use them as divers—put them in space suits and ferry them down here, two at a time. The Manta can be flooded, and once we get them here inside the core, the pressure is low enough. A rigid suit can easily stand up to it." She smiled. "It's still the greatest archaeological find in history, Professor. Even though it is full of water."

20

"I don't want to take up space here with yet another description of all the wonders of Amalthea. There have already been enough docu-chips and photograms and maps and learned disquisitions upon the subject—my own bookchip, by the way, will soon be published by Sidgwick, Routledge & Unwin—but what I would like to give you instead is some impression of what it was like to be one of the first humans ever to enter that strange watery world. . . ."

Bill Hawkins turned in his sleep, making himself more comfortable in his loose sleep restraint, and resumed his murmurous dream soliloquy. "Yet I'm sorry to say—I know this sounds hard to believe—that I simply can't remember what I was feeling when the Europan submarine ejected me into blackness. I suppose I could say that I was so excited and so overwhelmed by the wonder of it all that I've forgotten everything else. . . ."

In his dreams, Hawkins was a marvelous speechifier, throughout it all remaining fluent, suave—but humble, of course—although his audience constantly shifted, from packed lecture hall to intimate video studio to a circle of evening-jacketed, bearded men in a map-lined drawing room of a vaguely imagined Explorers Club. . . .

"Certainly I do recall the impression of sheer size, something which mere holos can never give. The builders of this world, coming from a world of waters, were giants, at least four times the size of humans—or so we guessed from the dimensions of their entranceways and corridors, which were easily big enough to admit the submarine. We were tadpoles wriggling among their works.

"We never got below the outer levels, so we met with few of the scientific marvels which later expeditions discovered. That was just as well; we had enough to keep us busy. We assumed we were exploring residential areas and control rooms and the like, but the architecture was so strange and haunting we were never perfectly sure what we were looking at—we might have been swimming in an octopus's garden. Oh, there were inscriptions aplenty, millions of characters of them, and I spent most of my time trying to decipher just enough to get their gist. Most were unimaginably dull, mere lists of supplies, or labeled diagrams for incomprehensible devices.

"But there were no representations of the creatures who had written them, no sign of the creatures who lived in these intricate halls. We knew from the Martian plaque that they were not without vanity, but nowhere did they keep pictures of themselves, or even surfaces smooth and flat enough to serve—as the Martian plaque and the Venus tablets might have served, had they not been covered with symbols—as mirrors. . . ."

Hawkins muttered and grumbled. In his dream he was looking into a mirror inscribed with a thousand alien characters, and behind them a face stared back at him, not his own. . . .

The face resembled that of the woman psychiatrist he'd been required to interview before he was accepted for the expedition.

"I *could* say that I was excited and overwhelmed

by the wonder of it all . . . but that would be inac-
curate." His dream statements became fussy, his
words precise. The dream psychiatrist regarded him
skeptically. "Actually, the first time Inspector Troy
heaved me out of the tight little Manta into the
warm fluid interior of Amalthea's core—pushed me
out rather roughly, in fact, with surprising strength
for a woman of her size—my mind was so filled
with thoughts of Marianne that I wasn't paying attention to the job I'd traveled so many hundreds of
thousands of . . ."

A new face confronted him in his dreams. He
moaned aloud. His eyes sprang open in the darkness.

His heart was thudding in great slow beats and
his forehead was beaded with sweat. He groped in
the pouch on the wall beside him and found a tissue, which he used to wipe the sweat carefully
away. Hawkins would never be able to eradicate
the memory of Marianne's horribly blackened and
bloody face as she lay blind and barely conscious
inside the wreck of the Moon Cruiser.

But less than twenty-four hours later—he'd kept
watch until the professor had ordered him to go to
sleep—all the burst cells and infused blood of her
ruined face had been carried away and digested,
and her skin was again as fresh and new as a ten-
year-old's. Her beauty hurt his heart.

Hawkins shared the tiny sleeping compartment
with the professor—he'd moved into the professor's
cabin when Sparta moved in with Blake—but the
work of exploring the great world-ship had required the crew of the *Ventris* to work in shifts, and
for the moment Hawkins had the place to himself.
He knew he would not be going back to sleep soon.
His dream had been too vivid.

He had not given any thought—consciously, anyway—to what he would make of his experiences
once he got back to civilization. There were the var-

ious confidentiality agreements and contracts he'd signed before coming aboard, but these merely limited him to clearing public statements with the professor until the scientific results of the expedition had been published. Forster had promised that he had no intention of delaying publication and no inclination to muzzle his crew.

It occurred to Hawkins that there was going to be a big demand for the memoirs of those who were actually on the scene, including his own. Certainly having Randolph Mays close to hand did nothing to discourage fantasies of fame.

Maybe his dream was trying to tell him something. As long as he wasn't going to sleep anyway, it wouldn't hurt to start making some private notes. He reached for his chip recorder, switched it on, and in the creaking darkness of the sleeping compartment, began to whisper into it. He started where his dream left off.

"Barely more than another hour had passed before both of them, Marianne and that odious Mays, were awake and talking—Mays doing almost all of it. As there was no room in the clinic, I watched all this on the monitor—a good thing, as I doubt I could have kept my hands from Mays's throat. His television persona is pretty well known, but it's misleading. In the flesh he is a tall, rather cadaverous man with thinning hair and an attitude of bonhomie which one knows to be only skin-deep, the protective coloration of someone who has to be friendly with too many people. Underneath he is a *carnivore*, as I had already learned.

" 'I *expect* this is as big a surprise to *you* as it is to *me*,' he said to us with a wholly inappropriate attempt at heartiness, as if he'd just shown up for a dinner invitation a day early. 'I see you've already made the acquaintance of my . . .'

"There was just the slightest pause before Mays's next word, but it was more than long enough to make me see red—'*assistant,*' he said, 'Marianne Mitchell.'

" 'Indeed, we have been pleased to make her acquaintance,' the professor said to him with a straight face, throwing his insincerity back in his face. 'And what brought you here? A spot of trouble, obviously. Why don't you tell us about it?'

"Mays went on to tell us a tale of innocence and modest heroics—about his Herculean efforts to improvise a program for the capsule's malfunctioning maneuvering system, in hopes of bringing them down softly on Amalthea. We already knew it to be a pack of lies. And no doubt Mays *knew* we knew he was lying, but there was nothing he could do about that, for he also well understood that the ship's recorders were picking up his every word and that anything he said could be held against him at the inevitable Space Board inquiry into the crash.

"The professor blandly let him hang himself. When Mays finally ran out of steam I waited for Forster to confront him with his lies; instead the professor said, 'You'll be up and about within a few hours, I'm glad to say. Unfortunately we won't be returning to Ganymede for a while, and Amalthea is still under Space Board quarantine. So I'm afraid you are stuck here with us.'

"Mays did his unconvincing best to appear crushed by this news. The professor went on, 'But when and if you feel up to it, we will welcome any help you and Ms. Mitchell care to give us'—you can imagine my consternation, hearing this!—'for you see, Sir Randolph, we have recently made a most extraordinary discovery. And by an even greater coincidence, here you are to share it with us. . . .'

"I glanced at Marianne, who floated in her life-support harness almost as naked as the day she was born—a fact I would not mention were it not for my acute awareness that the horrid and ancient Mays hovered in that same state beside her. Something atavistic in me was stirred. I wanted to cover her, a throwback to the attitudes of the last century. I was reminded of my humiliation, and I resolved not to let matters stand where they stood when we left Ganymede.''

Hawkins paused long enough to rub his sweating face. ''But that's off the track. In any other circumstances, given what we'd stumbled upon, we would have been glad of the extra help, but Sir Randolph Mays was a snake, and the professor knew it. Granted, Mays wasn't going anywhere without the *Ventris*, but there was some question as to whether we could legally deny him access to communications.

''The professor grasped that nettle firmly. As soon as he was back in the wardroom, out of earshot of the people in the clinic, he took us aside and said, 'I hope we can all get along together. As far as I'm concerned they can go where they like and record what they like, as long as they *don't take anything*—and as long as they don't transmit anything before we get back to Ganymede.'

'' 'I don't see how we can stop them,' McNeil said, in that deceptively languid way he has, so that you know he's scheming something. 'What if he tries to fix his capsule's radio? Especially since it's not really broken.'

'' '*Out* of the question,' Forster said with relish. 'For one thing, that would be tampering with evidence.'

''I'd been woolgathering, still stewing over Marianne, but at about that point I rejoined the conversation. 'Aren't we even going to let Ganymede know what happened to them?'

''Forster allowed me a hint of a smile. 'No, Bill, I suspect we too are going to suffer a communications breakdown—of the same kind that Sir Randolph's capsule did. Unfortunately the news will get out, within a day or so, that we are no longer under Space

Board protection here. But meanwhile, if we can delay interference from the outside worlds, we'll have an opportunity to get to know our guests better.'

"Ever since the whole incident began, I'd been playing the moralist—for Marianne's sake, or so I'd told myself. Until this point. For suddenly I found myself confronted with new possibilities. Marianne and me, incommunicado . . .

"But Forster wasn't through; he had another trick up his sleeve. 'Before we lose communication with the rest of the solar system, however, I'm going to register a claim to Amalthea. It will be back to Ganymede and on to Manhattan and Strasbourg and the Hague before Mays and his, hm, assistant get themselves free of their medical accoutrements.'

" 'How can you do that, sir?' Me again. Leave it to me to state the obvious. 'Space law prohibits private parties from claiming astronomical bodies.'

"Forster gave me that patented crooked grin of his, one bushy brow up and one down. 'I'm not annexing an astronomical body, Mr. Hawkins. The core of Amalthea is a derelict spaceship. In the name of the Cultural Commission, I've put in a claim for *salvage*. If Mays tries to take any souvenirs, he'll be stealing from the Council of Worlds. I'll explain the situation to him before he gets any bright ideas.'

"And that was that. For the last three days the professor has been working all of us so hard I've hardly exchanged a private word with Marianne."

Through the hull of the *Ventris* Hawkins heard hatches banging and the hiss of gasses. Shift change already. It was time for him to drag himself into his spacesuit. He made a final remark into his recorder: "But I haven't had time even to think as much about her as I expected I would. The levels of the world-ship we've seen so far will require a lifetime's exploration. And this afternoon we found the Ambassador. . . ."

21

Diving through the now shallow water to the core was like diving through bouillabaisse, thick with life. The core's great heating towers simmered and stirred the soup steadily, as if they had been working in the kitchen since eternity. Fewer than a dozen revolutions of Jupiter remained before the mirrored surface of the core lay sterile in space, all the life it had spawned having boiled away and perished in vacuum.

Inside the cool core the Manta—iridescent black, gill-breathing, its skin slick with slippery goo to make it slide easily through the waters, its searchlights like cold eyes in the night—was at home in the liquid darkness. Alongside, explorers in bulky, white-canvas spacesuits bobbed like drowned dolls.

They were the most fortunate archaeologists in human history; they had come upon a spaceship as big as a dozen cities of Earth, each wrapped onto a sphere as thin as a balloon, one inside the other, and all these nested spheres filled with water. Frozen to near-absolute zero for a billion years, this ship-as-big-as-a-world had been perfectly preserved.

Now it seemed utterly deserted; the simple aquatic life that swarmed in the water outside was nowhere evident in the sterile, warmer waters inside. Presumably the inhabitants of the great ship had set forth to colonize our solar system more than a billion years ago, yet so vast was it that no one could say whether some recently thawed specimen of alien intelligence would be found just around the next bend of one of its endlessly looping, winding, cavern-like corridors. Thousands of huge chambers gave an impression of natural undersea formations, except that there was no life in them. Left behind were quantities of artifacts—tools and instruments and what may have been furnishings, and inscribed objects, and plain objects, some simple, some complex, some whose purpose could be guessed, some baffling . . . too much for a mere half dozen humans to begin to catalogue.

Forster, with Sparta piloting the sub, discovered the "art gallery" on the morning of the second day, during a rapid survey of the south polar hemisphere. The term came spontaneously to his mind, and indeed there was no better name for the building, because there seemed no mistaking its purpose. "As somebody or other said," he grumbled to the group—his fatigue was beginning to rub up against his enthusiasm, and he was uncharacteristically imprecise—"the art of a people reveals its soul. In these compartments we might find a key to the soul of Culture X." He decreed that the expedition should concentrate all their energies upon it.

They took six precious hours to move the *Michael Ventris* as close to the south pole as they dared without exposing themselves to the constant onslaught of Jupiter's radiation. Then they used the Old Mole for the last time, to punch another opening in the markedly thinner ice.

Forster split his people into three teams; for an archaeologist, he was capable of occasional insights into the behavior of living humans, so he made it a point to separate Mays and Marianne Mitchell and to separate Marianne from Bill Hawkins. Two of the

Ventris's crew—Walsh, McNeil, and Groves—always stayed aboard, one asleep, one awake, while the remaining crewmember worked with the others. Inside the core, the "world-ship," one person was always supposed to stay in the Manta while the other two worked in their spacesuits. It was a good plan, and it worked—for at least the first couple of shifts.

Forster and Josepha Walsh and Randolph Mays made up the first team, Blake Redfield and Angus McNeil and Marianne Mitchell the second, Tony Groves and Bill Hawkins and Ellen Troy the third. The Manta's trips to the surface grew ever shorter as Amalthea's arctic-like ocean rapidly boiled away.

Then the *Ventris* developed a problem in its superconducting radiation shield. Even in the shadow of Amalthea the shield was vital to the safety of all of them, and if out of commission would require their immediate departure for Ganymede—so Walsh and McNeil had to be detailed to work it out, a process which took up a whole day and stretched into a second.

Forster's schedule was soon in shambles; he made up exploration teams from whoever was fresh enough to work.

The structure he called the art gallery was huge, even by the standards of the race that had made the world-ship. There was nothing cold or mechanical about its architecture, although like the other structures in the world-ship it was constructed of the gleaming semi-metallic stuff that had defied human analysis for decades, since the first sample of it was found on Mars. The building's topmost peak climbed half the distance between the two innermost levels—the greatest open space in all the core—and though it was easily taller than the Eiffel Tower it was shaped like the apse of Notre Dame, buttresses and all.

Sir Randolph Mays, his natural tendency toward

grandiosity stimulated by this chance resemblance, insisted upon calling it "The Temple of Art." No one had found any trace of anything that looked even vaguely religious aboard the world-ship, but Mays's name for the place seemed not inappropriate, and it stuck.

After a day of exploration, Forster was ecstatic. "Empty out the best museums of Earth, empty them of all their legitimate, indigenous treasures and all their ill-got, stolen loot as well, and you could not begin to approach the numbers of pieces at the levels of quality we are finding here." His rough estimate put the number of exhibits in the temple at between ten and twenty *million;* what slice of the cultural variety of an alien civilization these represented no one could know, but at the least presumptuous guess they were the best harvest of a race whose history had been much longer, before it vanished, than the history of humans upon Earth.

Two more days passed. With Forster's original schedule inoperative, Tony Groves was in the sub and Bill Hawkins was in the water with Marianne. It was the first chance he'd gotten to be completely alone with her since the crash—although underwater, with both of them in spacesuits, even a last-century patriarch would have found a chaperon redundant.

Their work gave them plenty to talk about without trespassing on the sensitive subjects. Hawkins was grateful for her warmth, approving of her grasp of the subject, tremendously impressed by the skill and competence she demonstrated, having in short order learned to maneuver in her suit and do the work required of her. Like him, she had started at a disadvantage; if anything, she was a faster learner.

They were recording a long frieze of colored metals, bronze and gold and silver and green-encrusted copper, partly incised, partly fused, an effect that

reminded Hawkins of the late 20th-century tech-
nique of high-explosive bonding. Hawkins made a
note to ask Blake about that; in casual conversation
Blake had revealed that he knew quite a bit about
explosives. The frieze depicted an ocean floor and
a rich assemblage of sea creatures—a scene from nature, not the artificial interior of the ship—but
though it looked as familiar as a coral reef off Aus-
tralia, nothing depicted in it was quite the same as
one would find in the seas of Earth. Beside many
of the plants and animals were incised words—
names, perhaps, like the names in spiky old Greek
letters beside the portraits of saints in gilded icons—
here labeling corals and worms and spiny things
and fishes of the reef and the floating umbrella-like
and ribbon-like and many-armed creatures in the
waters above, and the teams of big animals like
sharks or dolphins, diving together, which displayed the universally streamlined, torpedo-shaped
bodies of fast swimmers. Hawkins easily read off
the sounds of the words, but the results had no
equivalents in any of the languages of Earth with
which he was familiar.

The glinting images of the wall reflected his dancing torchlight back to Hawkins as he drifted silently
past them in the dark water, entranced. Before he
noticed, he'd gotten himself into a space too narrow for the Manta to follow.

"Tony? Where'd I lose you?" He got no reply.
And at the same moment he noticed that Marianne
was no longer with him.

He turned back. The spacesuits weren't equipped
with sonar, and the suitcomm radios didn't work
well underwater, especially among highly reflective
surfaces. Hawkins wasn't worried; he couldn't have
strayed too far from the Manta. And Marianne
would be near the sub. As game as she was, and as
quick to learn, she was sensible too, and generally
careful to stay within easy reach of help.

The narrow passage bifurcated, then trifurcated. All the surfaces of the diverging corridors were covered with intricate metallic relief and intaglio. The angle of Hawkin's torch fell on the walls in the opposite direction from a moment before, and although everything looked familiar nothing was the same.

He was sure he must have come through . . . where? That left-hand passage. But just as he was about to enter it, he thought he caught a flicker of white, at the edge of vision and at the farthest extent of his torchlight, some ten meters down a different corridor. "Marianne?"

He pushed his way into a different passage, following a will-o'-the-wisp that might be nothing more than his own reflection, and a moment later came into a small circular chamber, which was itself the meeting place of six radiating corridors. He felt the first stab of worry—

—just as his beam fell upon the statue.

The moment when one first meets a great work of art has an impact that can never again be recaptured; the alien subject of this work exaggerated the effect, made it overwhelming. Here, cast with superb skill and authority in metal whose soft color and luster resembled pewter, was a creature obviously modeled from life. Hawkins was the first human, so far as he knew, to see what a representative of Culture X actually looked like.

Two refracting eyes gazed serenely upon him— eyes made of crystal, as the Greeks had made the eyes of their incomparable life-sized bronzes. But these eyes were thirty centimeters apart, set in a face three times the size of a human face, a face without a nose and with a mouth that was not human, perhaps not a mouth at all, but rather an intricate folding of flesh. Nevertheless, the effect was one of serene and embracing emotion.

If there was nothing human about the face or

body, the figure moved Hawkins profoundly, for the artist had spanned the barriers of time and culture in a way he would never have believed possible. There were many things humans did not share—could not have shared—with the builders of this world, but all that was really important, it seemed to Hawkins, they would have felt in common. "Not human," he thought, "but still humane."

Just as one can read emotions in the alien but familiar face of a dog or horse, so it seemed to Hawkins that he knew the feelings of the undersea being whose unseeing eyes stared into his own. Here was wisdom and authority, the calm, confident power that is shown—Hawkins's art-historical mind rummaged for a suitable example from the great oceanic powers of Earth—in Bellini's portrait of the Doge Leonardo Loredano of Venice, diffused with pearly light from unseen windows overlooking a foggy sea. And there was sadness also, the sadness of a race which had made some stupendous effort and had made it in vain.

Hawkins floated transfixed before the creature, which appeared hooded in its own flesh. Like a giant squid, a tall mantle stood up above its face, and it was girdled with tentacles, but unlike a squid its body plan was long, a narrow ellipsoid, its lower half equipped with powerful fins. Gills marked its mantle with chevrons; their water intake was above the face, separate from the seeming mouth, crowning the being's "forehead" like a diadem.

Why this solitary representation of the Amaltheans, as Hawkins had come to think of them? He did not know; he only knew that this one was set here on purpose, to bridge time, to greet whatever beings might one day enter the great ship. That it was set inside this chamber, isolated from the exterior by narrow corridors, suggested that creatures no bigger than themselves were expected—or were to be permitted inside.

"Bill, it's lovely," said Marianne's voice in his suitcomm.

Startled, he made a floundering attempt to turn. She was floating only three meters behind him, having approached in silence.

"How did you get behind me?" he asked abruptly. "I thought I saw you going that way."

"Oh? Well, you couldn't have been following me. I've been following your torchlight." She sounded a bit miffed. "You scared me to death. I was all alone for . . . it seemed like an hour."

"More like five minutes," he said, "but I do owe you an apology. We'll have to be more careful. I . . . I'm afraid I was simply carried away."

Marianne's shining gaze was fixed on the statue. "It's wonderful," she breathed. "Just think of it waiting here in the darkness all those millions of years."

"More than a few million. At least a thousand million . . . a billion, as you say in North America."

"We ought to give it a name."

"That seems a bit presump—"

"It's a kind of envoy, I think, carrying a greeting to us," she went on, ignoring his objections. Her attention was fastened on the statue. "Those who made it knew that one day someone else was bound to come here and find this place. There's something noble about it, and something very sad, too." She turned her enraptured gaze on Hawkins. "Don't you feel it?"

He had been watching her face through her faceplate, lit only by the reflected glow of their torches, and at that moment he was convinced that his first of impression of her had been the right one: notwithstanding any of the unfortunate events on Ganymede or since, she was still the most beautiful woman he had ever met.

And the most loveable. In the moment when she turned her green eyes upon him, he felt that familiar pain, which only seemed to get worse, where his heart ought to be—

"The Ambassador," she said. "We'll call it the Ambassador."

—and really, quite possibly the most intelligent . . .

Hawkins, reminding himself of where he was, abruptly looked at the statue again and found that Marianne's reaction to the . . . the Ambassador was virtually identical to his own.

"Bill, don't you think we ought to take it back with us?" she whispered. "To give the people of Earth and the other worlds some idea of what we've really found here?"

"The professor's not against removing a few artifacts to the *right* museums, eventually"—too bad Marianne didn't understand, but she was not, after all, schooled in the archaeological disciplines—"but not until all the data's been gathered."

"How long will that take?"

"Well, it means the total context of each find, which in the case of Amalthea, is just not going to be recorded in the brief time we've got remaining to us. It will take hundreds of people, maybe thousands, a good many years to do what needs doing here."

"If it were the *only* piece removed, surely it wouldn't ruin the record-keeping," she said.

Hawkins thought about that. She might be right, in fact, or close to. The removal of a single statue, after it had been photogrammed and hologrammed, probably wouldn't make much difference to the archaeological understanding of Amalthea. But he didn't want to encourage that line of thinking. "It must mass a tonne. It will just have to wait."

She was genuinely puzzled. "It doesn't weigh anything," she protested. "No more than we do."

"Weight is one thing, inertia's another . . ." he began.

She bridled. "I'm certainly aware of that."

"Okay. And I'm no physicist. All I know is, Walsh says we can't afford the fuel—especially since we're taking you and Mays back to Ganymede with us. Not to mention your Moon Cruiser." He looked at her nervously. "Better take it up with the professor."

She gave him a small smile. "Don't worry, Bill, I'm not going to press it."

And that, for the time being, was the end of it. The way out of the maze was simpler than the way in, and they found Tony Groves waiting for them in the Manta only a few meters away, not even having had time to worry about them.

They made their way out without incident—that is, except for Bill Hawkins's second glimpse of something pale in the watery distance, flickering quickly in and out of visibility—something definitely not Marianne, for she was swimming ahead of him, well armored in her bulky suit . . .

"Randolph! I think *you* could persuade Forster to take it back. . . . It's the most moving thing I could have imagined."

Marianne and Mays found themselves alone in the corridor outside the equipment bay as she was coming off shift, peeling off her wet spacesuit, and he was just coaxing himself to full consciousness with a hot bulb of coffee McNeil had thoughtfully brought to him.

"Your young friend Hawkins is right, Marianne. If it's as *massive* as it sounds, there's no way to bring it back. At least without jettisoning our little Moon Cruiser."

"The Moon Cruiser! Why is Forster so insistent on taking *that* awful thing back."

"*Vendetta* against me," Mays whispered. "As

much as he's needed our help, I think he still would like to make us appear at fault at the inquiry.''

"But how can he *do* that?" She was genuinely indignant.

Mays shrugged. He was thinking of something else. "This Ambassador of yours—it is the *crux* of the biggest story of the age . . . and I'll lay odds Forster intends to keep it a secret."

"A *secret?*"

"Forster's not a legitimate archaeologist, Marianne. I won't repeat myself; you and I have discussed that enough times. Even the *name* of his vessel is a clue, this Michael Ventris he admires so much, the fellow who deciphered Linear B. But Evans, the fellow who discovered the Minoans, refused to *publish* his hoard of Linear B tablets for thirty years! Until other discoveries forced his hand. We've got to *force* Forster's hand, Marianne. We've got to make our own holograms of the Ambassador and send them over a tightlink *now*, to make sure *nothing* stands in the way of their publication."

As Mays already knew, Marianne could not have agreed more. "How can we do that?" she asked.

Mays breathed a sigh of relief that she had gotten into the practical questions before her subconscious could nag her with his illogic. Luckily, *Forster admires Ventris, but it wasn't Ventris who suppressed the tablets* was a thought that never formed in her mind. "Come into the sleeping compartments with me," he whispered urgently. "Everybody's out, we can *talk* a moment. It's a *bold* thing, but I believe it can be done. . . ."

He must always remember that Marianne was smarter in mind than in experience. He started to rough out a plan, relieved that his early-morning brain had not succeeded in tripping itself up.

PART
5

JUPITER FIVE
MINUS ONE

22

On Ganymede, one week earlier . . .

The commander's height, only occasionally notable in Manhattan, made him impossible to miss in the corridors and alleys of Shoreless Ocean, where his close-cropped gray head rose above a sea of shiny black hair as he pushed his way through the crowds. He made no concession to security except to wear a plain tan business suit instead of his blue uniform. Security was the least of his worries.

He found the Straits Cafe and Luke Lim inside it, sitting at his customary table beside the aquarium wall. The commander's attention was momentarily split between Lim, the most sinister-looking young Chinese he had ever encountered—but then, having followed him for days, he'd already gotten used to that—and what was certainly the ugliest fish he had ever seen, peering over the fellow's shoulder. The commander almost smiled, thinking that maybe Lim was attracted to this table because the fish was even uglier than he was.

The commander made straight for his table. "Luke Lim," he said in his gravelly voice. "I'm the one who called you."

"Hey, you recognize me, I'm impressed. Don't we

all look alike to you?" Lim grinned evilly, displaying enormous yellow teeth.

"No. This is not a secure location, Mr. Lim. We know that the owner, Mrs. Wong, has reported details of your meetings with Blake Redfield to Randolph Mays."

"O my goodness, that naughty Mrs. Wong." Lim launched an eyebrow into orbit. "Any harm done?"

"Maybe you'll help me assess that. But we should talk elsewhere."

Lim shrugged. "Long as you're buying."

As they left the restaurant Lim suggested they stop by his living quarters, nearby; he wanted to pick up his guitar. The commander eyed the inside of Lim's rooms suspiciously, expecting the worst; the walls were solid with shelves of books and magazines in a mix of European and Chinese languages, everything from Eastern and Western classics to Eastern and Western pornography. Hand-welded furniture took up too much of the scarce space, and high-tech toys lay in various stages of assembly in the corners and on the expanses of tabletop that seemed to serve Lim as desks, workbenches, chopping blocks, and dining tables, indiscriminately intermixed. Bright red and gold posters on the wall called for Ganymede's independence from the Council of Worlds; on them, Space Board officers were depicted as round-eyed, jackbooted thugs.

Lim and the commander bought skewers of soy-barbecued pork from a corridor vendor and walked to the ice gardens, making their way down slippery wet steps to the bottom of an artificial canyon, where a stream trickled at the feet of giant sculptures carved from the old, hard ice of Ganymede. Here were fierce Kirttimukha, rotund Ganesha, bloodthirsty Kali, smiling Kwan-yin, and a host of other supernaturals towering fifteen meters over the wandering sightseers below, under a black and icy "sky" six stories up, deeply carved with an enormous looping, writhing rain dragon.

The two men sat on a bench beside the smoking stream. Lim cradled his twelve-string guitar and picked out a passable solo version of the *Concierto de Aranjuez* while the commander spoke in a low voice that sounded like stones in the surf: ". . . through Von Frisch, Mays made a contact at Rising Moon Enterprises. Two days ago Mays and the Mitchell woman took the standard cruise. Twelve hours ago their capsule departed from the programmed path. Looks like they crashed on Amalthea."

"*Looks* like?" Lim strummed energetically on the ancient and honorably beaten-up classical instrument, his expression an exaggerated mask of disbelief.

"Whether anyone survived, we don't know." The commander focused his sapphire stare on Lim. "Not to be repeated: we've lost communication with Forster's expedition." Which was true, although there had been one last, puzzling communication from Forster after the crash—but it had had nothing to do with Mays or Mitchell, and the commander didn't intend to mention it to Luke Lim or anyone else who didn't have a need to know.

"What are you doing about them?"

"Nothing. The Space Board have put out a cover story, claiming we've been in touch with them, that Mays and Mitchell are safe and recovering from minor injuries. Eat it later if we have to."

Lim hit the guitar strings hard and glared at him, wide-eyed and disbelieving. "*Aieee*, all this bureaucratic garbage! Why *lie*, man?" *Thrummy-thrumm*.

The commander's jaw tightened. "First, we haven't got a cutter on hand. Little slip-up or, as you put it, bureaucratic garbage. Take us two days to get to Amalthea on one of the local tugs, and . . ."—he

held up a hand to forestall Lim's contempt—
"second, the Space Board don't get along all that
well with the Indo-Asians. Can't go to them for help
and understanding. Seems they think we're nothing but a bunch of racist blue-eyed guys looking out
mainly for North Continental interests."

Lim stared straight into the commander's blue
eyes as he picked out an intricate, Moorish-flavored
arpeggio on the mellow old instrument. "Yeah,
some of our wilder radical types have occasionally
whispered words to that effect in my ear."

"Won't claim it's wholly unfounded. Thing is"—
the commander was usually very good at conceal-
ing discomfort, but it now revealed itself in the slight
flaring of his nostrils—"I stuck my neck out, personally made sure there would be no cutter on hand
to go to Forster's rescue. Didn't want to tempt anyone to force the issue."

Lim was beginning to see what that issue was.
Thrummy-thrummy-thrummy-thrumm. "So Sir
Randolph-Pride-of-England-Mays has gone and
shipwrecked himself in the last place you guys want
him, and a sexy American white girl with him. But
he's not playing *our* game." *Thrummy-thrumm.* "If
we were trying to force the issue, we'd have crashed
this year's raven-tressed, purple-nippled Miss Shoreless Ocean." Lim considered matters a moment,
while the commander patiently waited. *Pickety-
pickety-pick.* "And me with her," Lim said at last,
nodding curtly. *Thunka-thrumm.*

The commander tried to hide his disappointment—Lim was refusing to get serious. "You were
Forster's agent here," he said, changing the subject.
"You arranged the sale of the Europan sub. We
don't think Von Frisch ever said anything to Mays
about it. Yet we know they were thick as thieves
over the Rising Moon business—Von Frisch probably sold him the Moon Cruiser codes. So why didn't
Von Frisch sell him the information about the sub?"

Lim grunted. *Strummm . . . strummm . . .* "Maybe because of *my* money—Forster's actually. I offered Von Frisch a two percent bonus if he kept his mouth shut."

"Why didn't you tell Forster that?" The words grated in the commander's throat.

"Didn't think he'd have to pay." Lim looked mournful, as if he'd sadly misjudged one of his fellows; his fingers plucked out the mournfully introspective melodies. "Von Frisch never blabbed? Not at all like the guy."

The commander said nothing.

Finally Lim sighed and seemed to relax. Abruptly, he stopped playing and put his guitar aside with a hollow, discordant boom. "Why me, Commander? Why are you trusting me with all this information I could use—if I were a political animal—to get the damned Space Board off our backs?"

"Well, this is a deniable conversation."

"How do you know I haven't got a chip-corder in my earring?"

But they both knew Lim wasn't wired. The expression that played at the corner of the commander's lips was not quite a smile. "Blake trusted you. I trust him."

Lim nodded and said, "I think you want me to confirm what you already know. Von Frisch probably *did* spill his guts to Mays. If Mays didn't broadcast it, it's because he's not a reporter, maybe not even a full-time history prof. So whatever mighty secret about Amalthea you—you personally, Commander, not the Space Board—are trying to keep, he's on to it."

"Yeah? What secret might that be?"

"I don't know and I don't care. But if I were you, man, I'd worry about those people of yours. I get vibes off of Mays."

"Vibes?"

"The man's a tiger. A hungry one."

* * *

On Amalthea, in real time . . .

"Ellen. Professor. Time to go. The place is coming to pieces over our heads."

Blake was piloting the Manta, shepherding the lone white figure of the spacesuited professor as he made a final bubble-trailing dash through the Temple of Art, recording in passing what he had no time to study.

"Right now, sir, or we'll get ourselves in trouble."

"All right," came the grudging reply. "I'm coming aboard. Where's Inspector Troy?"

"Here I am." Sparta's voice was attenuated in the depths of the waters. "I'm not going back with you."

"Say again?"

"Blake, you must explain to the others," she replied. "Reassure them."

"What are you saying, Troy?" Forster demanded.

"I'll be staying here through the transition," she said.

"What transition?" Forster asked.

"The ship will soon shed its waters. I'll be aboard it through that transition."

"But how will you . . . ?"

"Professor, come aboard *right now*," Blake said sternly. "I'll explain later."

"All right then."

Blake clapped on an air mask and hit the valves. Water rushed into the Manta's interior, filling it—except for a few reluctant bubbles that weren't sure which way was up. Blake hit the switch and the sub's aft hatch swung open.

Forster maneuvered himself to the hatch and pulled himself into the sub. Blake closed it behind him and hit more switches: the pumps throbbed again and high-pressure air began forcing the water out. He let his mask fall slack as Forster unlatched his helmet. The Manta flapped its wings and headed for the world-ship's south polar waterlock.

Blake tried to raise the *Ventris* on the sonarlink. "We're headed in," he said. "Come in, *Ventris*, do you read us? We're headed back." But he got no answer. He turned to the professor. "They must have lost the cable, or pulled it up. We'd better hurry."

"What *is* Troy doing? You said you'd explain."

"She's not *doing* anything, sir. Things are happening. Her place is down here. Ours is up there."

The dome of the south polar lock was not as big as the equatorial dome to which the school of squid-like animals had originally led Sparta and the professor, but it was still big enough to admit a terrestrial aircraft carrier. As its molecular layers peeled off, or retracted, or at any rate became magically transparent—in that process which the human explorers had not begun to understand, but which they had rapidly come to depend upon—Blake and Forster saw through to the seething sea outside, filled with the ruddy opalescence of Jupiter-light which shone through the fast-subliming ice.

"They're coming inside!" Forster exclaimed. Against his fatigue, he could still respond to new wonders.

The Manta was swimming upward against an inflowing tide of luminous sea creatures, luminous squid and shrimp and jellyfish and plankton by the millions, pouring into the core ship in orderly formations that streamed in the water like columns of smoke in the wind.

"They certainly act as if they know what they're doing, don't they?" Blake remarked.

The professor said, "It's as if the ship were drawing them in . . . into its protection."

"Or into the stock pens," Blake said dryly.

"Hm." Forster found that notion distasteful.

"Clearly they are responding to some programmed signal."

"Could simply be equilibrium conditions. Inside and outside pressure and temperature are just about in equilibrium at the core surface."

"Very rational," said the professor. "And still a miracle."

Blake smiled privately. Professor J.Q.R. Forster was not given to speaking of miracles. But then, any sufficiently advanced technology . . . Blake suspected that they were on the verge of encountering one or two more miracles.

The sleek black Manta was outside the lock now and beating its wings in a swift climb toward the surface. The lock remained open below them as the sea creatures swam swiftly down into the huge ship; above them, the last hard layer of Amalthea's ice rind was fracturing into ever smaller plates.

Blake still could rouse no one on the *Ventris*. He found the hole in the ice without trouble; the passage through the shaft was fraught with risk, but the sub flew cleanly through it and shot through the boiling interface between water and vacuum.

The *Ventris* stood off half a kilometer from the seething surface of the moon. Flying as a spacecraft now, the Manta sought the hold of the freighter with quick bursts of its rockets.

"It's beginning to look like a Halloween party down there," said Blake.

"A what?"

"Like a fake witch's cauldron—a tub of water and dry ice."

Beneath the flying sub, lanes of black water were opening in the cracks in the ice, and from under the jostling ice floes great round bubbles full of milky vapor rose up and burst into puffs of mist. Ahead of the Manta the equipment bay of the *Ventris* stood wide open, its metal interior bright against the stars—open, bright, and empty.

"The Moon Cruiser's gone," said Blake. "Communications are out, radiolink too."

"What's happening?" Forster demanded.

"Better put your helmet back on, Professor. We may have trouble ahead."

Without help from the commlinks, Blake eased the Manta cautiously into the open equipment bay, managing to dock the sub without trouble. His remote controls still functioned—the great clamshell doors closed quietly over the sub. As soon as they were sealed, air rushed into the bay. A few moments later, the hatch to the *Ventris*'s central corridor opened, audibly clanging against its stops.

Blake tried the commlinks again. "Jo? Angus? Anybody hear us? What's the situation here?" He peered around through the bubble, but could see nothing amiss. That no one had appeared in the hatch was perhaps a bit odd, although not in itself unusual.

The sub's gauges told him that the air outside was almost at normal pressure. "Okay, Professor, I'm going to open up. We're pretty wet in here, so this thing is probably going to fog up good. Let me go first."

"Why should you go first?"

"I can move faster. I'm not wearing a spacesuit."

"Do you believe something is seriously wrong?"

"I don't know what to think. It just smells funny."

He popped the Manta's lock and winced as his eardrums were hit by the pressure difference. The inside of the Manta instantly filled with fog, which misted the surface of the polyglas sphere. They were blind inside. The fog dissipated quickly, but the condensation on the sphere remained. Blake squeakily wiped at the curved polyglas, clearing a space to peer through. He saw nothing.

He wiggled himself around so that he could go head first through the hatch in the rear of the sub.

He got his head and shoulders into the cold, dry air of the equipment bay—

—when something brushed the exposed skin of his neck. He flipped himself over to see Randolph Mays crouching weightless on the back of the Manta. In his right hand Mays held a pistol-shaped drug injector.

Mays's enormous mouth curved in an obscene grin. "Bad *call*, I believe you say in North American football. Unfortunate *tactical* error. You should have sent the professor out first—my little mixture of chemicals would have been quite *useless* against a man in a spacesuit. . . ."

But Blake didn't hear the rest. He was already asleep.

Inside the Manta, Forster struggled to reverse his orientation in the cramped cabin.

Mays's voice came to him through the open hatch. "You next, Inspector Troy. Or should I call you Linda? Have I given you time enough to put your helmet back on? Need a few more seconds? How about you, Professor? I must say your body is a *marvel*, sir. Outwardly the very *picture* of youth. When not swathed in a spacesuit, of course. Just think, in the wake of that very nearly successful attempt to firebomb you on Venus"—Mays's tone sounded oddly regretful—"well, your *surgeons* are certainly to be congratulated. But your poor old bones! Your muscles *and* organs! Unhappily they must have suffered the wear and tear *appropriate* to your, what, six-plus *actual* decades? And with what cost to your resilience? To your *endurance*?"

Forster had now thoroughly got himself stuck in the narrow passage, curled up as if halfway through a somersault.

"You can come on out whenever you think you're ready, Inspector Troy; you'll find *me* quite ready for *you*," Mays said cheerfully, "and as for you, Professor, please, just rest a *moment* while I explain the situation. Like our friend Blake here, all your crew are taking little *naps*—but unless I have a reason to keep them asleep, their drowsiness will wear off in another hour or two. And I've put your *external* communications hook-up out of commission. Quite thoroughly, I'm afraid. And you *have* been keeping us incommunicado for reasons of your own, eh? Having to do with me? How did you plan to *explain* that?"

Forster had himself turned around now, and could see out the open hatch to the bare metal walls of the equipment bay. But Mays was keeping out of sight.

"So I've given you the perfect *excuse* to cover for your own transgressions, d'you see?" Mays paused, as if something had been left out of his script. "You *are* with us, Troy? You must be. You know it all, don't you? *All* of it." Another pause, but despite his apparent hopes to the contrary, Mays was not interrupted. "As for you, Professor, after all, antennas are always getting themselves sheared off, what a pity! Don't bother to *thank* me. I'll tell you how to make it up to me."

Forster reached for his helmet, and found it jammed against the passage wall below his knees. He would have to back up into the sphere to get enough room to bring it up over his head. He was beginning to breath loudly now, so loudly that he had difficulty hearing Mays.

"All I want, you see, is what you illegally tried to deny me. I want to broadcast to the *inhabited* worlds the nature of our—yes, *our*—finds here at Amalthea. And especially I want to tell them about the Ambassador. That *magnificent* statue."

As if repelled by Mays's insistence, Forster had got himself back up into the front of the Manta, into the polyglas sphere . . . and at last his helmet was free. He rolled it over in his gloved and trembling hands, trying to find the bottom of it, aiming to pull it onto his head—

"But to *do* that," Mays was saying, "you have to lend me this nice *submarine*. For just the briefest moment. There are certain angles and points of view—certain effects of lighting, you understand—that are useless for your business, that of the archaeological *scholar,* but quite essential to mine. . . ."

At last Forster had his helmet properly aligned. "No, Mays. Never," he said defiantly, surprised at the hoarseness of his own voice. He pulled the helmet toward him. Once it was on his head, Mays's drugs could not harm him.

Just then an arm and hand came into view in the small opening of the hatch, holding a pistol.

The pistol dispensed an aerosol spray this time, and Forster had barely a fraction of a second in which to realize his mistake in speaking out. Not long enough to get his helmet sealed.

As he flew the Manta through the fog above the boiling icescape, immersed in the submarine's incongruous smells of fresh human sweat and billion-year-old salt water, Mays's mind ignored immediate sensations and ranged ahead across a plane of abstraction, reviewing possibilities. His plan had already gone awry, but he was a brilliant and highly experienced tactician who found something exhilarating about improvising within the strictures of an unfolding and unpredictable reality. He had accomplished most of what he'd set out to do; it was what remained undone that could undo all the rest.

Inspector Ellen Troy was *missing!* She hadn't been aboard the Manta—nor aboard the *Ventris* earlier, when he'd gassed the others. Surely Redfield and Forster wouldn't have left her in the water! But just as surely Redfield had intended to park the sub permanently, with *no* intention of making another trip.

Was she in the water—even inside the alien ship? He had to *know*. He had to *deal* with her.

He plunged the Manta with uncanny skill through a temporary opening in the ice, handling the machine as if he'd been trained in its use. He steered it through black water, empty of life, toward the south polar lock of the world-ship. No one could reasonably expect to find a single person within the world-ship's millions of kilometers of passageways, its hundreds of millions of square kilometers of space and rooms. But Mays was willing to bet that he knew where the woman was.

And if she was not there, what matter? What could she do to him then?

Through the great ship's mysterious lock, which always seemed to know when entry and exit were wanted . . . through the black and winding corridors . . . through water positively *filled* with squirming creatures, so thick as to make visibility impossibly low . . . nearly to the Temple of Art itself . . .

Mays drove the Manta on beating wings to the heart of the temple, until it could go no further in the narrowing labyrinthine passageways. He was preparing to pull his suit on and go into the water when he thought he saw a flicker of white. . . .

There was a wider passageway, away from the center of the temple, off to one side. He drove the Manta into it at full speed. The rounded embossed walls, weirdly lit in the white beams of the lamps, slid past the sub's wings with centimeters to spare; still he rushed on. He came around a sharp curve—

—and she was there in front of him, her white suit blooming so brightly in his lights he had to wince. She was wallowing helplessly in the dark waters, trying to swim away from him. He drove into her at full speed; he felt and saw the back-breaking impact of her body against the polyglas sphere of the sub's nose.

He couldn't turn the Manta around in the narrow corridor, but some meters further along he came to a round hub of passageways and circled the sub. He made his way slowly back down the corridor from which he'd come.

There she was, floating slack in the eddies. Her helmet glass was half opaque, but through it he was sure he saw her upturned eyes. And there was a huge, very visible gash below her heart, cut clean through the canvas and metal of her suit. Tiny air bubbles, silver in the sub's light, still oozed from the wound.

Mays chuckled to himself as he steered the Manta past the floating body of Inspector Troy. His second task was done. One or two more still to accomplish. . . .

Shrouded in writhing fog only a kilometer away from the *Ventris,* Moon Cruiser Four was safely parked in Amalthea's radiation shadow. More than three hours had passed since Mays had left Marianne alone to safeguard it. He approached it with caution.

Transferring from the Manta to the Moon Cruiser in open vacuum was a tedious business, requiring both Marianne and himself to don spacesuits and depressurize the capsule. When at last they were safe inside the dark little cabin, with air pressure enough to get their helmets off their heads, he found her in a bad mood.

"God, Randolph, this is the worst," said Marianne.

"Not quite the *greeting* I'd hoped for, I must confess."

"Oh, I'm glad you're safe. You know that's not what I meant. But three *hours!* I didn't know where you were. Or what was happening. I almost went

over there, but . . . I didn't want to spoil everything."

"You did precisely the *right* thing," he said. "You
trusted me and *waited.*"

She hesitated. "They're safe? They're awake
now?"

"Yes, all lively and *quite* talkative. As I assured
you, it was a harmless hypnotic, only briefly effective—just long enough for you and me to get this,
our little home, away from them. They don't even
show signs of hangovers."

"They agreed, then."

He lowered his sad eyes and concentrated on taking off his gloves. "Well, I suppose the short reply
is . . ." He glanced up at her mischievously. *"Yes!*
After much rather heated discussion, during which
I assured Forster that you and I would *testify* that
he had held us incommunicado against our wills,
Forster gave me the submarine."

She seemed more relieved than excited. "Good.
Let's use it right now. Let's make the transmission.
Once that's done we can go back."

"I *do* wish it were that easy. They agreed to let
me make my own photograms of the Ambassador.
Here are the chips"—he fished them from his inner
shirt pocket and handed them to her. "They agreed
to let us tightbeam the images. But just *minutes* ago,
when I spoke to the ship and sought to establish
communication, they *claimed* that their long-range
radiolinks were still out of service."

She moaned, low in her throat. "They wouldn't
let you send the damn . . . the pictures?"

"No, darling. But I have some *experience* of the
ways of men and women, and I was prepared for
their *bluff.*"

"O God, Randolph, O God O God . . . what have
you done now?"

He regarded her, judiciously concerned. "Please

don't upset yourself, my dear. All I did was move the statue.''

''What? *What!* You *moved* it?''

''I had to do just that *little* thing, don't you see? I hid it to assure that after our account is published *no* one can contradict us. For only *we* will be able to produce the thing itself!''

''Where did you hide it?''

''Since it is inside a very big spaceship, it would be rather difficult for me to expl . . .''

''Never mind.'' Marianne stared sullenly at the flatscreen, now blank, that had so recently been the source of profound deception. She wiped at her eyes, as if angry to discover tears there. ''I'm really not sure what to think about all this.''

''What do you mean?''

''You say one thing. They say the opp . . .''—she cleared an obstruction in her throat—''something different.''

''By 'they' you mean young Hawkins, I suppose.''

She shrugged, avoiding his prying gaze.

''I *won't* stoop to demean him,'' Mays said righteously. ''I believe that he is an honest young man, although a thoroughly deluded one.''

Marianne turned her dark-eyed gaze upon him. ''You meant to come here all along.''

''Your meaning is unclear, Mari . . .''

''Bill says that you must have monkeyed with the computer, the maneuvering system, of this capsule. And ruined the communications gear so we couldn't call for help.''

''Does he say all that? Is he a navigator? A physicist? A specialist in electronics?''

''He heard it from Groves and the others. After they inspected it.''

''Forster and his people will say anything to keep the truth from getting out. I'm convinced they are *all* members of the evil sect.''

Marianne pulled her seat harness tightly about her, as if in memory of what had been wiped from her conscious mind, the horrible moments of the crash into the ice.

"Marianne . . ."

"Be quiet, Randolph, I'm trying to think." She stared at the blank screen, and he nervously complied with her demand. After a moment she asked, "Did you tell them you had hidden the statue?"

"Yes, of course."

"What did they say to that?"

"What *could* they say? They simply cut me off."

"Randolph, you told me—and I quote—'the eyes of the solar system are fixed upon us. Even now a Space Board rescue cutter is standing by, prepared to come to the assistance of the *Ventris.*' "

"Yes."

"Well, I'm telling you I'm not going to sit out here in this stinking tin can and wait for rescue. If you're holding so many cards, I want you to start playing them. I want you to get out in that submarine and get on the horn with Forster—or even go back to the *Ventris* if you have to—and get down to serious bargaining. And I don't want you back in here until you've made a deal."

"What if I *were* to confront him personally?" Mays asked with unaccustomed timidity. "What's to keep him from locking me up? Or even *torturing* me in some . . . subtle fashion?"

She looked at him, for the first time in their brief relationship, with a suggestion of contempt. "Well, I'll tell you, Randolph, it's because it won't do them any good. You've given me the chips, and now you're going to draw me a map of exactly where the statue is. So they'll have to kill both of us, *partner* . . . isn't that the way they put it in the old viddies?"

For a man of his experience, Randolph Mays found it hard to keep from laughing out loud at this moment. Marianne had asked him to do exactly as he had hoped she would. If he had written her script himself, she could not have said it better. For a long moment he mulled her suggestion before he said, soberly, "They *would* have rather a difficult time explaining that to the Space Board, wouldn't they?"

But it was *her* idea, and that was how she would remember it—when they faced the inquiry together, the sole survivors of J.Q.R. Forster's expedition to Amalthea.

23

Sparta rose naked out of the foam, higher through the milky mist into hard vacuum, her skin reflecting the diffuse and coppery Jupiter-light.

Something odd about the *Ventris*, not quite where she'd left it, and apparently deserted, all its lights blazing, lit up like high noon. . . .

That something was wrong was no surprise. She'd smelled the return of the Manta in the waters of the core and had gone to investigate. In the deserted corridor she'd found her empty spacesuit, broken and gashed, the last bubbles of its depleted oxygen stores oozing from a gaping tear. Someone, imagining that she was inside the suit—a very reasonable assumption—had tried to kill her.

Who else had that someone tried to kill?

Sparta reached the *Ventris*'s equipment bay airlock and went inside. She had steered herself by hanging on to her spacesuit's borrowed maneuvering unit; she left that beside the hatch but did not bother to shed the bubble suit of silvery mucous that clung close to her skin. Shining like a chrysallis, she would have seemed hardly human to any casual observer as she made her way through empty bays and corridors, felt her way through the ship—until she came to the crew module.

There she came upon an eerie scene. Josepha Walsh was limp in her acceleration couch on the flight deck, with Angus McNeil hanging half out of his own couch on the other side of the deck. Tony Groves was in the sleeping compartment he'd been forced to share with Randolph Mays, neatly bundled into his sleep restraint. In the compartment across from him, Hawkins was similarly enmeshed. Blake and Professor Forster were resting lightly on the floor of the wardroom; it appeared that they'd been having a friendly game of chess. Sparta had never seen Forster playing chess.

Mays and Marianne Mitchell were gone, along with the Moon Cruiser capsule in which they had arrived so precipitously.

The unconscious people still in the *Ventris* were alive, their vital signs robust—steady respiration, strong heartbeat and the rest—but they had been massively dosed with anesthetic. Sparta bent to absorb samples of their breath through the thin membrane that isolated her from the outer world. She allowed a telltale whiff of the drug to diffuse through the protective mucous; its chemical formula unfolded itself on the inner screen of her mind. It was a benign narcotic of the sort that would soon vanish, leaving hardly a trace. They would all wake up eventually, having slept soundly for perhaps three or four orbits of Jupiter, without even hangovers to show for it.

She took a few moments to check the status of the ship. The first anomaly was obvious: the radiation shield was down again, after Walsh and McNeil had sworn they'd fixed it for good. But to the casual eye nothing else was amiss.

PIN spines slid from beneath her fingernails, puncturing the shining film that coated her; she inserted the spines into the ports on the main computer and let tingling data flow straight to her brain. Nothing to be seen or heard here out of the ordi-

nary, but amidst the tangy data an odd aroma—
something off, something metallic, coppery-sour
like sucking a penny, or an acrid whiff of potas-
sium—under the baked-bread smells of normalcy.

Ah, there, there in the maneuvering control system . . . Everything just as normal as could be, and
only this slightest hint of a leak in a valve . . . a
trickle of fuel, venting under pressure through—remarkably bad luck!—a trio of external nozzles, so
positioned on the hull that the *Ventris* was being
pushed ever so slowly into the full force of the radiation slipstream that blew past Amalthea.

Once into that belt, and without any radiation
shield whatever, a mere couple of orbits of Jupiter
would do the whole crew in. Even with all their
antiradiologicals, by the time they woke up they'd
be too far gone to save themselves.

Sparta hardly took the time to think about what
to do. She corrected the ship's positional problems
first. Then she moved unhurriedly to the clinic and
opened its well-equipped pharmaceutical cabinet.
She visited the sleeping crew in the order of their
need, injecting each with what she had determined
was sufficient to bring them safely awake—about
one day sooner than the clever saboteur had
planned.

Randolph Mays flew the Manta close to the *Ventris* and parked it in vacuum. The *Ventris* seemed
not to have moved as much as he would have expected, but such things were almost impossible to
judge by eye. Ships and sub and satellites were
whirling around Jupiter in ever-adjusting orbits as
Amalthea boiled itself into nothing, a few meters
below them.

He floated into the equipment bay through its
clamshell doors, open to space as he had left them.
He parked the Manta and climbed cautiously out of
it. He went carefully through the hatches of the in-

ternal airlock, sealing it behind him so as not to
disturb the condition of things inside, keeping his
spacesuit sealed.

Not that he feared the crew; they were safely
asleep, even unto eternity.

He drifted through the ship's corridor, while inside his helmet his amplified breath sucked and
hissed in his ears.

He passed the sleeping compartments. Hawkins
was unconscious, wrapped in his sleep restraint; little Tony Groves was still asleep in his, in the compartment he and Mays had shared.

Through the wardroom. Forster and Redfield
were there, huddled over the chessboard, having
drifted only a few centimeters from where he'd left
them.

On up to the flight deck—Walsh inert in her
couch, McNeil in his. Nothing on the big console
different from the way he'd left it.

Above the flight deck there was storage space and
tanks of maneuvering-system fuel and an overhead
hatch which the expedition rarely used, preferring
the more convenient airlock through the equipment bay. Mays was not a careless man; he checked
these spaces again. Still no one there.

He moved down through the ship, past the sleeping men. Everything was in place. Mays had
sketched out many a mystery scenario in his lifetime, but none was more perfect than this. Marianne's testimony . . . all the physical evidence . . .
every last detail would confirm his special version
of the truth.

He'd just about made it to the bottom of the corridor when he sensed a presence, a flicker of
shadow along the corridor wall. Someone behind
him? He wheeled around. . . .

"Why don't you say a bit more, Sir Randolph?"
Forster was prodding him hard, with a forefinger

that felt as thick as a cricket bat. "About why you felt you had to gas us all. About why you felt you had to sabotage the communications systems. About what has become of your . . . of Ms. Mitchell."

Mays was surrounded—rather closely, given the confines of a working spaceship—by the people he had gassed. All of them. His legalistic arguments were having no effect—

—but it was not his purpose to change any minds, as they all understood. It was his purpose to have his statements recorded by the ship's recorders—now that they were functioning again, evidently—and to stall for time. "*You* sabotaged the communications, Professor," he said loudly, "not I. Marianne and I took what measures we felt were necessary to *escape*."

"Escape from what?"

"It will take us a little longer than it will take *you*, perhaps, but we can get back to Ganymede without your help. We've made contact with the Space Board. They are on their way."

"You've radioed them from your capsule?" Bill Hawkins blurted. He'd forgotten, or never learned, that the first rule of negotiation is to show no surprise.

"Yes, by dint of great *effort* I managed to repair the capsule's communications gear," Mays said with a wide-mouthed, big-toothed grin. "Although I wouldn't attempt to contact Marianne, if I were you. I've instructed her to ignore *anyone's* voice but my own. Until all of us here have come to terms."

Hawkins cried out in anguish, "Does anyone here think she's actually fond of this blackguard?" He pushed his limp blond hair out of his eyes so vigorously that he drifted halfway across the room.

"Bill," Josepha Walsh murmured uncomfortably, "let's leave that kind of thing for later, what say?"

Hawkins turned away in anguish, unable to bear Mays's unruffled complacency. Hawkins could not know that beneath his calm exterior, Mays was a desperate man. Had Troy done this? He'd *killed* her!

Forster, meanwhile, had been studying his adversary. "Well, you're here with us again. So we'll just go fetch Ms. Mitchell and . . . hold you both captive, as you put it, until we get back to Ganymede—or until the Space Board arrive. Whichever comes first. Then let the bureaucracy sort it all out."

"Fine. You'll never *find* the Ambassador again, of course."

Forster's eyebrows shot up. "Never find the Ambassador?"

"After I took the photogram views I wanted, I moved it." Mays paused just long enough to let the news sink in. "Oh, I *do* exaggerate. You *might* find it again, with enough time. But I assure you it won't be easy."

"Pray, what was the point of that?" Forster inquired civilly.

"My *estimate* of the situation has not changed since the last time we talked, Professor," said Mays. "You have illegally held me and my associate, Ms. Mitchell, *incommunicado.*" It was becoming his favorite word. "Everything I've done has been in my . . . in our self defense. I want merely to communicate the news of this extraordinary discovery. I claim it as our right."

Forster slowly reddened. "*Sir* Randolph," he said acidly, "you're not only an attempted murderer but an unmitigated crook, and accordingly I've no compunction left in dealing with you."

"What's that supposed to *mean*, sir?" Mays inquired cheerily.

"I'll tell you shortly. Tony. Blake. You, Bill. Come with me."

They caucused in the corridor, outside the lock to the equipment bay—in the same place Mays and Marianne had plotted their downfall.

"I want to go with Blake," Hawkins said hotly, after hearing Forster's plan. "There's no reason I can't go."

"There is, Bill, which I will presently explain to you. I understand your feelings. But if you do what I suggest, you'll have a much better chance of, mm . . . getting what you want."

So it was that they sent Blake out alone.

Blake piloted the Manta to within half a dozen meters of the lonely Moon Cruiser. Even in the milky fog he found it readily enough by its radar signature.

Blake was wearing his spacesuit sealed, and having prepared for the event by leaving the hatch of the Manta open, he slipped free of the craft and pushed himself gently through the white night toward the burned black capsule. He had a moment's rush of sympathy for the lonely young woman inside who, despite Mays's assertions, could not see out, could not hear anything, did not know that her capsule was even now drifting out of a narrow and rapidly diminishing zone of radiation safety.

Mays must have planned it that way, Blake thought; he'd meant to let her fry. He meant to leave no stone unburied.

He clipped an acoustic coupler to the hull. "Marianne, this is Blake. Can you hear me?"

"Who is that?" Her voice was full of strength, and of fear.

"Blake Redfield. Since your commlink is out, I'm here as a go-between. For the negotiations, I guess you'd call them. What you say can be heard on the *Ventris*."

"Where are you?"

"Right outside. I've clipped an acoustic coupler to your hull. It's feeding through the Manta's radiolink to the *Ventris.*"

"What are you planning to do? Where's Randolph?"

"I'm not going to do anything. Whatever happens to Sir Randolph is between you and Professor Forster."

"I won't tell you where the statue is," she said defiantly.

"Whatever you say. I'm not in on that; you'll have to talk to the professor. I'm going back to the sub."

"Ms. Mitchell, do you hear me?" Forster's voice intruded on the link, coming through clearly. "Sir Randolph has explained what he's done, Marianne. All of us feel strongly that all of this . . . complication is completely unnecessary. We have treated you both as colleagues, and as such we still regard you. We've asked only that Sir Randolph obey the most basic rules of scholarship and ethical conduct."

"Does that mean you're willing to call it off?" Marianne asked. "I hope so. I'm getting so . . . bored."

"Ms. Mitchell, I would like you to give Redfield permission to tow your capsule back here to the *Ventris.* In a very little time, we may have to move our ship. I'm concerned for your safety."

"I *won't* tell you where the statue is," she said. "Not unless Randolph tells me to."

"He's not willing to do that," said the professor.

"Well . . ." Her sigh was almost audible through the jury-rigged sound link. "No."

"It's apparent that you don't take me seriously," Forster said sternly. "Therefore I've arranged a rather drastic demonstration—to indicate that *I* at least am serious. In order to have his way, Sir Randolph has exposed you and the rest of us to extreme dangers. Now it's his turn."

"What do you mean?" she replied. She tried to sound merely cautious, though her apprehension was apparent in her voice.

"I'm not sure how much you know about celestial mechanics, but if your onboard computer is functioning at all, I'm sure it will confirm what I'm about to tell you."

"Just say what you mean, please."

"I'm trying to impress upon you our curious, indeed our pre*car*ious position. If your videoplate were functioning—alas, another deficit you might want to ask Sir Randolph about when you see him next—you would have only to look at it to remind yourself how close to Jupiter we are. And I need hardly remind *you* that Jupiter has by far the most intense gravitational field of all the planets."

She was quiet a moment. Then she said, "Go on."

He was alert to the edge in her voice, and continued with less condescension. "You, and we, and what's left of Amalthea are going around Jupiter in a bit more than twelve hours. A well-known theorem states that if a body falls from an orbit to the center of attraction, it will take point one seven seven of a period to make the drop. In other words, anything falling from here to Jupiter would reach the center of the planet in a little over two hours. As I said earlier, your computer, if it is functioning, will confirm this."

There was a long pause before Marianne again said, "Go on," in a voice that seemed drained of expression.

"A fall to the center of Jupiter is of course a theoretical case. Anything dropped from our altitude would reach the upper atmosphere of Jupiter in a considerably shorter time." When she did not immediately reply Forster added, a bit viciously, "I hope I'm not boring you."

"Uh," said Marianne, then, "Just get on with it."

"We've worked out the actual time, and it's about an hour and thirty-five minutes. You've worked with us long enough, Ms. Mitchell, to notice that as the mass of Amalthea boils away and the moon shrinks beneath us, what was a weak gravitational field to begin with has grown considerably weaker. Computer tells us that escape velocity is now only about ten meters per second. Anything thrown away at that speed will never come back. Your own experience will confirm the truth of that, I think."

"Yes, of course." Her voice revealed no impatience, for she was quick and may already have seen where Forster was leading.

"I'll come to the point. We propose to take Sir Randolph for a little spacewalk, until he's at the sub-Jupiter point—immediately under Jupiter, that is. We've disabled his suit's maneuvering unit. We can operate it, but he can't. We're going to, ah, launch him forth. We'll be prepared to retrieve him with the *Ventris* as soon as you give us the detailed directions to the whereabouts of the statue, which Sir Randolph himself assures us that you have."

Marianne hesitated, and then she said, "I want to talk to Randolph."

"I'm sorry, that's impossible."

Blake, listening in, thought Forster's eager anticipation was almost too evident; this was the moment he'd been waiting for.

"Is Bill on the flight deck?" she asked, oh so softly.

"Hawkins? Mm, actually, yes . . ."

"Let me talk to him."

"Well, if you . . . if you wish."

Hawkins came on the link. His voice was frantic with guilt and fear. "I objected, Marianne. I'll lodge a formal protest, I promise. But Forster is adamant. He . . ."

Forster cut him off angrily. "Enough of that,

Hawkins. And no more digressions, Ms. Mitchell. After what I've told you, I'm sure you appreciate that time is vital. An hour and thirty-five minutes will go by rather quickly, but if you could observe what is happening to Amalthea, you would agree that we have little more time than that in which to confirm any information you choose to give us."

"You're bluffing," said Marianne.

Blake was alarmed. This wasn't according to plan.

Then she went on. "I don't believe you'd do anything of the kind. Your crew won't let you."

Blake relaxed. She was trying to convey toughness and doing a creditable job of it, but mingled horror and disbelief underlay her words.

The professor emitted an expressive sigh. "Too bad. Mr. McNeil, Mr. Groves, please take the prisoner and proceed as instructed."

McNeil's solemn "Aye-aye, sir" was heard in the background.

"What are you doing now?" Marianne demanded.

"Sir Randolph and friends are going for a little walk," Forster said. "Too bad you can't see this for yourself."

Blake's cue: he broke in excitedly. "Professor, what's to keep Marianne from thinking this is all a colossal bluff? She's gotten to know you in the past few days—you saved her life, after all, and she doesn't believe you'd really kill the guy, throw him into Jupiter. And even if *you* would, she knows Angus and Tony—she probably doesn't think *they'd* do it." Pause . . . "Right, Marianne?"

She said nothing.

Blake went on, "Well, she probably figures she's seen through the bluff, and we're left looking mighty foolish."

"What do you suggest?" Forster said.

"I think we ought to let her come out of that tin can and see for herself. She knows we're not interested in grabbing *her*—if we were, I could have towed her all the way back to the *Ventris* by now. And she'd never have known it.''

That suggestion took about four seconds to sink in—little more than the time it took Marianne to seal her helmet. All the explosive bolts of the capsule's hatch blew off at once and the square hatch went tumbling straight off into heaven. The massive capsule itself recoiled and drifted slowly backward as Marianne clambered out of the open hatch.

Evidently she'd already determined that the Moon Cruiser was a useless relic of games past. The new game would be played here in vacuum; no matter who won or lost, whoever went home would be going home in the *Ventris*, if not in a Space Board cutter.

She looked around, noting the spiraling umbilical cable that connected the acoustic link on the capsule to the Manta, which drifted a few meters off—Blake's face was visible through the sphere, but she spared him hardly a glance—and noting, too, the distant bright reflection of the *Michael Ventris* floating above the glowing fog. The vast curve of Jupiter rose above them all, turning the tendrils of mist to fleshy pink in its backlight.

Three white doll-like figures were just then leaving the *Ventris*'s open bay.

''She's out, Professor,'' said Blake.

''Now that you're not shielded in the capsule, Ms. Mitchell, can you hear me in your suitcomm?''

''Yes. I hear you.''

''If you use the magnifying visor plate on your suit helmet, you'll be able to reassure yourself that Angus and Tony aren't dragging an empty suit between them. They'll be over the horizon in a minute, but you'll be able to see Sir Randolph as he begins to, er . . . ascend.''

Marianne said nothing, but she reached up and pulled the visor over her faceplate.

Time seemed to stop then. The aether was silent. Forster said nothing; Marianne said nothing but only watched the sky; Blake lay in the Manta saying nothing, apparently studying his fingernails, deliberately sparing Marianne his curious stare.

She kept her silence. Was she waiting to see how far the professor would go?

Amalthea's diffuse horizon was ridiculously close. Marianne made a tiny involuntary gesture that upset her equilibrium; she had seen the exhaust of McNeil's and Grove's maneuvering systems drawing thin, straight lines against the orange backcloth of Jupiter. She adjusted quickly, in time to see the three figures rising into space.

As she watched, they separated. Two of them decelerated and started to fall back. The other went on ascending helplessly toward the ominous bulk of Jupiter.

"He'll die," she whispered. "You've thrown him into the radiation belt."

Forster said nothing—perhaps he hadn't heard her—so Blake took it upon himself to allay that particular horror. "We'll take care of that on the ship. We've got the enzymes to clean up the dead cells, repair the damaged ones. You know from your own experience that even twelve hours' exposure won't kill you if you get treatment."

"Twelve hours . . ."

"Yeah," Blake said, not without a hint of satisfaction, "Mays knew *that* when he crashed the two of you. He counted on us to save your lives. And we did." Almost immediately, Blake regretted his words. This was not the time to discourage her sympathy for Mays.

Forster's voice came over the link. "I hope I don't need to impress upon you the urgency of the situation. As I said, the time of fall from our orbit to the upper atmosphere of Jupiter is about ninety-five minutes. But of course, if one waited even half that time . . . it would be much too late.''

Marianne floated there in space, arms akimbo, head tilted back, and Blake thought that even in obvious anguish, swathed in a bulky spacesuit, she was an image of dignity and natural grace. Watching her, Blake sighed. He felt sorry for her. And for Bill Hawkins. Love gets people into the worst tangles.

24

Deep in the darkest waters of Amalthea's core, Sparta swam without light, sliding through the cold as strong as a dolphin but with less effort, as slick and quick as a fish.

To see, she did not need light in the so-called visible spectrum, for she could easily see by the infrared emanations of the great ship's crystalline tissues; everywhere the pillars and walls transmitted the vibrant heat from its unseen inner heart. Warm light pulsed around her with the deep beating of that heart.

Even in the visible spectrum the waters were literally alive; around her sparkled galaxies of tiny living lights, Amalthea's bounty, animals of blue and purple and startling orange.

Sparta was one with them, unencumbered by canvas and metal, needing no bottled oxygen. As she moved naked through the water, dark swollen slits opened on either side of her chest, from beneath her Adam's apple to the wings of her collar bones; water pushed into her and pulsed out again through flowering petals of flesh that opened beneath her ribs, the blue white of skin on the outside, frilled inside with throbbing gills that in longer wave-lengths would have revealed their rich and blood-swollen redness.

Although she had spent far more hours exploring the alien ship than all the other members of Forster's team together, even she had seen no more than a fraction of it. Millions—millions at least—of intelligent creatures had once inhabited these empty grottoes and corridors; millions upon millions of other animals and plants, trillions upon trillions of single-celled creatures, uncountable as the stars in the galaxies, had filled the innumerable niches of its watery ecology. She had formed a clearer picture of who they were, what they had been about, why they had lived the way they did, where they had gone and what they had done. She was a long way from knowing how they did it.

Yet every minute that she swam alone in the darkness she learned more, for the colorful plankton and larvaceans and medusas and ctenophores, even the anemones that coated the walls in some parts of the ship, all sang a rhythmic song coded in the pumping of their stomachs and hearts, the beating of their tentacles and wings. The ship as big as a world was also a world as coordinated and purposeful as a ship, a ship made not of titanium and aluminum and steel—or not exclusively—but of calcium and phosphorus and carbon and nitrogen and hydrogen and oxygen as well—and of forty or fifty other elements, in significant percentages—assembled in uncounted varieties of molecules, in proteins and acids and fats, some of them simple as gasses, some of them huge and entwined upon themselves beyond immediate comprehension. There were familiar shapes here, DNA and RNA and ATP and hemoglobin, keratin and calcium carbonate and so on and so forth, the stuff of earthly nucleus and earthly cell, earthly bone and earthly shell. And there were molecules never yet seen, but seeming not so odd here, not so illogical. There was everything a living being needed to extrude a cloak about itself, thick with life, a shining suit of mucous tough enough to withstand the depths or the vacuum. Or to go naked in the warm, shallow waters.

Sparta inhaled the creatures as she swam—and ate a good many of them—which is how she knew these things. They did not mind; individually, they had no minds. Tasting them and smelling them, almost without her willing it whole arrays of chemical formulas appeared on the screen of her mind. She stored what information she could analyze—far from everything, for her means of analysis depended almost wholly upon stereochemistry, upon the fit of her taste buds and olfactory sensors to the shapes of the molecules presented to them—in the dense tissue of her soul's eye, there to be sorted and compared against what was known.

Thus she learned the world-ship, and—if not yet its purpose—its organization.

Professor Forster's teams had gone in along two axes, one equatorial and one polar, and had generated maps of the two narrow cone-shaped regions of their exploration, showing that the ship was built in shells, one within the other. Forster had pictured them as nested ellipsoid balloons. Sparta knew that the ship was at once simpler and more sophisticated than that; it was more like a spiral, more like a nautilus's shell, but not so easy to compute. The volume of each subsequent space outward from the center did not increase in a simple Fibonacci sequence, as the sum of the two preceding values, but according to a curve of fractal dimension. Nevertheless, it had grown according to rules which, if not wholly predictable in their production of detail, were so in result, at the cut-off.

She had never swum the fifteen kilometers down to the center of the ship. Her body would have been unperturbed by the pressures and temperatures; like the sea lions or the great whales, she had had built into herself the mechanisms of heart and blood vessels that she needed to force oxygen into her brain and organs at depth. She knew that the engine of all that had transpired since the *Kon-Tiki* expedition had entered the clouds of Jupiter was centered there. The power that had melted Amalthea and the intelligence that had ordered the resurrection of the ship's life were centered there. The potential of whatever was yet to come was centered there.

But she had not had the time to make the trip. Something in the Knowledge held her away from the place. The Knowledge, that torn scrapbook of enigmas, had revealed much as it had unfolded itself in her memory, but it left as much unrevealed.

She returned time and again to the chamber within the Temple of Art where the Ambassador rested in stasis. She was drawn back to the immense statue not only by her natural curiosity and appreciation of it, but because of expectation. . . .

Thowintha had been alone in the singing darkness for a hundred thousand uncounted circuits of the sun, undreaming.

It was not the darkness that first dissolved; that came later. What came first, was that the oneness of the world formed an edge—for as the myriad creatures say, the edge of oneness is time.

There was a beating as of a great heart. Thowintha was far from awake, or even alive as the myriad creatures are alive, but the oneness of the world had formed a way of knowing something of itself: its great heart was beating and Thowintha, without consciousness, knew that it was beating. The world was marking its time.

Next there was a beating inside and a beating outside, and they were not the same. Indeed, Thowintha was the world's way of marking its time, and—while of the world still—Thowintha marked a separate time as well. Thus the darkness began to dissolve.

Thowintha's eyes grew transparent to the light that seeped from the walls of the world, beating with the world's heart. The walls were not black, although the light of them did not travel far through the waters. Brighter than the stars in heaven were the myriad creatures that filled the sweet waters.

Thowintha did not move or need to move, but only to wait and savor the delicious waters. All things were dissolved in the waters. In the waters were life and the memory of life. In the waters was the state of things.

The world was waking as it had been meant to: in this there was joy, as the first designation had foretold. The most perilous circuits of the sun, feared with reason by the delegates that came after—for when they saw the state of things on the natural worlds they were plunged into sorrow—had been endured by the myriad creatures. Now their representatives, those who had been designated, had arrived. All was well.

They had arrived. The smell of them was in the water, an acceptable smell—indeed, a fine smell—but nothing that had been foretold by the first designates. For these creatures were not water-breathers.

No matter. The nature of these creatures—abstract thinkers, machine-makers and life-tenders, storytellers—had been discovered by the second designates. What seemed wondrous to Thowintha was how few of them there were. There was so little taste of them in the water! They had so little variety! Their numbers were less than a bundle of feelers.

Where were their great vessels? Why did the myriad creatures of the natural worlds not come in their thousands and millions to occupy the spaces that had been prepared for them? For the world had been set in order for them when it was seen that the great work had failed, that the natural worlds *must fail. The second designates, who came after, had said there was hope still, that all would be well even yet, that they would arrive, having developed that capacity for abstract thinking, not only for machine-making but for life-tending, for storytelling, without which it would be unthinkable to carry them onward. . . . But the moment had come. The world was awake and soon would move. If these were all there were to go with it, so it must be.*

In the water nearby Thowintha tasted one of them now, the one who came most often. By the beating of three hearts, by the marking of time, Thowintha knew it was time to exchange stories.

Swimming long hours alone in life-spangled darkness, she had begun to understand deeply the place the Knowledge had played in the myths and legends of the Bronze Age, from which so many contemporary religions had descended. She knew why so many heroes had spent so much of their time under the sea. She knew why Genesis described heaven and Earth, in the beginning, as "without form and void; and darkness was upon the face of the deep," and why "the Spirit of God moved upon the face of the waters."

For the Hebrew word that the scribes of King James had translated as "moved" was *merahepeth,* "to brood." In the beginning the Spirit of God brooded, as eagles brood or as salmon brood, whether above or below the waters. . . .

Sparta flickered whitely through the corridors of the Temple of Art where the walls glowed most warmly and nebulas of shining life swarmed most thickly. She came to the inner chamber. The Ambassador rested there on its pedestal, unchanged, giving no visible hint of life, much less of awakening consciousness. By the taste of the water she knew better. The acids that had bathed its cells in stasis were flowing away, out of its system.

She hovered before the Ambassador in the water, her short straight hair drained of color, gently swaying in the beating current, her gills opening and closing as gracefully as the waving of kelp in the slow sea surge.

You are awake. She blew air—borrowed from her gills, stored in her lungs—through her mouth and nose and made clicks deep in her throat, speaking in the language known to those who had reconstructed it as the language of Culture X.

A single click echoed in the water around her. *Yes.*

How are you called?

We are the living world.

How do you wish to be addressed?

The sounds that came back were hollow poundings, like wooden gongs struck under water. *In this body, the form of address is Thowintha.*

You are Thowintha? The volume of Sparta's body was a fourth the Ambassador's; as much as she tried, she was unable to reproduce the sound of the name precisely.

You may call us Thowintha. We would not call ourselves this, but we understand that you have a different impression . . . a different outlook. How are you called?

We—all of my kind—call ourselves human beings. In this body, most who know me call me Ellen Troy. Others call me Linda Nagy. I call myself Sparta.

We call you Designate.

Why do you call me that?

You are like the other humans who have come here, and those we observed before, but also different. You have learned ways to make yourself more like us. You can only have learned these ways from designates: thus you are designated.

Please explain these matters. Sparta emitted an

impatient sequence of clicks and hisses. *I want to know your impression.*

We will tell each other many stories. We will tell you as much as we can of what happened before we last visited you. You will tell us of all that has happened since. With each phrase, water flowed in and out of the Ambassador's mantle; life was rippling through its body. *There will be more time later. But there is little time now. Where are the others?*

They are in our ship in nearby space.

You wish them to be destroyed, then. The Ambassador's impassive "face" gave no hint of approval or disapproval as it subtly drifted free of the gleaming pedestal and the nest of writhing microtubules that had fastened it to the ship. *You wish to come with us alone.*

No! A reverberating click. *They must not be harmed.*

All must come. There is little time. Very soon there will be no time.

I will tell them, if you will show me how.

Come and we will show you how.

The equipment-bay airlock of the *Michael Ventris* opened slowly. Marianne came inside first, followed by Blake. She pulled her helmet from her head before proceeding on up the corridor to the crowded flight deck.

She arrived with fire in her heart and fire in her eye, needing only a bloodstained axe to fit her for the part of Clytemnestra. Her first words were not for Forster, however, who floated expectantly before her, but for Bill Hawkins.

"You could have *stopped* them," she said angrily. "Or at least tried. You *want* him to die."

He looked her in that fiery eye. "No, Marianne, I don't. And he won't."

"Because I gave in," she said. "Obviously *he*

didn't. If I hadn't made him tell me where he hid the statue, he would have gone to his death for his principles. He acted like a ma . . . a grown-up. But *you*, Bill . . .''

''Plenty of time for recriminations later, Ms. Mitchell.'' Forster interrupted before she said the harder words. ''We have business to settle.''

''Here,'' she said, and pushed a graphics pad at him. On it was a crude sketch-map of a section of the Temple of Art, with an X to mark the spot. ''That's the best I can do.''

''That will be fine,'' said Forster, glancing at it briefly. He passed it to Blake. ''Blake, I believe you indicated you wanted to take care of this.''

''Sir.'' Blake took the pad and immediately left the flight deck.

''Well, now that that's over with''—Forster moved to Fulton's empty couch and bent over, rummaging in a canvas sack beneath the console. He came up with a glass bottle plastered with peeling labels, filled with a dark amber liquid. One of his treasured Napoleons—''Why don't we relax and have a drink to forget all this unpleasantness?''

''A *drink?*'' Marianne's outrage carried almost palpable force. She pointed at the time display on the console behind Forster. ''Have you gone crazy? Randolph must have fallen halfway to Jupiter!''

Professor Forster regarded her disapprovingly. ''Lack of patience is a common failing in the young,'' he said, which sounded odd coming from his youthful-appearing self. ''I see no cause at all for hasty action.''

Marianne flushed red but as quickly became pale again; real fear had temporarily pushed aside her anger. ''You promised,'' she whispered.

In Bill Hawkins's expression, menace was replacing anxiousness. ''Professor, you told me . . . well, I don't see there's any point in prolonging this.''

Seeing their emotion, Forster realized he might

have gone a tad too far; he'd had his little joke, after all. "I can tell you at once, Ms. Mitchell—Bill knows this already, which is why he is justly angry with me—that Randolph Mays is in no more danger than we are. We can go and collect him whenever we like."

"Then you *did* lie to me," she said instantly.

"No, I certainly did not. *Mays* has lied to you repeatedly, but what I told you was the truth. Granted, you jumped to the wrong conclusions. So did Bill here, until I explained it to him—his outrage on your behalf, and on Mays's, was quite genuine, and I doubt we could have restrained him had we not convinced him that we were telling the truth."

"Which is?" she demanded—and added with a hiss, "If you're ready to cut the self-serving bull."

Despite himself, Forster flinched. "Yes, well . . . when I said that a body would take ninety-five minutes to fall from here to Jupiter, I omitted—not accidentally, I confess—a rather important phrase. I should have added, 'a body at rest with respect to Jupiter.' But we are not at rest with respect to Jupiter. Sir Randolph shares our orbital speed, which is about, mm, twenty-seven kilometers per second."

She was quick even when the ideas were strange, so the moral force of her anger was slightly sapped by a suspicion of what Forster would say next; the best she could do was display her contempt for his self-satisfaction. "To hell with your numbers. Will you for God's sake get to the point?"

"Mm, yes, as you say." Remarkably he was looking almost sheepish by now. "We did throw him completely away from Amalthea, toward Jupiter. But the extra velocity we gave him was trivial; he's still moving in practically the same orbit as before. The most he can do, computer says, is drift about a hundred kilometers inward. In one revolution, twelve hours or so, he'll come right back where he started. Without us having to do anything at all."

Marianne locked eyes with the professor. To the other two watchers on the flight deck, Walsh and Hawkins, there was no doubting the meaning of the exchange: Forster was ashamed of himself, but defiant, for he believed that what he had done needed doing; Marianne was relieved, but frustrated and annoyed at having been duped.

"Which is why you wouldn't let me talk to him," she said. "Randolph's smart enough to realize that he's in no danger. He would have told me that."

"That's why I wouldn't let you talk to him, yes," Forster admitted. "As for his sophistication with orbital mechanics, I warned you of that myself. Indeed, Sir Randolph was so confident of his ability in that regard that he risked *your* life without compunction."

She turned to Hawkins. "You knew."

Hawkins steadily returned her accusing gaze. "What the professor hasn't told you, Marianne, is that Mays tried to murder us all. And made you his accomplice. You two didn't knock us out for just a few minutes; you gassed us good. Then he set the ship to drift into the radiation belt."

The blood drained from her face, but she said, "So what? Radiation effects are curable." It came out with more defiance than she felt. "I have firsthand knowledge of that fact, too."

"So long as someone's awake to administer the cure. You two dosed us to keep us unconscious for a long time, too long to save ourselves after we woke up. He kept you alive to support his story—but he made sure you wouldn't really witness a thing."

Marianne stared at Hawkins, her face slowly creasing with the horror of what he was saying. She shifted her wavering gaze to the professor. "Then . . . why would he bother hiding the statue?"

"He didn't bother, of course," said Forster. "I gave your map to Blake to put under seal with the rest of the evidence against him. Mays told you an involved tale so that *you* would send him back here to the *Ventris*. It was all your idea, Marianne. *You* are the guilty party; the innocent Sir Randolph Mays would never have done it on his own. Or so he would have told the Space Board."

"If you knew, why did you go through with all of this?" Marianne asked.

Forster said quietly, "So that you would know too."

25

"We've got you, Sir Randolph. You'll have been listening in, I suppose."

"Yes."

McNeil and Groves closed on Mays an hour after Forster told them to retrieve him; he was only twenty kilometers up, and they located him without too much trouble by tracking the radio beacon on his suit, which they'd left intact when they disabled his suit-comm. His radiation exposure would be no worse than that of his rescuers.

"No need to make the long round trip after all. Ms. Mitchell valued your life too much," said Groves.

"Yes, well . . . good-hearted person. Quick study. Have to give her that."

"I'm afraid you've rather shaken her faith in you."

Mays made no reply.

Of the two crewmen, quick little Tony Groves was more inclined to play Mercurius, the psychologist; it seemed to him that something had gone out of Sir Randolph Mays, some dark force of resistance, for he came down with them very listlessly out of the bronze-colored, Jupiter-dominated sky.

It occurred to the navigator to suggest to Professor Forster, that famous rationalist, that now would be a good time to question Mays more closely. Perhaps the historian-journalist was willing to admit, if not defeat, something closer to the unvarnished truth about himself.

First they had to get back to the *Michael Ventris*, a barely visible speck of light alongside the glowing fluff-ball of Amalthea, which was virtually plummeting through the night, visibly shifting against the background of fixed stars.

Even as they watched, diving full speed toward the satellite on their suit maneuvering systems, Amalthea's aspect changed. The last of the icy husk melted into hot water, and the last of the hot water boiled away in a flash. A rapidly dissipating whiff of vapor slid away, ever so slowly, like the silk scarf of a magician lifting in interminable slow motion and with exquisite grace, to reveal—

—what they had known was there but could not have seen with their own eyes before now, the mirror-finished spacecraft, the world that was a spaceship. The diamond moon.

Just then, Jo Walsh's voice broke in on their suit-comms: "Angus, Tony, get back here as fast as you can. We've got an emergency on our hands."

"What's up, Jo?"

"Give it all you've got, guys. Bleed Mr. Mays's maneuvering gas if you must. Looks like the neighborhood is about to go critical, if our informants know what the hell they're talking about."

And on the flight deck of the *Ventris*:

". . . bring the *Ventris* into the one-eighty equatorial hold. I can't be sure, but I think you've got only about twenty minutes to accomplish this," Sparta's quiet voice was saying over the speakers.

"Twenty minutes," Marianne exclaimed softly. She looked about as if someone could save the situation. But Forster and the captain were staring at the blank videoplate as if by force of concentration they could see Sparta on it. Hawkins was chewing his lip, looking at Marianne helplessly. Even Blake, whose normal impulse in emergencies was to go out and blow something up, stood glumly by, inactive.

Forster said, "We're still missing McNeil and Groves, Inspector Troy."

"Mays?" came Sparta's voice on the link.

"Yes, he's with them."

"Are you in contact?"

"Captain Walsh has just now instructed them to make all possible speed, but we estimate that they are perhaps fifteen minutes away from our current position."

On the bridge of the *Ventris* all was silent for a moment, until Sparta's voice spoke again from the radiolink. "You will have to enter the hold now. They'll have to come in when they arrive."

"Their *maneuvering* fuel . . ." Marianne began.

Sparta's voice continued. "There seems to be no leeway here—it's my sense of the situation that the . . . the world-ship is in an automated countdown. And that we've already gone past the point of no return."

"But Inspector Troy . . ."

"Sorry, sir, give me a moment"—Walsh interrupted Forster's reply with a hired captain's diplomatic firmness, which under her politeness brooked no contradiction—"I'll be getting the ship underway, alerting the men. You and Inspector Troy can carry on your debate again shortly."

Walsh busily communed with the computer of the *Ventris*—it was a bit more work than usual to get the ship started without the help of her engineer—and programmed it to head for the equator of the diamond moon. "Better strap in, sir. Blake, please take the engineer's couch. Ms. Mitchell, Mr. Hawkins, down below, please. Secure for course adjustment."

A moment later the maneuvering rockets went off like howitzers, hard enough and loud enough to give them all headaches. The *Ventris* curved smartly inward, toward the black hole that was even then spiraling open in the side of the glistening world-ship.

McNeil looked at Groves. They'd just been briefed by Walsh over their suitlinks. "Any help, Mr. Navigator?"

"Well, Mr. Engineer, I've just run a rather preliminary estimate on my sleeve"—he tapped the computer locator pad on his suit's forearm—"and it puts us in a bit of a bind. To make the vector change, we've got to save what fuel we've got. But if we save what we've got, we arrive, oh, a tad late."

"We haven't got the delta-vees, then?"

"That's putting it succinctly."

"Any recommendations?"

Inside his suit, Groves visibly shrugged. "I say, let's go like bats out of hell and hope somebody thinks of something before we run out of gas."

McNeil looked sideways at their captive. "S'pose you should have a vote, Mays. Not that we have to count it."

Mays said, "No matter. I've nothing to add."

They hit their suit thrusters then, and dived toward the diamond moon.

The *Ventris* entered the huge dome originally explored by Forster and Troy in the Manta submarine. Its cathedral-like space was a filigree of ink and silver, drawn with a fine steel needlepoint—for it was full of vacuum now, not water, and its intricate architecture was severely illuminated by inpouring Jupiter light.

From the floor a bundle of gleaming mechanisms, flexible and alive as tentacles, sprang up to grasp the *Ventris* and draw it inward. They turned it as they carried it, so that finally it lay on its side, firmly entangled in a nest of sucking tendrils like a fish that had blundered into the grip of an anemone.

The *Ventris* was aligned so that it was parallel to the axis of the world-ship, pointed in the direction of what they had called the south pole. On the flight deck, what feeble gravity there was tended to draw people to one wall instead of the floor, but the force was so slight that the sensation was not so much like falling as drifting sideways in a slow current.

"The Manta's got fuel," Blake said to Walsh. "I can ride it out toward them and abandon it, use my suit gas to help them come in."

"Sorry, Blake," she said shortly. "You'd use up your suit gas and more, just matching their trajectory."

"I insist upon making the attempt," Blake said, with all the angry dignity he could muster.

"I refuse to have four casualties instead of three."

"Captain . . ."

"If there were the slightest chance"—Walsh was rigid; two of her long-time companions, her oldest friends, were among the men she proposed to abandon—"but there is not. Run the numbers, if you like. Please prove me wrong."

Forster—strapped into his couch and brooding, his face in his hands—had stayed out of the dispute. Now he lifted his sad gaze to Blake. "Do as the captain suggests, Blake. Run the numbers."

"Sir, computer is using its own fuel estimates. I suggest . . . I'm saying they're low."

"Or high," Walsh shot back at him.

"Run the numbers, Blake," Forster said. "Leave Mays's mass out of the calculation."

Walsh looked at Blake without saying anything. She was asking him to take the burden.

"Sorry, Jo. Professor," Blake whispered. "I won't

say I'd be sorry to see them make that choice for themselves. But . . .''

Walsh turned to the console and tapped numbers into the computer manually; it was not the sort of thing you told the machine to do in voice mode. The numbers came back, and the potential trajectories were graphically displayed.

Walsh and the rest of them stared at the plate. ''Well,'' she said, ''let's hope that when the idea occurs to them, they're less squeamish than . . . than I am.''

''What are you talking about?'' Marianne demanded. She and Bill Hawkins had at that moment arrived on the flight deck.

Forster didn't look at her, but he spoke loudly and flatly, ''With Mays's fuel—but without his mass—McNeil and Groves have a chance to make it back here before Inspector Troy's deadline.''

''A rapidly diminishing chance,'' growled Walsh.

Marianne sifted that. ''You want them to abandon Randolph?'' she said.

''I wish they would.'' Forster looked her in the eye. ''But I doubt that they will.''

Marianne could have expressed outrage or horror. But she didn't.

Inward toward Jupiter, Tony Groves said, ''We just passed it, mate. Point of no return,''

''Meaning if nobody comes to our rescue, we sail on forever,'' said McNeil.

'' 'Fraid so.''

For a moment their suitcomms were filled with nothing but Jupiter static; then Mays spoke. ''You've got my suit fuel. Just get rid of me. Perhaps you can still save yourselves.''

''Not the sort of thing that's usually done,'' said Groves.

''And of course you're the sort who always does the *usual* thing,'' Mays said spitefully.

"I think he's trying to provoke us, Angus," Groves said.

"Won't do him any good. All *déjà vu* to me," said McNeil. "Sure, kill off the odd inconvenient fellow and you may live a bit longer. Then try living it down."

Groves clucked his tongue. "I say, was that a pun?"

"Clever you."

They sailed on into space, their suit rockets pushing them toward the diamond moon that now almost filled their sky—knowing that they would have no way of stopping, or even of turning, once they reached it.

"*Frankly*," said Mays, "it doesn't really matter to me whether you two live or die. I would like to make a statement before *I* die."

"We're listening," said McNeil.

"Not to you two. To . . . to Forster, I suppose. To that woman Troy, or whatever she calls herself these days."

McNeil keyed his suitcomm. "Can you still pick us up, Professor?"

The answer came back so clear that Forster might have been in a suit next to them. "I've been listening in, Angus. Say what you have to, Sir Randolph."

"I'm listening too, Sir Randolph," Sparta said, as clearly as Forster.

Mays sighed deeply, and took a deep breath of his suit's cold air. "My name is not Randolph Mays," he said. "You may know me by other names. William Laird. Jean-Jacques Lequeu. I am none of these. My name does not matter."

"That's right, your name doesn't matter," Sparta said, her voice as close as if she were inside his head—and to him the sound of her must have been like the hissing of a lizard, for he had been foolish enough to believe she really did not know him.

"You thought you had killed my parents. You thought you had *created* me. But nothing you did made any difference. None of it mattered, Mr. Nemo. Neither do you."

"We *do* want to hear what you have to say," Forster said hastily.

"Well, you will hear it," Mays said wearily. "The cursed woman is right: I don't matter anymore. But we *prophetae* were not mad. We preserved the Knowledge, the Knowledge that made her what she is . . . that brought all of us to this place."

We committed horrible crimes in the name of the Knowledge.

Perhaps you think it strange that I can admit this so plainly. Conventional thinkers—most people— believe that the daring criminal, the outrageous criminal, the man or woman who murders innocents in cold blood, blows them up in some anonymous bombing or slaughters them with a machine gun, never having seen them before, not knowing anything about them, that such an implacable murderer, as opposed to the congenial spouse-killer or child-butcher, could not possibly be possessed of a conscience. How pitifully mistaken.

Mays flew alone through space, reciting his macabre soliloquy while the shining bulk of the world-ship expanded to one side. McNeil and Groves were alone too, some distance away—not out of any sense of privacy or decorum, but because they had released their grip on him and in the course of several hundred meters had simply drifted way. All three spacesuits were depleted of maneuvering fuel; the men drifted and turned randomly, sometimes facing each other, sometimes staring away into empty space, or at the mirror surface of the thing that had been Amalthea, or into the awesome cloud-cauldron of Jupiter.

We prophetae knew well what we did. We ached

for those we sacrificed. The ancient primitives who prayed for the souls of the deer they ate were no more devout than we.

We committed horrible crimes and kept our good cheer, as those before us had done for milleniums. In the end, we believed, the sum of history and the fate of humankind would exculpate us; men and women would bless us.

None of us hoped to live forever, and if a few— or a great many—innocents had to die before Paradise arrived, it was all to the good, for Paradise would arrive that much sooner; that many more would benefit in future.

And so, in the name of the Knowledge, to hurry the day when the Pancreator would return, we made another attempt to realize the Emperor of the Last Days, the feast of the gods. We created her.

Or, as my colleagues and contemporaries insist upon reminding me, I created her. But I cannot take all the credit. Her parents—those subtle, lying Hungarians—sold her to me. Under my direction, a few modifications were made. She refused to cooperate. She, this child, knew the Knowledge better than the knights and elders, she insinuated. Too bad I was unsuccessful in disposing of my failure.

After she escaped, only a fistful of years passed before she showed us that seven thousand years of the Knowledge were, to phrase it mincingly, incomplete. The Venusian tablets revealed that our translations were in error, especially our translation of the Martian plaque. There would be no signal from the homeworld in Crux. The Doradus, the mainstay of what was to be our final assault, was thrown away by that fool Kingman.

The monstrous woman went further, striking at us in our most secret strongholds—I myself came within a hair's-breadth of death at her hands. Then Howard Falcon, who was to have been the new Emperor, failed to rouse the Pancreator on Jupiter;

the so-called world of the gods was only a world of elephantine animals. None of us had foreseen the significance of Amalthea; there was not a word of it in the Knowledge. Our plans and our pride were cast in the dust.

We knights and elders of the prophetae—those of us who survived—lost courage at last. We faced the bitter truth, that everything we had worked for and believed was in error. We had earned no privileges by virtue of our false secrets; if Paradise did come to Earth, we were not among the chosen.

I refused to enter the suicide pact with the others. They heartily cursed me, but at least I did them the service of scattering their ashes in space.

For me, three things remained. I would gaze upon the face of the Pancreator. I would bring death to the terrible woman I had helped create. Then I would die myself. To this end I resurrected the useful personality of Sir Randolph Mays and did all that you know about and can infer.

I have seen the Pancreator. What you call the Ambassador is the being for whom seven thousand years of my tradition had prepared me. I was not even prepared for the inevitable disappointment. He, or she, or whatever it is, is not an ugly thing, but neither is it a god.

At last Mays fell silent. If he was done, he had timed his speech well, for the three drifting men were passing as close to the world-ship as they were likely to come. They were no more than half a kilometer from the still-gaping opening of that equatorial hold into which the *Ventris* had settled, but helpless to stop or turn in their onward rush.

Mays could not resist adding a final, unnecessary comment. "My hopes for revenge have also been disappointed. At least I will not be cheated of my own death."

"Think again, Nemo." Sparta shattered any dignity which might have clung, mold-like, to Mays's self-pity. "The Ambassador has a name. Thowintha is many things—the pilot of this ship, among them— but not what you choose to call the Pancreator." She laughed, low in her throat. "And you aren't dead yet."

A second later the three men understood her. From the cavity of the world-ship's enormous hold, three almost invisibly fine silvery tentacles had emerged and were rapidly feeling their way through space. They moved unerringly, with the quickness of rattlesnakes, as if with their own perception and intelligence.

"Ahh . . . easy there!" McNeil cried out, as one of the tentacles hooked his leg and jerked him upside down.

"Whoops!" Groves exclaimed at almost the same moment—a boy's gleeful shout; a tentacle had him by the arm.

Mays merely grunted in surprise as the third tentacle wrapped itself around his middle.

Immediately the silvery fibers were taut, although they were still playing out of the hold faster than a fishing line spinning off a reel. The total difference in velocity between the ship and the men was that of a well-thrown skipping stone on Earth, and the ship's smart tentacles did not mean to dismember their prey by taking up the slack all at once. But within three hundred meters the men were momentarily motionless with respect to the ship; the ship instantly started reeling them in.

Sparta's calm voice came into their suitcomms: "You are going to be put into the airlock of the Ventris—it's open for you. You will have very little time to prepare for acceleration, a few seconds at most. Don't stop to take off your suits, just head for the wardroom and lie flat on the floor. I can't say how many gees we're going to pull. Regard any delay as potentially fatal."

The tentacles seemed to have a very precise

knowledge of how much acceleration and deceleration a human's body could be expected to withstand without serious injury. They pulled hard and fast, stiffened within a couple of dozen meters of the hold, and dragged the men in through it as the dome was already knitting itself back together. Side by side, the men cleared the dome just as it snapped shut, only a little more than the height of their helmets above them.

The *Ventris* appeared ridiculously tiny where it lay inside the kilometer-wide lock. Within seconds the whiplike tentacles had shoved the men through the *Ventris*'s open equipment bay—one, two, three, they were deposited and released—and the tentacles snatched away out of their sight. Even Randolph Mays, who had so recently recited his own funeral oration, scurried through the double hatches and sought a flat place to lie down.

The world began to move even before they had gotten down on their knees. But Sparta—who surely had known what she was doing, intending to hurry them along—had exaggerated the awesome capabilities of Culture X. Even the alien vessel did not have the capacity to translate itself—an ellipsoid thirty kilometers long and filled with water—with an instant acceleration of one Earth gravity.

No, the incredible column of fire that burst from its "north" pole, pointed directly at Jupiter, moved the world-ship slowly at first, just enough to make the floor of the *Ventris*'s wardroom feel more like a floor than a wall. Indeed, after a few seconds, Angus McNeil got up to make himself more comfortable, unlatching his helmet and throwing it aside, struggling out of his suit.

He moved prematurely. By the time he'd gotten his top half off, the world-ship was accelerating at one gee; by the time he'd gotten the bottom half halfway down his legs it was moving at five, and he could no longer support his own rapidly increasing weight. He crashed to the padded floor and lay there, his bulk crushing the fabric.

Sparta's voice came into the helmets of Tony Groves and the man who had called himself Randolph Mays. "I'm given to understand that acceleration will continue to increase for five more minutes and then cease. By then we will be well on our way to our destination."

Groves, the navigator, forced a question out of his collapsing chest. "Where might that be, Inspector?"

"I don't know. However, I take it we are going to meet Sir Randolph's Pancreator after all."

On the bridge of the world-ship—what the explorers had mistaken for an art gallery—little Sparta and big Thowintha studied the living, shining murals and charted their course thereby. They floated close to each other, turning and gliding through the waters of the control space, communicating with the schools of myriad helpers, as if they had known each other for a billion years and were water-dancing to celebrate their long-delayed reunion.

But even as she danced with the alien, an unimaginable event which she had imagined countless times in her dreams, she thought of Blake, her true mate. . . .

He brooded in the hold of the *Ventris*. He thought he must be getting old, very old. And it was true, he'd changed: the older he got the more like a responsible adult he became. In this whole trip he hadn't found an excuse to blow anything up.

Epilogue

At Ganymede Base they had been tracking these events throughout. A Space Board vessel—a creaking old tug—had been launched in a token attempt at rescue of the Forster expedition, which, having ceased to communicate (by now everybody knew it), was surely in distress.

But the blazing forth of the silvery egg took all the watchers by surprise. On Ganymede, on Earth, on all the inhabited worlds, they saw the titanic engines ignite. They saw the kernel of a moon move against the grasp of mighty Jupiter. They followed its course, fully expecting it to aim itself out of the solar system, toward the most distant stars.

It was with suspicion—then with disbelief—then with wonder that they finally believed the evidence of their own computers.

On Ganymede, the commander watched it with a grim, unyielding expression. Too late he'd tracked down the last of the *prophetae*, the last mole within the Space Board's delicate presence on the shore of the Shoreless Ocean. Whatever these pitiful conspiratorial pensionaires of the Free Spirit had to tell him was worthless in the face of an unfolding future.

On Earth, Ari and Jozsef watched the spectacle.

272

Tears streamed from Ari's eyes, tears of joy and anger, that it was happening, that her daughter had helped it happen—and that she had been excluded from its happening.

For what was left of Amalthea—its gleaming core, the world-ship, the diamond moon—was not headed for a destination somewhere in the constellation Crux. It was coming to a rendezvous with Earth.

The Diamond Moon
an Afterword by
Arthur C. Clarke

I have already described, in the Afterword to *Venus Prime 4: The Medusa
Encounter*, the story of my life-long fascination with the greatest of all planets.
Only since 1979, however, has it been
discovered—to the delighted amaze-
ment of astronomers—that Jupiter's wonders are
matched by those of its many satellites.

In 1610, Galileo Galilei turned his newly invented
"optic tube" upon the planet Jupiter. He was not
surprised to see that—unlike the stars—it showed a
perceptible disc, but during the course of the next
few weeks he made a discovery that demolished
the mediaeval image of the universe. In that world-
picture, *everything*—including Sun and Moon—
revolved around a central Earth. But Jupiter had
four faint sparks of light revolving around it. Earth
was not the only planet with a moon. To make matters even worse—Jupiter had not one, but *four*
companions. No wonder that some of Galileo's
more intransigent colleagues refused to look
through his diabolical invention. Anyway, they argued, if Jupiter's satellites were *that* small, they
didn't really matter, and the heck with them . . .

Until the 19th century, the four "Galilean" moons—Io, Europa, Ganymede, and Callisto—remained as no more than featureless pinpoints even through the most powerful telescopes. Their regular movements (in periods ranging from a mere 42 hours for Io, up to 17 days for distant Callisto) around their giant master made them a source of continual delight to generations of astronomers, amateur and professional. A good pair of modern binoculars—*rigidly supported*—will show them easily, as they swing back and forth along Jupiter's equatorial plane. Usually three or four will be visible, but on rare occasions Jupiter will appear as moonless as Galileo's opponents would have wished, because all four of the satellites will be eclipsed by the planet, or inconspicuously transiting its face.

There was no reason to suppose, before the Space Age opened, that the four Galilean satellites would be very different from our own Moon—that is, airless, cratered deserts where nothing ever moved except the shadows cast by the distant sun. In fact, this proved to be true for the outermost satellite, Callisto: it is so saturated with craters of all sizes that there is simply no room for any more.

This was about the only *un*surprising result of the 1979 *Voyager* missions, undoubtedly the most successful in the history of space exploration. For the three inner moons proved to be wildly different from Callisto, and from each other.

Io is pockmarked with volcanoes—the first active ones ever discovered beyond the Earth—blasting sulphurous vapors a hundred kilometers into space. Europa is a frozen ice-pack from pole to pole, covered with the intricate traceries of fractured floes. And Ganymede—larger than Mercury, and not much smaller than Mars—is most bizarre of all. Much of its surface looks as if scraped by gigantic combs, leaving multiple groves meandering for thousands of kilometers. And there are curious pits from which emerge tracks that might have been made by snails the size of an Olympic stadium.

If you want to know more about these weird places, I refer you to the numerous splendidly illustrated volumes that were inspired by the *Voyager* missions. Stanley Kubrick and I never dreamed, back in the mid-sixties, that within a dozen years we would be seeing closeups of the places we were planning to send our astronauts: we thought such knowledge would not be available until at least 2001. Without the *Voyagers*, I could never have written *Odyssey Two*. Thank you, NASA and JPL.

In addition to its quartet of almost planet-sized moons, the *Voyager* spaceprobes discovered that Jupiter also has Saturn-type rings—though they are much less spectacular—and at least a dozen smaller satellites. As befits such a giant, it is a mini-solar system in its own right, whose exploration may take many centuries—and many lives.

The short story *"Jupiter V"*, the genesis of this novel, takes place on a satellite which was discovered by a sharp-eyed astronomer, E. E. Barnard, back in 1892. Now officially christened Amalthea, Jupiter V was long believed to be the moon closest to Jupiter, but even smaller and closer satellites were detected by the *Voyagers*. There may be scores, or hundreds, or thousands more; some day we'll have to answer the question: "How small can a lump of rock be and still qualify as a moon?"

Written in 1951, and later published in the collection *Reach for Tomorrow* (1956), *"Jupiter V"* is one of the few stories whose origins I can pinpoint exactly. Its first inspiration (explicitly mentioned in the original version) was Chesley Bonestell's wonderful series of astronomical paintings, featured in a 1944 issue of *Life* magazine.* Later reprinted in the volume edited by Willy Ley, *The Conquest of Space* (1949), they must have made thousands of people realize for the first time that the other planets and satellites of the Solar System were real *places*, which one day we might visit.

Chesley's paintings—when published in *The Conquest of Space*—inspired legions of young space cadets, and this somewhat older one. Little did I know, to coin a phrase, that one day I would collaborate with Chesley on a book about the exploration of the outer planets *(Beyond Jupiter* [1972]: see Afterword to *Venus Prime 4: The Medusa Encounter).* How glad I am that Chesley—who died, still painting furiously, at the age of 99—lived to see the reality behind his imagination.

The second input to "*Jupiter V*" was somewhat more sophisticated. In 1949, during my final year at King's College, London, my applied mathematics instructor Dr G. C. McVittie gave a lecture which made an indelible impression on me. It was on the apparently unpromising subject of perturbation theory—i.e., what happens to an orbiting body when some external force alters its velocity. At that date, nothing could have seemed of less practical importance; today, it is the basis of the multi-billion dollar communications satellite industry, and all space rendezvous missions.

The conclusions that "Mac" illustrated on the blackboard were surprising, and often counterintuitive; who would have thought that one way to make a satellite go faster was to slow it down? Over the next few decades, I used perturbation theory in

---

*Just a few years earlier, he had done the matte work for what is widely regarded as the greatest movie ever made, Orson Welles's masterpiece *Citizen Kane.* His widow has just told me (October 1989) how much he would have enjoyed the *second* San Francisco earthquake, knowing he had a great time in the first. . . .

a number of other tales besides *"Jupiter V"* and it plays a vital role, though in very different ways, in the finales of both *2010* and *2061*.

In March 1989 the Royal Astronomical Society, of which Dr. McVittie had long been a leading Fellow, gave a special symposium in his memory, and I took pains to tell the organizers about his contribution to my own career.

But back to Jupiter V—Amalthea. In 1951 I felt perfectly safe in making it anything I wished, for it was inconceivable that we would get a good look at it during this century. Yet that is just one of the feats accomplished in the *Voyager* missions.

Well, perhaps not a *good* look, but *Voyager*'s slightly blurred image, though from several thousand kilometers away, completely demolished my description: "There were faint crisscrossing lines on the surface of the satellite, and suddenly my eye grasped their full pattern. For it *was* a pattern; those lines covered Five with the same geometrical accuracy as the lines of latitude and longitude divide up a globe of the Earth. . . ."

I'm not worried: the real Amalthea looks even weirder. It's a delicate shade of pink—probably as a result of spraying by sulphur dust spewed out from nearby Io. And it has a matched pair of prominent white spots, looking very much like protruding eyes.

Maybe that's just what they are—we should know when *Galileo* arrives there in 1995. . . .

Arthur C. Clarke
23 October 1989

ARTHUR C. CLARKE'S VENUS PRIME

by Paul Preuss

VOLUME 1: BREAKING STRAIN   75344-8/$3.95 US/$4.95 CAN
Her code name is Sparta. Her beauty veils a mysterious past and abilities of superhuman dimension, the product of advanced biotechnology.

VOLUME 2: MAELSTROM   75345-6/$3.95 US/$4.95 CAN
When a team of scientists is trapped in the gaseous inferno of Venus, Sparta must risk her life to save them.

VOLUME 3: HIDE AND SEEK   75346-4/$3.95 US/$4.95 CAN
When the theft of an alien artifact, evidence of extraterrestrial life, leads to two murders, Sparta must risk her life and identity to solve the case.

VOLUME 4: THE MEDUSA ENCOUNTER
                                75348-0/$3.95 US/$4.95 CAN
Sparta's recovery from her last mission is interrupted as she sets out on an interplanetary investigation of her host, the Space Board.

VOLUME 5: THE DIAMOND MOON
                                75349-9/$3.95 US/$4.95 CAN
Sparta's mission is to monitor the exploration of Jupiter's moon, Amalthea, by the renowned Professor J.Q.R. Forester.

Each volume features a special technical infopak, including blueprints of the structures of Venus Prime

THE CONTINUATION
OF THE FABULOUS
INCARNATIONS OF IMMORTALITY
SERIES

PIERS ANTHONY

FOR LOVE OF EVIL
75285-9/$4.95 US/$5.95 Can

Coming Soon
from Avon Books

AND ETERNITY
75286-7

RETURN TO AMBER...
THE ONE *REAL* WORLD, OF WHICH ALL OTHERS, INCLUDING EARTH, ARE BUT SHADOWS

ROGER ZELAZNY

The New Amber Novel

KNIGHT OF SHADOWS   75501-7/$3.95 US/$4.95 Can
Merlin is forced to choose to ally himself with the Pattern of Amber or of Chaos. A child of both worlds, this crucial decision will decide his fate and the fate of the true world.

SIGN OF CHAOS   89637-0/$3.50 US/$4.50 Can
Merlin embarks on another marathon adventure, leading him back to the court of Amber and a final confrontation at the Keep of the Four Worlds.

The Classic Amber Series

NINE PRINCES IN AMBER   01430-0/$3.50 US/$4.50 Can
THE GUNS OF AVALON   00083-0/$3.50 US/$4.50 Can
SIGN OF THE UNICORN   00031-9/$3.50 US/$4.25 Can
THE HAND OF OBERON   01664-8/$3.50 US/$4.50 Can
THE COURTS OF CHAOS   47175-2/$3.50 US/$4.25 Can
BLOOD OF AMBER   89636-2/$3.95 US/$4.95 Can
TRUMPS OF DOOM   89635-4/$3.50 US/$3.95 Can

Magic...Mystery...Revelations
Welcome to
THE FANTASTICAL
WORLD OF AMBER!

ROGER ZELAZNY'S
VISUAL GUIDE to
CASTLE
AMBER

by Roger Zelazny and Neil Randall
75566-1/$8.95 US/$10.95 Can

AN AVON TRADE PAPERBACK

Tour Castle Amber—
through vivid illustrations, detailed floor plans,
cutaway drawings, and page after page
of never-before-revealed information!